BATTLING BOXING STORIES

Borgo Press Books by GARY LOVISI

Battle Boxing Stories: Thrilling Tales of Pugilistic Puissance
  (Editor)
Driving Hell's Highway: A Crime Novel
Gargoyle Nights: A Collection of Horror
Mars Needs Books!: A Science Fiction Novel
Murder of a Bookman: A Bentley Hollow Collectibles Mystery
  Novel
Violence Is the Only Solution: 3 Vic Powers Crime Tales

BATTLING BOXING STORIES

THRILLING TALES OF PUGILISTIC PUISSANCE

GARY LOVISI, EDITOR

THE BORGO PRESS

MMXII

BATTLING BOXING STORIES

FIRST EDITION

Published by Wildside Press LLC

www.wildsidebooks.com

DEDICATION

To all the authors whose fine stories have made this book possible

CONTENTS

INTRODUCTION
BATTLING BOXERS

Do you know the name of the heavyweight champion? There was a time not so long ago when every one of us knew his name. The great boxing champions were in all the newspapers and on TV, their names indelibly burned into our collective memory as true giants, powerful men who were larger than life itself—John L. Sullivan, Jack Johnson, Jim Tully, Jack Dempsey, Joe Louis, Rocky Graziano, Muhammad Ali, Joe Frazier, George Foreman, even Iron Mike Tyson. These men—and many others I have not named here—are the ones we remember today; men who lived and fought in a tough and often dirty, corrupt sport. Many of them we admired—some more than others. We wanted them to triumph, and while some failed, each one gave it their all to thrill us in the boxing ring and we were there cheering them on.

Today, I doubt many of us can name the champions of any weight division. There seems to be little meaning or magic today in modern boxing, at least to the general public. These days traditional boxing has been somewhat eclipsed by other more violent aspects of sport, such as mixed martial arts (MMA), kick boxing, and cage matches. It is sad. The idea of boxing has been truly noble. It offered many young men who came from nowhere the opportunity to be someone, you didn't need a degree or an uncle in the business. You just had to be able to keep standing, while your opponent fell. There are many boxing stories and legends, and they are as individual as is each man who put on gloves and stepped into the ring.

In the old days—in those far away traditional times—the game seemed to possess elements that were virtually magical, and that is what the stories in this book are all about and what they seek to capture. Boxing *is* a magical sport. The stories can be as heroic and as full of triumph and tragedy as anything Homer ever wrote. The sport pits two men *mano a mano*. One man against another man—but also today with women boxers—it pits one person against another with nothing to interfere with their battle royale. Nothing except that which is deep within themselves, their inner secrets and fears, or the plans of those around them—to stop them.

Boxing can be art, heroic majesty, and dark magic all wrapped up in a bloody maelstrom of passion and sheer violence. It has been captured well in classic films like *Somebody Up There Likes Me*, *Requiem for a Heavyweight*, *Raging Bull*, even *Rocky*, and so many other fine boxing flicks. However, most of that is mere fantasy, they are not like the *real* game. Books fare better, especially non-fiction books. However, the actual boxing game is far tougher and meaner than any film, darker and grimmer than anything written in books. Short stories, however, can tell these tales extremely well because they capture that short-burst intensity and hyper-emotion and turmoil very effectively—few feature-length films or long novels can ever sustain that. I believe the short stories in this book do that extremely well, each one offering its own sharp, powerful vision of a particular aspect of the game—and an individual boxer in a specific time or place.

As good as a film can be, no mere *film* can ever capture the real action and excitement of some of the classic boxing bouts that make up the exciting history of this sport. The old news-reels and videos of classic bouts are the best, staggering in their raw intensity and passion—but too often grainy, shot poorly, or sometimes missing key action. However, fiction in a short story can also hit the mark, putting the reader right there in the ring with the champ—or the chump—making him or her feel the impact of every blow; the pain, the hurt, and the crying bitter rage of anger or betrayal. It's all there and more in the stories in this book by a host of fine writers who tell their particular tale with passion, violence, action, anger—and the most important ingredient of all—sheer brutal truth. However the stories in this book also show the other side of that coin. They give us noble men and women winning against the odds, men who fight the good fight in the ring and in their life, people who celebrate a passion for the sport and a passion for life and...even love. These are heroes who rise up against tragedy to do what is right, to protect those they love, to care for someone other than themselves, or to fight the toughest fight there can ever be—battling their own inner demons. Sometimes they win, sometimes they lose, but they always give it their all. That too, is all part of the game.

I am proud that the traditional boxing stories in this book chronicle all manner of battles, both inside the ring and out. Some of them offer unabashed pulp action with real heart, others raw reality and truth. There is certainly magic in each one of these tales and maybe even just a touch of fantasy, but no outright magic or fantasy. Here you will find no bouts with human boxers duking it out with aliens; no men fighting wizards, monsters, zombies, vampires, or even superhuman robots—none of that nonsense. So have no fear on that score here. Perhaps that might be fodder for some other book—*but not this one!*

The fifteen stories in this book also do *not* offer a how-to manual on the boxing arts, they're not instructional tales devoted to process. These are stories created solely to entertain you, to grab the reader, to offer some measure of that magic and truth found in the boxing ring. They do that quite well. These stories are as real as their authors could make them, they're stories with heart and soul, depicting pain and triumph by fascinating and unforgettable characters entangled in the eternal warfare of the boxing arena. These are stories with impact, and they'll hit you like a cold smack to the face. They may shock you with their intense violence, sheer brutality, and bitter rage; but they will also lighten your soul with their heartfelt emotion, humor, and even outright depictions of love; where sometimes sweet, sometimes rough, and sometimes decent characters struggle to triumph, battling for their very dignity and humanity—their own special story of *boxing magic*!

Gary Lovisi
Brooklyn, New York
January 5, 2012

QUICK HANDS

BY WAYNE D. DUNDEE

Usually they just put some brute up against him—the strongest, toughest miner from whatever camp they happened to be visiting. Powerful men with massive shoulders and thick arms, men who could load more ore and out-arm wrestle any other man in the camp. Experienced brawlers at best...but possessed of little or nothing in the way of punching basics or actual boxing skills.

This kid tonight, however, was something of an exception. He was smaller, though not by much, and considerably faster. He'd already proven he could move and dodge, rather than wade in right away like so many of them did and try to finish everything with a thrashing windmill of uppercuts and roundhouses. McMahon actually appreciated this. Those other types too often punched themselves out before the end of the first round. And then it was up to McMahon, in order to make sure the crowd got its money's worth, to carry his opponent (sometimes almost literally since the dumb clods were practically too exhausted to stand) until it reached a point where it was okay to put them down.

As they went into the second round now, McMahon could see his opponent still had quite a bit left. He was showing some wear, sure, breathing hard and sweating—just as McMahon himself was—but the lad was far from being played out. In the corner, between rounds, Professor Hanratty had razor-slit McMahon above his left eye and then held ice against it so it wouldn't start leaking right away. "Take a punch or two, let him get you bleeding good for the crowd," he'd instructed. "Then go ahead and finish this rock-chopper before the round ends."

McMahon nodded his agreement. He had no doubt he could end this contest whenever he wanted—the lad wasn't *that* much different than the others. Yeah, he was in better shape and had a few moves; but he couldn't counter-punch worth a damn and, judging from the big openings McMahon had allowed earlier for the sake of gauging exactly what he was up against, the kid didn't know how to throw combinations and he was seldom able to get full weight into his harder shots for maximum effect.

So, when it was time, after a sticky flow of blood was smeared down the side of his face and the crowd's excitement was sufficiently stoked, McMahon went to work and did what he was trained to do. He cut off the ring, backed the kid into a corner, began rocking him with lightning-fast flurries. The kid ducked, bobbed, got his arms up to block a lot of these blows. But the relentless peppering crowded him, didn't give him a chance to breathe, and the repeated shots to his arms quickly started to make them heavier and slower to rise in defense. That's when McMahon went head-hunting and started to throw high, hard, jarring combinations....

"It's the combinations that'll score you a knockout every time, especially coming from those amazing quick hands of yours," coached the professor. *"Generally speaking, it's almost impossible to knock a man unconscious when he can see the punch coming, no matter how hard it lands. It might knock him down, it might rattle him all the way back to his ancestors, but he'll still be conscious. Only when you throw combinations as fast and hard as you do, Mackie-boy, one of them is bound to be the blind punch that gets the job done."*

...And tonight that blind punch was a final shattering right cross to the jaw. The young man went down, hard, and everybody watching knew he wasn't going to be get back up—at least not under his own power—any time soon.

The audience of grim-faced miners, gathered tight around

the makeshift ring erected specially for this event, had been eager and loud and boisterous right from the get-go. The sight of McMahon's blood had brought them to a near frenzy. And now, even as McMahon started to turn things around, their excitement level remained high. Although he was whittling down one of their own, they nevertheless harbored a grudging respect for his brutal, methodical skill. Once it was over, in their minds they had seen a hard-won fight, had gotten their blood lust slaked, and therefore turned away satisfied.

McMahon had done his job. Once again.

* * * * * * *

"Ah, it's those wonderful quick hands of yours, Mackie me boy. Never in my born days have I seen a big man like you with quicker hands. If only our paths had crossed sooner, I could have taken you to the best training camps in the country and managed you to becoming a contender right up there in the championship ranks. Even the great John L. would be taking notice! Why, we'd be the toasts of both coasts and every important city in between."

The boxing bout was nearly an hour past now. Professor Hanratty was speaking as he treated the bruises to McMahon's face and the cut over his eye. The fighter sat stoically through this, his hands soaking in a bowl of stinging salt brine. They were inside a large tent that had been put up between their two traveling wagons. Soft lantern light filled the enclosure with a golden glow, night shadows seeping in to claim only the corners. A low wind was building outside, moaning down out of the higher mountain range, lifting the tent skirts here and there and allowing cold drafts to swirl in. The day had been unseasonably warm. The temperature had been dropping steadily since sundown, though, and the feel of approaching winter was once again unmistakable in the air.

Professor Hanratty's spiel, his marveling about McMahon's quick hands, was standard after every fight. And as he made his reply, McMahon was aware that his words had become pretty standard by now, too.

"Never had that much of a hankerin' to see the coasts. And I damn sure got no desire to get caught in the crush of any of those big 'important' cities you keep yammerin' about," he said. "Far as John L., he's gone to gloved fightin' these days under those Marquess of Queensberry Rules that all the swells are so keen on. Me, I'm strictly a bare-knuckler and too old to change.... Besides, suits me fine the way things are goin' for us just like they are."

"I don't mind the way things are, either," spoke up Molly from where she sat on the opposite side of the folding table, counting up the money from tonight's take. "'Cept I really hate it when you have to cut Mac the way you done again tonight, Professor. Don't he get bruised up and split open enough by those fellas he fights without you havin' to add to it?"

Hanratty sighed dramatically (which was how he tended to do many things). "For the hundredth time, my dear, the answer is no, on occasion Mac does *not* get cut open enough by his opponents. That's a sorry part of it, I know, but it nevertheless remains a fact. A large part of what we do—just like the way I carry on during my medicine spiel about your foot and Hugo's misfortune—is showmanship. We *have* to do that in order to draw sufficient customers.... Without showmanship, that tidy sum of cash you have before you there would be a mere fraction because too few would be interested enough to shell out for what we are pitching."

Now it was Molly's turn to sigh. "I suppose you're right," she allowed. "You know a lot more about a lot more stuff than I probably ever will.... But I still don't like seein' Mac get cut up all the time."

"Thanks for the concern, sweetie," McMahon said, favoring the girl with a weary smile. "But gettin' busted up some is part of what I signed on for. Like the professor said, it's sort of necessary to the show. If I went out there and whupped all the fellas that step forward in these towns we visit and made it look too easy—without givin' 'em some reason to believe they had a chance, or not let the crowd get worked up over thinkin' it might be *me* who was goin' down for the count—why, where would be the draw in that? What's more, it might make those tough ol' miners downright displeased to pay out their admission money and lay down their side bets only to see me plunk their boy without hardly breakin' a sweat. How bad a shape you think I'd end up in if a whole passel of 'em *rioted* on us, maybe rode me out of town on a rail?"

"I seen a crowd riot once," Hugo said from the other side of the tent, where he was bundling up the ring posts and ropes that he had dismantled after the fight. "It wasn't a pretty sight. Nossir. I wouldn't want to see another one, and that's for sure."

These four now gathered in the tent comprised the full make-up of *Professor Hanratty's Traveling Medicine & Health Show.* In its present incarnation, Hanratty's troupe had been working the mining camps along the front range of the Colorado Rockies for closing on three years. The centerpiece of the whole endeavor was Hanratty's Astonishing Elixir, which the professor had been marketing for two decades. Truth be known, Alphonse Herschel Hanratty's "professorship" had come in the mail for ten dollars sent to a Boston print shop—alas now burned to the ground—specializing in authentic-looking degrees and licenses of any type desired. Yet while the credentials for his title might be lacking, his dedication to purpose was not; he genuinely believed that his elixir had health benefits. Over time he worked to refine and improve the concoction even as he worked to enhance his techniques for selling it. Over that same period of time he had gradually accumulated the others about him.

Hugo was the first. That was back when the professor had been peddling his elixir and other wares on a circuit running through high plains towns and settlements between Cheyenne and Denver. He had come upon the gentle, feeble-minded young giant cleaning spittoons and gutters at a nameless saloon in the middle of nowhere, working for so-called room and board that consisted of being allowed to sleep in a drafty old woodshed out behind the main building and getting thrown table scraps twice a day, like a dog on a chain. In addition to this neglect, the poor wretch—whose brains had been fried to irreversible damage by an adolescent fever—was subject to daily taunts and frequent physical abuse by the saloon owner, his hag of a wife, and numerous regular customers of the establishment. When Hanratty's wagon rolled away from that vile place, Hugo was riding on the seat beside him. The old peddler didn't have much to share, but what he had was a lot more than Hugo was used to getting and it came with a friendly smile and nurturing words in place of further abuse.

Molly was next. Hanratty and Hugo happened across her on a street corner on the edge of Cheyenne's red light district—an instantly heart-wrenching sight to see, this skinny, dirty, ragged, club-footed little nine-year-old holding out a battered tin cup and begging passer-bys for spare coins. They learned that her prostitute of a mother would send her out to the corner each morning, as soon as she returned from putting in her own hours on the street. There Molly would remain until her mother fetched her back home in the evening, where she was fed a supper of corn bread and molasses (occasionally accompanied by an overcooked sausage link or a glass of half-sour milk) and then left alone in their hovel of an apartment while the mother went out to once more ply her trade through the night. The cycle would repeat the next day. The mother's earnings were sparse due to her foul temperament and hardened looks so much of the time it was only the money from Molly's cup that carried them through. Even still, when Hanratty offered the woman fifty dollars to take the girl away from the squalid life they were leading, the money was seized with only minor hesitation and the mother's parting words regarding her daughter were, "Be good to get the hungry-mouthed little cripple off my hands."

Last came McMahon. The medicine wagon rolled into the town of Bitterroot one morning just in time to see the struggle that was taking place as three deputies from the town marshal's office were trying to arrest a man for vagrancy. The deputies were all stalwart fellows armed with billy clubs while the target of their attention was weaponless. Reining up his wagon to watch, Professor Hanratty was quick to marvel at the vagrant's rapidly flying fists and the accuracy with which his punches landed. Having trained in the art of pugilism during his privileged youth, before the corrupt practices and eventual suicide of his father destroyed the family fortune, Hanratty immediately saw the potential for an added element to his traveling medicine show. Therefore, after the billy clubs inevitably took their toll and the vagrant was thrown behind bars, Hanratty came forward with a proposition: He would go the man's bail and pay any related fines if the fellow would agree to join the professor's show and travel with them for a minimum of one year. The prisoner, who called himself McMahon, extended a battered right hand through the jail bars and they shook on it.

Not long after that Hanratty added a second wagon and the necessary equipment for a boxing ring to his show, and they began working the mining camp circuit. The first year had long since come and gone with never a mention of McMahon taking leave after his obligation was fulfilled.

While his embrace of these misfits and cast-offs, these lost souls, stemmed primarily from genuine compassion on Hanratty's part, there nevertheless was a practical side to him that recognized they also needed to contribute something to the overall good of the group. And since the main thing sustaining all of them was the sale of Hanratty's Astonishing Elixir, it followed that each would have to play some role in the medicine show presentations that drew the paying customers.

Having demonstrated early on a natural way with animals, Hugo immediately took over the duties of lead teamster and the general care and feeding of the wagon mules (contrary-minded but necessary beasts that Hanratty had been fighting a running battle with for years). At Hugo's gentle coaxing, the animals responded with only rare instances of the stubbornness they had so regularly exhibited for the professor. By virtue of his size and raw strength, Hugo also handled most of the heavier chores—lugging barrels of ingredients, loading/unloading cases of bottled elixir, setting up and striking the boxing ring, etc.—associated to putting on a show.

Additionally, Hanratty called upon this same physical power to utilize Hugo in a brief segment of the show itself. Explaining to the audiences (in the exaggerated, fictionalized way that made up most of his spiel) how he had first found Hugo riddled by the remnants of a devastating fever, the professor would go on to claim that it was the administration of his amazing elixir that had nursed Hugo not only back to full health but to the mighty physical specimen who now stood before them. Alas, Hanratty would add sadly and dramatically, the effects of the fever on the young man's obviously stunted mental capacities could not be reversed as successfully. After all, even his vaunted elixir had its limits. But still, he would insist, the physical results could not be denied—and at this point he would call upon Hugo to perform some pre-arranged but quite legitimate feats of strength that included bending iron bars and lifting one end of a loaded ore cart.

Nobody seemed to remember exactly how Molly had assumed the roll of banker/ accountant, but she did and did a superb job at it. Everything was always balanced to the penny, a budget was set and adhered to, funds were available and promptly paid out when needed, and a tidy savings stash (especially after McMahon joined up and started drawing bigger paydays for the troupe) was accumulating. In addition to that, Molly also did most of the traditional female chores for the troupe. Laundry, mending, cleaning, doing dishes...everything but cooking. No matter how hard she tried to learn and how hard the professor tried to teach her, disastrous would be a charitable way of describing her results.

As far as Molly's performance part of the show, Hanratty once again took an obvious flaw, in this case her clubbed foot, and spun it into an exaggerated tale of how afflicted the poor girl's entire body might have become had he not found her in time to administer copious amounts of his amazing elixir. A portion of each show's earnings, he would be sure to mention, went into a savings fund intended to one day pay for an operation that would correct the impaired foot. And then he would call Molly onto the stage where she would proceed, accompanied by the professor's banjo strumming, to do a simple little dance routine that demonstrated her high-spiritedness yet at the same time also showed the restrictions placed upon her by the foot as it was. After that, she would close the show with a liltingly beautiful rendition of *Greensleeves*, Hanratty this time accompanying on a violin. By the time she was done there unfailingly were hardened miners in the audience with a tear on their rough cheeks and they would be the first in line to buy a bottle or two of elixir, accompanied by the admonishment: "Be sure a share of this goes toward little Molly's operation."

Hanratty was not exempt from feeling pangs of guilt over exploiting the maladies of both Hugo and Molly in this manner. But, strictly from a practical standpoint he told himself, a person had to do whatever it took to survive and prosper on this rugged slice of the frontier. Each of his wards understood this, too, and neither had any qualms about what they were called upon to do because each also understood that their lots in life were immeasurably improved since taking up with the professor. Furthermore, the plan to one day have enough money to get Molly's foot operated on wasn't mere sales hype—it was a very real goal of everybody in the troupe, even though Molly (who secretly longed for that day more deeply than anyone) always insisted she was fine the way she was and didn't rate any special treatment over the others.

When McMahon joined the troupe, the paydays from their performances and thereby the chances for getting Molly's foot corrected increased significantly. Hanratty had always wanted to add something to his show, something special, something to give it an edge over the dozens of other snake oil-sellers prowling the region. At one point he'd tried to use Hugo in a wrestling-challenge format, offering fifty dollars (and taking bets on the side, of course) to anyone willing to try their luck at pinning the powerful young giant. That plan quickly backfired when it turned out that Hugo, for all his raw strength, had no warrior's heart when it came to actually *fighting* anybody, for fear of maybe hurting them. Which meant he was the one who ended up on his back and Hanratty ended up shelling out money instead of raking it in.

With McMahon and his lightning fists, however, it was a whole different story. Hanratty had already seen proof the man was willing to fight. It took practically no time for the professor to formulate the rest of the concept that became part of each show: First McMahon would come out and demonstrate the accuracy of his quick hands by striking down fist-sized burlap pouches of pea gravel thrown at him from a distance of thirty feet. (Since baseball was fast becoming a popular sport all across the country, this distance was widely recognized as being only half that of a pitcher throwing to home plate.) Would-be hurlers were invited to pay twenty-five cents for a pouch of gravel to throw as hard as they could at McMahon's head and shoulders. They could try as many times as they wished, providing of course they purchased a new pouch each time, and if one of their throws eluded McMahon's fists within a reasonable reach zone their entire expenditure would be repaid double. This naturally segued into the inevitable challenge for a boxing match to take place later that night—$150 offered to any man who could go three rounds with McMahon and still be on his feet at the end. Admission to see this event was fifty cents and once again Hanratty was available to take side bets.

All of the hoopla for this, of course, was liberally laced with claims that McMahon's physical prowess was due largely to faithful daily doses of Hanratty's Astonishing Elixir. In truth, the boxing challenges quickly became popular and profitable quite apart from the rest of the show and how much they actually added to sales of the elixir no one could be sure. But what was certain beyond any doubt was that *Professor Hanratty's Traveling Medicine & Health Show* was seeing profits like never before and the day of having enough money set aside for

Molly's operation was close at hand.

* * * * * * *

The next day they departed the nameless mining camp and headed on up the line toward their next destination, which was likely to be the final stop of the season before the snows of winter chased them down out of the mountains until spring.

The four riders appeared right after they'd begun their descent into a narrow gorge with the shadows of late afternoon starting to stretch across the rocky trail. At the other end of the gorge was a campsite where they'd planned to spend the night. But, suddenly, the way was blocked by two of the riders dancing their horses out from behind a jagged outcropping and then reining them to a halt directly in the middle of the trail. From behind came the other two riders, galloping up fast, the clatter of their horses' hooves announcing their arrival until they too reined up short and blocked the trail from behind.

Hugo brought the first wagon to a halt and McMahon, driving the second team, followed suit. Each of the riders promptly produced a Winchester rifle from his saddle scabbard and made a show of jacking a round into the chamber, the sound of the levering mechanisms echoing hollowly off the surrounding rocks.

From the wagon seat beside Hugo, Hanratty scowled fiercely and demanded, "Here now. What is the meaning of this?"

One of the front riders, evidently the leader of the bunch, a wedge-faced specimen with shaggy brows and a prominently displayed set of gnarled yellow teeth, replied calmly, "For an educated man, Professor, that sure seems like a stupid-ass question.... What the hell do you *think* the meaning of four armed men blockin' your path might be?"

"Is this an attempted robbery, you knave? Is that what you are about?"

Gnarled Teeth flashed a coyote's grin. "No, you phony bag of wind, this ain't an *attempted* robbery...this *is* a damn robbery.

Now start shuckin' your hardware—guns and knives and such—and tossin' 'em down to the ground."

"We are not armed hooligans like you. We are simply—"

"More stupid talk," Gnarled Teeth cut him off. "Only a bunch of fools would try to pass through these mountains unarmed against wild critters and the like. Don't try to tell me you don't have a rifle or two somewhere in those wagons. Now shuck 'em out and be quick about it or you'll force me to show you the hard way that we mean business and ain't to be trifled with."

"Better do as he says, Professor," advised McMahon.

Moments later an old Henry rifle and a shotgun had been withdrawn from the wagons and tossed to the ground.

"What about sidearms? Short guns?" Gnarled Teeth wanted to know.

"Surely you can see we are not shootists to be armed in that manner," said Hanratty.

"No, that's just it.... I *can't* see. Stand up, each of you, and open your coats wide. Do it slow and careful."

When that demand had been satisfied, Gnarled Teeth motioned for them to re-seat themselves. "Now," he said, "we get to the fun part.... Leastways for me and my pards. Time for you to hand over all your valuables and the money sack or strongbox or whatever it is you keep your hard cash in."

"You miserable wretch," Hanratty seethed. "We're nothing but a poor traveling show barely eeking out an existence. Your take will be pitiful when split amongst the four of you and you'll leave us facing starvation with winter coming on."

"Stow that poor-mouth shit, I ain't buyin' it," responded Gnarled Teeth. "I been watchin' you. I've seen you put on your show two or three times now. Includin' again last night. You draw big crowds and you take in plenty of cash, so don't pretend you ain't got a sizable wad stashed somewhere. You'll cough it up, too, and do it mighty fast or my pards and me will start throwin' lead to encourage you. You push us, we'll start with that big ox sittin' right there beside you—blowin' his pumpkin off won't matter much, anyway, what with it bein' nothin' but empty space to begin with."

"You leave Hugo alone!" protested Molly.

"Shhh. Pipe down, girl," McMahon admonished her.

The riders at the rear edged up closer.

Gnarled Teeth swung his focus to McMahon. "Yeah, you tell her, boxer man. Tell her like it is. Bullets start flyin', they ain't necessarily gonna care if it's a lame-brain or a cripple that gets in their way."

McMahon's eyes blazed with hate. "You're a cowardly dog," he rasped.

"I truly am sorry you feel that way about me," said Gnarled Teeth. "You see, I sorta admire you. Like I said, I've seen your show. Seen you box. You got real quick hands for a big man, maybe the quickest I ever saw. I admire a fella who takes a natural ability like that and trains it into a special skill like boxin'."

"Step down off that horse, I'd be happy to give you a personal demonstration."

Gnarled Teeth chuckled throatily. "Yeah, I bet you would, wouldn't you? Tell you what, though.... I got me a skill of my own. You see, I happen to be pretty good with a gun. And you know what? The best punch you ever throwed in your life wouldn't amount to shit up against the punch from one of my Winchester slugs." Gnarled Teeth's expression suddenly turned cold. "Now you tell this phony old bastard up here in the front wagon to get his ass in gear and start handin' over what I asked for and nobody has to get hurt."

"All right, all right," the professor said hurriedly. "No need for violence. Please. Here, under my seat, is the strongbox you want." He stood up again, as did Hugo, and the two of them lifted the wagon seat so that it swung back on a hinge, revealing a hollowed out area underneath in which rested a black metal strongbox.

"Hand it down to them, Hugo," Hanratty instructed.

"Make sure you don't pull nothin' outta there but money," Gnarled Teeth warned, "or there'll be hell to pay."

"I've no doubt you'll be paying a debt in hell one day," the professor said calmly, "but unfortunately you won't be sent there by our hand. You have effectively stripped us of any weapon against you."

"Damned right. And best you remember that if you know what's good for you."

The second front rider had nudged his horse closer and now Hugo lifted the strongbox and held it out to him. As this was taking place, the professor pleaded with Gnarled Teeth. "Take whatever you want. Just get this over with and spare the lives of me and my people. I beg of you."

"Quit your whinin'. We'll get to the rest soon enough," Gnarled Teeth told him. "But first things first...Virgil"—speaking now to the rider who'd taken the strongbox from Hugo—"pop that thing open and let's see what we got."

Virgil slipped from his saddle and dragged the box down with him. A moment later he sent it crashing to the ground and then dropped to his knees beside it, forcing open the lid. Several loosely bundled bills spilled out.

"How much is there?" called one of the riders who had moved up alongside the rear wagon.

"Looks like a pretty good haul," Virgil answered, scooping up some of the bills. "Two, three hundred dollars here at least— maybe more."

"Chicken feed!" spat Gnarled Teeth.

All eyes swung to him.

"I'm on to your tricks, old man," Gnarled Teeth said to the professor. "How many times I have to tell you I been watchin' you. You think I don't know a plant when I see one? Your take from all these minin' camps you been hittin' has been a helluva better than that." He jabbed the muzzle of his rifle threateningly. "So you pitched out what you *wanted* us to settle for.... Now where's the *real* stash?"

"I—I don't know what you're talking about," stammered Hanratty. "We take in money, yes, but there are expenses—feed for the mules, ingredients for my elixir—"

Gnarled Teeth swung his Winchester and fired a round into the nearest mule, shattering the poor beast's brain. Molly screamed as the shot rang out. The stricken animal emitted a soft snort and then its legs buckled and it collapsed heavily to the ground. The mule harnessed next to it pawed and jerked wildly for a moment but was held in check by the weight of its fallen mate and by Hugo hauling back hard on the reins. "You murderer! You bastard!" Hugo wailed at Gnarled Teeth.

"There. Now I cut down part of your expense," Gnarled Teeth proclaimed. "Best shut up that loud-mouthed lame-brain, Professor, or my next bullet goes in him."

Molly fell against McMahon, sobbing. "Make them stop! No more shooting—Don't let them hurt Hugo."

"All right," McMahon said, patting the girl comfortingly as he addressed Gnarled Teeth. "That's enough. You win, you bastard.... You're right, there's more money to be had."

Hanratty looked aghast. "McMahon...stop and think...all we worked for, the money we put away for Molly's operation...."

McMahon shook his head. "It ain't worth it, Professor. What does any of that mean if this scum decides to cut us all down.... And he will, sure as can be, just as cold as he pulled on that poor dumb mule."

"Damn betcha I will," Gnarled Teeth confirmed.

"What's to stop him from killing us all anyway?" Hanratty protested.

"No guarantee," allowed McMahon, giving another faint head shake. "But it's damn certain he will if he thinks we're holdin' out on him."

"Ain't no thinkin' left to it now," Gnarled Teeth pointed out. "You done admitted you got more money hid away. The only question left...where is it?"

Grim-faced, McMahon said, "Let me climb down, I'll show you.... You and your boys hold easy on those triggers, right?"

Gnarled Teeth nodded. "Go ahead. Just move real slow and careful-like."

McMahon gave Molly another comforting pat before quitting

the wagon seat. "Everything's gonna to be all right, little girl," he assured her.

"It had better be," Gnarled Teeth said. "Just to be sure, O'Toole"—he gestured to the rider who had moved close to the rear wagon—"you train that rifle gun of yours right on the little cripple. If boxer man tries anything funny, you blow her clean out of that seat, you hear?"

Dropping lightly to the ground, McMahon walked forward to the front wagon. There, he stopped before a large rectangular storage bin that had been fastened to the sideboards on the near side. "What you're askin' for is in here," he said over his shoulder to Gnarled Teeth, as he began untying the ropes that were lashed around the bin to hold its lid shut.

"Mackie-boy, are you sure about what you're doing?" asked Hanratty edgily.

"Trust me, Professor. This is our best chance."

"That's right. Trust the boxer man," said Gnarled Teeth, "and while you're at it keep your whinin' trap shut."

McMahon wrestled off the lid to the storage bin and let it drop to the ground. Dust puffed up from the rocky footing and swirled in the cold wind. Then he began rummaging in the bin, in time scooping out an armload of small burlap pouches, which he turned and also dumped to the ground. He'd turned back to rummage some more when Gnarled Teeth called sharply.

"Hold up there! What foolery is that? What do you think you're doing?"

McMahon jerked his chin. "The money you want—it's squirreled inside some of those pouches."

"The hell you say! Didn't you hear me tell the old man that I been watchin' your shows? You think I ain't seen how those pouches get used—you knockin' 'em outta the air when they're throwed at you?"

"That's true enough," McMahon allowed. "But that don't mean they still can't have another use too. You never heard of hidin' something in plain sight, where it's least likely to be looked for? I'm tellin' you there are tight balls of money shoved down in the pea gravel inside several of these pouches—the ones tied with red string, the ones we never use as part of the show."

Virgil looked anxiously at Gnarled Teeth. "When he says it like that, it makes sense in a sneaky kind of way. Might be tellin' the truth.... Want me to check some of 'em out, Boss?"

Gnarled Teeth scowled suspiciously. "You go ahead and do that, Virgil," he finally said. "But you hear me, boxer man: I don't real soon see some money spillin' out amidst that pea gravel, I'm gonna take you tryin' to make a fool outta me mighty damn hard—hard on you!"

From where he stood, his right arm still dangling down inside the storage bin, McMahon said, "Let Virgil have his look...you'll get what you're askin' for."

Virgil left the spilled strongbox and went over to the pouches that had been tossed to the ground. He squatted beside them, laying his Winchester down beside his right foot.

"Want me to give him a hand?" asked O'Toole, a greedy gleam forming in his eyes as he watched Virgil reach for the first of the pouches.

That was the opening McMahon had been waiting for—the moment O'Toole shifted his attention off Molly. In a blinding blur of motion, McMahon's arm swung free of the storage bin. In his fist, as he extended the arm out to his right, was gripped a Colt .44 Peacemaker. Twice the gun roared, the shots coming so close together it was almost a single sound. Two bullets streaked out, the first splitting open the forehead of O'Toole, the second catching the other rear rider just under the tip of his nose and blowing away the bottom half of his face. Twisting at the waist, reaching cross-body now, the motion a continuing blur of speed, McMahon sent a third bullet up into the soft pad of flesh under Gnarled Teeth's chin—then on up through his brain, which blew messily out the top of his head, sending his hat flying in the process—before the gang leader even got his rifle raised. That left only Virgil, squatting nearly at McMahon's feet, He tried desperately to retrieve the Winchester he had laid down only moments earlier. McMahon blasted him at point-blank range and sent him flying backward to land in a sprawl.

It was over in mere seconds. Four bodies lay toppled to the ground, forever stilled, before the echoes of the shots were finished reverberating down through the gorge.

Professor Hanratty wore a stunned expression, his mouth hanging agape to the point of barely being able to form words. "Mackie-boy.... Lord, lord.... Where did you?... How did?... Did you kill them all?"

"Wasn't time not to," McMahon answered coolly, as his hands automatically busied themselves pressing out spent shells and then reloading the Peacemaker. He cut his eyes over to Molly. "You all right up there, sweetie?"

Molly, wide-eyed, answered, "I—I'm okay. I'm fine.... Gosh, Mac, where did you learn how to shoot like that?"

McMahon looked away from her questioning gaze and stared off up the gorge for a long minute. Then, in a low voice, he said, "Was a time...back before I joined the show...when my way was to take up the gun pretty regular. Don't care to go into it more than that, really. It's a life I left behind...until today." His eyes fell on Hanratty. "You see, Professor, quick hands are useful for some things other than boxing. For me, that other was drawin' and firin' a gun. But then I made my mind up to quit usin' 'em for that. Never meant to go back to it again, not if I could help it."

"Yet you had the six-gun in the storage bin. When did you put it there, Mackie-boy?"

"Not too long after we started ridin' the minin' camp circuit. Knew there were desperate men to be found on these same trails. Figured havin' a gun stashed close by might be an ace in the hole we'd need some day."

"Thank God for your foresight."

McMahon looked down at the gun in his hand. "Four men are dead because of it.... Don't rightly know if God wants in on any thanks for that."

"You did what needed doing, Mackie-boy. You did what *had*

to be done. It's a dreadful thing to contemplate but you know those vermin wouldn't have ridden away without leaving all of us dead." Hanratty's eyes flicked meaningfully toward Molly and then, in a lowered voice, he added, "...or worse."

* * * * * *

They camped right there in the gorge that night. The bodies of the four highwaymen were dragged away and buried under a pile of loose rocks tumbled down from a jagged shelf. Their horses were tied on behind the rear wagon to be sold off, along with the saddles, in the next mining camp. In the morning, just before first light, Hugo got up and began digging a proper grave for his slaughtered mule. It was grueling, hard work in the rocky ground but the powerful young giant was determined to see it done. McMahon pitched in to help. Once the carcass had been dragged to the opening and covered over, they stood in a circle and the professor said a simple yet sincere prayer. Hugo wept.

After that they struck camp and prepared to roll out. Part of the load from the front wagon, now pulled by only a single mule, had been lightened and transferred to the rear wagon. A cold, raw wind was howling down out of the higher elevations this morning and whistling into the gorge, pushing them on their way.

Bundled in a heavy blanket on the seat beside McMahon, Molly said, "How long before we get to the next minin' town, Mac?"

"Be there by evening, I expect," replied McMahon. "We'll do our show, then that'll be the end of it for a spell. We'll head on down to the flats somewhere and lay over until spring."

"I'm looking forward to that."

"Me, too, little girl."

Molly frowned. "But you'll still have to fight one more time. Tomorrow night. Won't you?"

"That's the way it works."

"I sure hope you won't have to get all cut up again."

They were rolling past the jumble of rocks covering the bodies of the would-be robbers.

Molly averted her eyes. But McMahon didn't. He fixed the spot with an icy glare and let it linger there. Then, facing front again, he clucked softly to the mules and said, "Don't fret over it, gal. Cuts got a way of healin'.... Most things do, in time."

A LITTLE TOO MUCH HEART

BY STAN TRYBULSKI

1.

"Think you're ready for another fight, Bobby?" I asked the kid.

"Sure, I should be on next Friday's undercard, what with all those bums and canvasbacks they have listed."

"You been in the gym lately?" McCarthy prodded him.

"Everyday. Run there and back, too."

"You finally learn how to slip a jab?" McCarthy asked him.

"I can slip yours," Bobby said. He was smiling but I could see he didn't especially like McCarthy needling him.

"How's your weight?" I asked, changing the subject.

"One-fifty-five," Bobby said. "I've been keeping it under one-sixty."

"Can you get it down quickly?" He fought as a welterweight.

"Why? You hear something?"

"Álvarez was cut sparring this morning. Over his left eye. His manager's talking it down but I hear it's a bad one. The promoter is looking for a substitute. I heard he called Harry, your manager."

"That's the main event at the Felt Forum. He's up against Georgie Adams."

Álvarez was a Mexican kid from Coney Island who loved

to mix it up. A real crowd pleaser who took chances and would take two punches to land one. Adams had been the welter title holder, losing by TKO last year to the current champ. He was on the comeback trail to a title rematch and Álvarez was the perfect opponent. Except, Álvarez liked to mix it up in the gym too and eyebrow cuts being what they are, he trained himself out of a good pay day.

The three of us, Bobby Colón, Mike McCarthy, and I were in McSorley's. There was a trio of tourists sitting at the next table to us. They had been drinking long before we got there and their table top was filled with empty ale mugs. They were two men and a blonde woman. The woman was sitting closest to Bobby.

"You a fighter?" she said, leaning towards him. Her words were slightly slurred from the ale.

He ignored her.

"You don't look like a fighter." She tapped him on the shoulder.

"Ease up, lady," I said. "We're just here to relax, so why don't you do the same."

"Fighter," she continued. "He's no fighter."

One of the men at the table looked over at me. "What kind of fighter trains on ale?"

Bobby still said nothing.

"You ever heard of Chuck Wepner?" McCarthy asked.

"The Bayonne Bleeder?" the man said. "He's before my time."

"Yeah, but not hers."

Richie the front room waiter brought us our ales, setting two mugs of dark each down in front of McCarthy and I, ginger ale in front of Bobby, then cleared away the mugs on the other table. He studied the trio of faces, trying to decide whether to give them refills or cut them off.

Bobby's cell phone went off and he reached into his trousers' pocket and took it out. Flipping it open, he held it to his ear.

"Great," Bobby said, "see you in the morning." He closed up the cell phone.

"Who was it?" McCarthy asked.

"Harry."

"Well?"

"He said to start losing weight."

"You mean he signed you to fight Adams?" I asked him.

Bobby grinned.

"He's a lefty," McCarthy said. "You've never boxed a lefty."

"There's a first time for everything," I said.

Before his last fight, Bobby had been training in a small gym up in the Bronx. He lost an eight-round decision on an Atlantic City casino undercard to Jersey Joe Kernan, a local kid who could sell tickets. He banged Kernan around the ring the first couple of rounds, ripping him with vicious body shots, but for some reason couldn't finish him off. Still, Bobby should have easily won the decision but was jobbed. Superstitious, he changed gyms and now trained at Biff's in Brooklyn. Biff's was a larger gym, occupying an entire two-story building under the shadow of the Brooklyn Bridge. It had better equipment and better fighters, which meant that the local promoters came around more often to check the talent out. So as far as I was concerned, the loss in AC had been a good thing for him. He seemed to agree, something had changed in him after that fight. He worked harder than ever in the gym and out of the ring, he was quiet, serious.

I bent down and scooped up a handful of sawdust from the floor. "Let's get out of here. It's getting too hot." I liked McSorley's and didn't want to get into a brawl here and I sure didn't want Bobby getting into a fight and busting his hands up on some boozed up clown's face.

"Pussy," the tourist keeps on, talking at Bobby's back as we headed for the door. "Drinking ginger ale like a little girl."

Outside, the afternoon sun was lower and the air felt cool and fresh. I was zipping up my leather jacket when I heard the tavern doors swing open and the drunk's sour voice. "Pussy. You're no fighter, you're a pussy."

I turned and saw him standing in the doorway, an empty

glass mug in his right hand. His buddy was just behind him. I reached into my pockets and took out a set of keys and tossed them to Bobby.

"Do me a favor," I told him. "My Cherokee is parked over on East 6th. Go get it and drive it around and pick us up."

"Are you sure?"

"Sure as the sun's going to come up tomorrow." He still hesitated. "Go on," I said, "it's okay." I watched him disappear around the corner and then I turned back to the other men.

"You must be the daddy," he said to me, "sending little sonny boy off before he gets hurt." He looked over at McCarthy. "And you must be the mommy." He stepped out onto the sidewalk.

"Why don't you just go back inside?" I said.

"After we kick your asses and you apologize for insulting my wife." He charged toward me, his hand holding the mug raised, ready to swing at my head.

I threw the handful of sawdust into his face and as he tried to wipe it away I landed a pro field goal kick to his groin. He fell to his knees and grabbed his crotch. I started to follow up with a kick to his head but stopped. He wasn't going to be a problem so I left him kneeling there, holding his crotch and making strange whooping sounds. McCarthy had waited for the other man to come toward him and when he did, McCarthy let him swing and stepped inside and ripped an uppercut to his nose. Blood exploded all over the sidewalk and the man squealed in pain.

"You broke my nose," he whimpered.

"No, I didn't," McCarthy said, planting his feet and landing a straight right. "Now, I did." The punch sent the man sprawling over a series of garbage cans and down a small flight of steps that led to a basement.

The street fell silent except for the strange whooping sound coming from the man who was holding his crotch. Then, I could hear the roar of an engine as my Cherokee came barreling down the block. Bobby braked when we reached us and we piled into the jeep and drove back to Brooklyn. Bobby wanted to hit Biff's steam room and try and take another half-pound off.

McCarthy was flushed from the street fight and on the way to Brooklyn he started needling Bobby again. "You'd have to make the jump to ten rounds," he said from the back seat. "You've never gone ten rounds. That's a big haul against a fighter like Adams. Ten long rounds. Of course, the fight might end sooner. Adams likes to pump his jab real fast. Doubles and triples it. You can't block them all."

"You don't know what I can do. Buy a ticket for the fight and see what I can do."

"I just might do that," McCarthy said. "Front row."

"I saw him get knocked out," Bobby said. "That fight took a lot out of him. He's thirty-four and after the fight he looked it."

"Oh, don't worry about him," McCarthy said, "he's well trained. He wants that title back."

"What makes you think I'm worried?" He stared at McCarthy. "Say, you're a southpaw. You want some work?"

"Sparring with you? Sure."

"Be here tomorrow at eleven a.m. Three rounds."

"Sure you don't want to go ten with me?"

"No, three will do," Bobby said. His voice was calm and I was relieved that McCarthy's needling hadn't got to him.

After McCarthy left, we went upstairs and Bobby got a fresh towel and stripped and put his clothes in the locker. I asked Bobby what else Harry had said on the phone.

"Twenty large," Bobby said. "Adam's manager said he saw me fight in AC and he liked my style, said he knew I would be fighting on short notice and offered twenty thou."

I had forgotten that Adams had managed one of the main event fighters on the Atlantic City card. He must have seen Bobby in the prelim. "I want you working my corner for this one," he said. "You're cut will be fifteen hundred."

"Is that okay with Harry?

"Screw Harry. He's just gets the fights. Your money is coming out of my end anyway. So if I say you get fifteen hundred, you get fifteen hundred."

I walked with him to the steam room. "No more than fifteen

minutes," I told him. "And don't rehydrate all the way afterwards."

2.

When Bobby and Mike entered the ring, Biff Tucker came over and stood next to me. "Heard Bobby's substituting next week in the Adams fight. Should be a good pay day for him."

Biff ran his gym like boot camp. The gym rules were posted on every wall and were to be obeyed. Dues were to be paid on the first of the month and on the second; any locker with unpaid dues had its lock clipped and the contents tossed in the trash. While Biff loved the boxing game, he knew it was a business and maintained that any fighter that didn't know it was a business didn't belong in his gym.

I went over to Mike's corner to talk to him before they sparred. He had a funny look on his face.

"You think he's still pissed off about last night? I was just cracking on him to have a little fun; I didn't mean anything by it?"

"Don't worry about it," I said. "I want you to stay out of range and double and triple your jabs when he closes, just like Adams will. Let's see what Bobby has today."

McCarthy nodded and slipped the mouthpiece in. When the bell sounded he was up but Bobby was already in the center of the ring. McCarthy circled, staying away, the funny look still on his face. Bobby was having none of it. He danced left, then right, each step closing the distance, cutting McCarthy off. Mike suddenly found himself near the corner and pumped out a double jab with his right, trying to keep Bobby away until he could move off. Bobby slid to his left just before the second jab and ripped a vicious hook to McCarthy's midsection, following with a second hook upstairs and that landed flush on McCarthy's head gear. Even through the padding Mike was stunned and when he tried to turn and face Bobby, his movement was awkward and off balance. Bobby threw a straight right that landed flush on McCarthy's cheek, driving him into the ropes.

"Move off the ropes, Mikey," I yelled at McCarthy, "You're getting paid for three rounds of sparring."

He tried moving away but Bobby was back in front of him, sending another left hook, this time to the liver and the sound made everyone in the gym stop and look towards the ring. Just in time to see the second hook come over the top and land again on the side of McCarthy's head, a sold thwack on the padding.

Bobby then threw a three-punch combination: a right, a left hook and another right, and when McCarthy tried to slip the first right, the left hook caught him flush on the nose and the right slammed into his cheek bone. Bobby danced back into the center of the ring and motioned at Mike to come after him.

"Just keep pumping that jab, Mikey," I yelled, watching McCarthy shuffle towards the center of the ring where Bobby was dancing, a smile on his face. He was measuring McCarthy, waiting for him to step inside the punching arc and when he sensed McCarthy was there, he double jabbed first, both punches hitting Mike on the nose, causing a bright red stream of blood to flow. McCarthy stepped back and pawed at his nose with a glove and stared at the bloody smear on the leather.

I knew now that the funny look on his face was the look of fear. Bobby knew it too and stepped in and threw two more jabs before sliding around the counter left McCarthy automatically sent back. Bobby bent underneath the extended arm and delivered a hard right hook that some might have called a kidney punch. McCarthy dropped to a knee and stayed there, unable to move, and the bell sounded.

Back in the corner, Bobby was breathing easily. I tilted the water bottle and he rolled the liquid around in his mouth. "Just keep slipping the jab," I told him, "but you don't have to unload on him with everything you have."

"Why not? I'm paying him to fight three rounds. So let's see the fat fuck fight."

"Let's see that he makes it then." I walked over to McCarthy's corner.

"How do you feel?" I asked him.

"My ribs hurt real bad, I think something's broke."

"Nothing's broke; you're just a little of out shape. Keep moving and jabbing but this time close the distance once in a while and hook and give him some straight rights. Let's see how he can handle that."

McCarthy nodded. He might be scared of Bobby's power but he wasn't a quitter. The bell sounded and he moved slowly off his stool and started toward the center of the ring where Bobby was waiting. This time he danced right, then left and moved in on Bobby first and snapped out a couple of jabs that hit Bobby's gloves. Bobby glided again around McCarthy's right, forcing him to turn and punch. When he did, Bobby threw the double left hook again, right to the solar plexus and upstairs to the nose. Blood started streaming again and McCarthy instinctively pawed at the swollen proboscis with his left glove. But as McCarthy turned Bobby had danced back around so that he was now at an angle where he ripped another solid left hook to the liver, and then again in the same spot. McCarthy dropped to both knees and rolled over.

Bobby stood over him for a moment and then walked away.

I jumped into the ring and ran over to McCarthy and waved my hands. "It's over for today."

A couple of fighters came into the ring and helped McCarthy back into the locker room. I walked over to the corner where Bobby was sitting, his head gear was off and a wide grin was spread across his face.

"You busted Mike up real good. He's through, he won't be back."

"I was sick of hearing his mouth anyway. So who's next, I'm just getting started."

"That's it, I don't have anyone else. So you're going to work the heavy bag for four rounds and then I want you to run afterwards. Since you're so hungry for a brawl, I'll have two sparring partners for you tomorrow."

That afternoon Harry showed up at the gym. Jack was in the steam trying to knock another half-pound off.

"How's he look?" Harry asked.

"Terrific. He ran five miles and then sparred three tough rounds. I used Mike McCarthy so he could have a lefty to punch at. Don't think McCarthy's coming back. Bobby busted a couple of his ribs."

Harry arched his eyebrows. "The line in Vegas has Adams as the 8-1 favorite."

"That's about right, if you haven't seen Bobby's workouts since his last fight. But the word'll be out about the beating he gave McCarthy today and it should narrow."

Bobby came out of the locker and walked over to us. He was dressed in a sweater and jeans and looked relaxed.

"How do you feel, kid?" Harry asked him.

Bobby smiled. It was a big boyish grin. "I'll be ready. More than ready."

"What did the scale say?" I asked.

"One-fifty-one."

"We've got four days left. You'll make the weight easy. Better lay off the steam room, you'll drop too much. Adams is a natural middleweight now and he's had weeks to come down. After the weigh in, he's going right back up."

"I'll send over another southpaw tomorrow," Harry said. "Someone built more like Adams. Go four rounds with him. Okay?"

Bobby nodded.

"Then go on home and eat a good meal and get a good night's sleep. We'll see you in the morning."

After he left, Harry asked, "Do you really think the odds are going to come down?"

"If you're going to bet on him, call your bookie now."

Word had spread quickly about the beating Bobby had given McCarthy. The next day two sportswriters and a photog showed up at the gym and watched the workout. I wouldn't let the newsies talk to Bobby so they interviewed Harry. He played it cozy, not talking Bobby up or down, only promising that Bobby would make it a good fight.

3.

When Wednesday rolled around, we took a cab to the Garden for the noon weigh in. One-forty-seven was the contract weight for noon, with any fighter not making the weight given until six p.m. to make it at a second weighing.

Bimmy Franco, Adam's manager came over and we shook hands. "This is a great opportunity for you, kid," he said to Bobby. "I know you can't win but make it a good fight. Crowd pleasers always get fights. Isn't that right?" he said that last to me.

"Other than you, who says he can't win?"

Bimmy grinned. "That's right; you gotta have confidence in your fighter. Now let's see what the scale says."

Bobby stepped up on the scale, the towel still wrapped around his waist. "One forty-six even," the official read. "Plenty to spare."

Adams approached the scale, sauntering with the upper torso of a middleweight on his way to becoming a light heavy. His shoulders and arms were massive, his left shoulder and triceps covered by a huge green dragon tattoo. He posed for the news photogs and the dragon's wings rippled as he flexed his muscles.

"Look at his face," I told Bobby, trying to distract him from the obvious size differential. "It's still all marked up from Soto slicing and dicing him for twelve rounds in the title fight. He's as easy to hit as Mike was."

Bobby grinned. "That was pleasure; this is business."

Adams stepped on the scale, smiling for the photog. "What's it say?" Harry asked.

"Just over one-forty-seven." Adams smiled and dropped his towel.

4.

I led Bobby into the arena, his head covered by the cape and his gloves resting on my shoulders and we danced down the aisle to the ring. In the ring, I pulled his cape back and he danced around, throwing combinations at the air.

When the fighters were introduced there was only a smattering of applause and lot of boos for Bobby. The cheers were all for Adams, after all he had been the champ and this was a comeback fight.

"Just fight him like you did Mikey," I told him. "Slip and hook, slip and hook."

Adams smirked as they touched gloves. Bobby just stared at him. Back in the corner, I told him again to take the first round slow, get a sense of his southpaw rhythm. The bell rang and Bobby danced out and met Adams in the center of the ring. Adams came in high with his left carried low, trying to entice Bobby into an early exchange. They circled warily; throwing jabs at each other, Adams landing a pair on Bobby's left cheek. They were moving along one of the sides, Adams keeping his left still low, flicking sharp rights out at Bobby's head and ribs. He was sure he was the faster fighter but was surprised when Bobby suddenly threw two right hooks, landing both of them, the second right under Adam's left ear, causing him to cover up against the ropes.

"Don't punch yourself out," I said to him in the corner. Jimmy rubbed extra Vaseline on his left cheek, covering the bright red spot where Adams's jabs had hit their mark. "And get your jab off first, force him to counter from that low position."

Bobby winked at me as he got off his stool for the second round, ready to go before the bell sounded. I could see Adams still seated on his stool.

Both fighters were still cautious, mainly trading jabs, looking for any weaknesses that they might exploit. Near the end of the round, Bobby double-jabbed at Adams's nose and Adams threw a counter right hook, catching Bobby on the left cheek. I could see the flesh swelling almost instantaneously.

"You're doing great," I said when he came back to the corner, his cheek looking a ripe peach. "Don't talk, just listen. Keep landing on the dragon, you'll bring his left down further. Then you can double hook him before he can get his arm up. And slip his jab, for chrissakes, you can't block them all."

When Adams came out for the third round, he was holding his right higher. Bobby's jabs were getting to him. I could see his nose and right cheekbone were swelling and if we were lucky, Bobby's hooks would rip the flesh wide open. Adams was smart though and even though he kept his hands high, he could sense when Bobby would try and slip his jab and move to the left and instead of doubling his right, hooked the second punch as Bobby slid to the side, landing solidly and driving against the ropes. He managed to land a three-punch combination to Bobby's head before being tied up. But he didn't show much after that, content to stay outside, jabbing and when Bobby would move forward, he grabbed at his arms, tying him up.

By the fourth round, Bobby was giving Adams a real contest. They were in close, trading jabs, and when Adams tried to clinch, Bobby slapped his arm down and threw a left and right hook to Adam's ribs. He was bringing the left up for a hook to the head when suddenly he stopped and sank down and then just as suddenly bounced back up and danced away. The referee waved Adams to a neutral corner and picked up the count.

"Did you see the punch?" I asked Jimmy the cutman. He shook his head.

"His knees didn't even hit the canvas," I said.

"I couldn't tell," Jimmy said.

"It was a slip," I yelled at the ref who was wiping off Bobby's gloves.

Adams was bouncing up and down in the neutral corner, smacking his gloves. The lust for victory filled his face.

"What happened? Didn't you see the punch?" I asked him at the end of the round.

"His kids," he sighed, as Jimmy toweled off his chest.

"Whaddya mean his kids?"

"His kids are at the fight. They're in the second row with his wife. I just saw them."

"So what?"

"I can't hurt a guy in front of his kids," Bobby said. "That's why I couldn't take Kernan out in AC. His wife and little girl were there. Otherwise, I could have ended it in the third round."

"Jeezus Christ," Jimmy said.

I said the same thing. No wonder Bimmy wanted Bobby as a substitute. He was at the AC fight and must have seen something in Bobby's eyes. Maybe Bobby had looked at Kernan's wife and daughter and then stopped slugging. Bimmy must have put two and two together and made sure that Mrs. Adams and the two little boys had seats up real close where Bobby couldn't fail to miss them. And it was working.

The ref came over to the corner. "He got clipped with a left hook," he said to me.

"In your dreams," I said.

The ring doctor was at the apron, leaning over the ropes and looking into Bobby's eyes with a flashlight.

"Put that goddam thing away," I said, "he wasn't knocked down."

The doc ignored me. "Well," he said quietly to Bobby, "how do you feel?"

"I'm all right, he didn't knock me down, he stepped on my foot and I tripped."

When the bell rang I looked away from Bobby's face, afraid to see what might be in his eyes. I pulled him off the stool, my eyes fixed on Adams's wife. She was holding one of her boys on her lap, the other seated next to her. There was no way Bobby wasn't going to see her.

"Jimmy," I said to the cutman. "Go find the usher for that section and tell him there's an emergency. That Adams's home is burning and that the police are looking for Mrs. Adams; she needs to call them right away."

"You got it."

I turned back to the fight. Adams had reached the center of the ring first. Bobby stayed outside his reach, jabbing, circling, trying to keep away, but Adams closed the gap and every time Bobby jabbed, the other fighter threw combination counter left hooks, landing solid punches to the body and head, making me wince as I heard the thuds.

"Move away!" I yelled. But Adams was still light on his feet, cutting the ring off, and had abandoned the jab, punching hard, trying to take Bobby out. He landed another double hook to the ribs, causing Bobby to hold on. I could see the body shots were starting to take their toll. The ref separated them and as soon as he stepped aside, Adams weaved back in, throwing a jab at Bobby's left cheek, followed by left and right hooks to Bobby's head. He was in danger of going down again when the bell rang.

"You've got to punch back," I told him in the corner. "He's standing straight, unloading from the outside, with his left all the way down at his waist. Just step to your left and get inside and upper cut him. It'll be lights out."

"I can't do it in front of his kids."

"This isn't Kernan you're fighting. This guy is going to take you out if you don't try and take him out first."

He nodded. "I know."

"Then start punching again, dammit."

When the bell rang he was back out there all right but it seemed his heart wasn't in it any longer. After taking a couple of jabs in the kisser, he clinched and was content to waltz Adams around the ring, oblivious to the boos coming from the crowd. That was pretty much the story of the whole round. Bobby taking jabs in the face and then clinching. The ref was looking at him as if he felt something might be wrong with him.

"How do you feel?" I asked him when he came back to the corner at the end of the sixth round.

"Great," he said, spitting out his mouthpiece.

He didn't look that great. The welt under his left eye was larger now and turning purple, swollen like an overripe plum ready to burst. It was forcing his lower eyelid shut and I was worried the ring doc would be back to check it out, saying Bobby couldn't continue.

"Look. Look out at the seats. His wife and kids are gone."

Bobby turned and squinted. "You're right," he mumbled. "They are gone."

"So get back out there and bust this guy up like you busted up Mike." I rubbed his legs while Jimmy pressed the endswell against the bruise. "Go for his body. You had it right when you said he was thirty-four. Age him, make his body feel every punch. He's thrown a lot of punches and he's tired. You can finish him."

Bobby nodded. The gleam was back in his eyes.

He was up before the bell rang and went right after Adams in the center of the ring. He threw a solid straight left to Adams's nose followed by a hard right hook that Adams couldn't duck. The fighter was wobbled and grabbed for Bobby's arms and clinched. Blood spurted from his nose where the left had landed. I could see Bobby looking out of the corner of his eye at the seats where Adam's wife and kids had been sitting. He winked at me.

"His nose is broken!" I yelled.

After the ref broke them up, Adams backpedaled, using up time, staying away from Bobby's punches, taking boos from the crowd instead.

At the end of the seventh round, Bobby was breathing hard, his rib cage one reddened mass from the punches Adams had landed. Condition was everything and I was worried. But Adams was no longer hooking or throwing straight rights, concentrating on protecting his smashed in nose and trying to go the distance for the decision. He was slower too and Bobby was slipping the jab and right-stepping him again. Just before the bell, he turned Adams and there was plenty of zip in his right hook when it landed solidly to the other fighter's side.

"Kidney punch, kidney punch," came the shouts from Adams's corner.

The ref waved them off but between rounds the corner kept it up, Bimmy screaming foul at the ref who ignored him.

In the eighth, Adams was retreating, trying to dance away. Bobby stepped in and hooked him with a left and tried to follow up with a right but Adams was inside him and reached up and pulled Bobby's head down. The referee separated them and gave Adams a warning as the crowd booed.

Bobby moved in again and slipped a jab, ripping another right hook to Adams's side and the fighter visibly slowed, his elbows down protecting his right side. Screams of kidney punch erupted again from Adams's corner and the ref cautioned Bobby to be careful with the right hook. The fighters were back in the center of the ring and Bobby took a couple of solid punches to the body from Adams so he could land one of his own to the other fighter's nose. Blood sprayed out over the crowd and I knew Adams wouldn't try that again.

At the end of the eighth round Bobby was slow as he came back to the corner. "It's close," I told him. "He's not looking good. He's slowed. He's more tired than you. The bleeding from his nose won't stop, you busted it up real good. He's going have to take you out if he wants that title rematch. You can't afford to cover up. But neither can he. He's going to have to stop protecting his nose and punch. I want you to counter with straight lefts and rights to the center of his face. Something will hit his nose. Then hook him with both hands. Can you give me a four punch combo? Can you do that?" I was yelling at him. "You can win this fight now, in this round, but you've got to go all out. He's not going to quit, you're going have to take him out. Four punches! Four fucking punches!" I held four fingers up in front of his face.

He nodded at me and smiled. I couldn't believe it. The kid had been in the fight of his life, had taken a terrific beating in the middle rounds and he was smiling at me. I had to smile back. The kid sure had a lot of heart.

The bell rang and I hauled him off of the stool, practically shoving him out into the ring. In Adams's corner, they were doing the same thing to their man. His massive shoulders were slumped and the blue of his boxing shorts was streaked with smears of wet blood. He was moving away from Bobby who was tried to cut the ring off and corner him.

"Oh, shit!" Jimmy yelled behind me.

I turned. He was pointing out into the seats, to the aisle where Bimmy was leading Mrs. Adams and the two kids back to their seats.

"Stop them before Bobby's sees them."

Jimmy jumped off the ring apron and went over to a vendor hawking beer to the crowd. He grabbed a large container and ran up the aisle and threw the foamy liquid in the Adams woman's face.

"You sonofabitch," Bimmy shouted while taking a swing at Jimmy. Mrs. Adams was wiping away the beer from her face while trying to kick Jimmy at the same time. The two kids started crying and I could see a mass of uniformed security rushing down the aisle toward the melee. Jimmy counterpunched Bimmy and then rammed his shoulder into him, sending him back into Mrs. Adams who fell down in the aisle with Bimmy landing on top of her.

The cops were all over of them, dragging Jimmy, Mrs. Adams, Bimmy and the two kids back up the aisle and out of the arena. Mrs. Adams, thoroughly infuriated by her dousing with beer, kept trying to reach over one of the cops to punch Jimmy, all the while screaming profanities that had the crowd laughing.

In the ring, Bobby was on his toes throwing straight lefts and right like I had told him. Adams must have heard his wife screaming, he was distracted for a moment and Bobby came down off of his toes, using a flat-footed stance to muster all the power he could in ripping two solid left hooks to the body. He tried following upstairs but Adams was kept his right glove high, protecting his nose.

Bobby was back on his toes, circling, then suddenly went flat footed again and threw another hook to the liver and followed with another hook to the head that again landed on Adam's glove. Adams tried jabbing to keep Bobby away but the jabs were tired, half-hearted and Bobby slipped around them as he had McCarthy's. I could see Adam's right side clearly now, there was sickly bulge like a thin inner tube protruding between a couple of swollen ribs.

"Four punches," I yelled at Bobby. "Give me four punches." The kid had the heart to do it, I just knew it.

Bobby had the angle and threw a left hook around the right jab, the solid noise booming through the auditorium, causing the crowd to gasp. Adams hunched over and Bobby glided two steps the other way and threw two right hooks to the liver. This time, Adams's left glove moved down in automatic response to the pain and Bobby threw another right hook that smashed Adams's nose against his cheekbone. Adams dropped to the floor, bent over, choking on his blood. He spit out his mouthpiece as the ref stood over him waving his arms that the fight was over.

I ran over to Bobby and lifted hum up in the air. "You did it kid, you've got more heart than any fighter I've worked with."

He was laughing. "Five. I gave you five."

"What?"

"You asked me for four more punches, I gave you five."

I started laughing too. "Like I said, you've got heart."

Harry was in the ring now, rushing over and pumping Bobby's hand. "The crowd loves you," he said. "You won them over."

Bob Arum was right behind Harry, shaking Bobby's hand. "Great fight, kid. You got a lot of heart." A broad smile was on his face. He turned to Harry. "Think your boy is ready for Margarito?"

"Does he have any kids?" I asked. Bobby might just have a little too much heart.

BLOOD FEUD

BY RON FORTIER

Danny Sinclair ducked under the flying right cross and brought his own right into his opponent's ribs with a powerful jab. His sparring partner, Jake Olivio, grunted and tried to cover up allowing Danny to follow up with a left hook to the head. Shaking off the blow, the bigger Olivio dropped his helmet covered head and charged. It was a familiar move, trying to push the younger fighter back into the ropes and negate his speed by shortening the ring.

Danny felt the rubber coated rope dig into his shoulder blades as Olivio began pounding away at his midsection, or attempted to. Danny pulled his arms in tight, elbows together to block the punches and lessen their effect.

"Come on, Danny, push him off!" Arnie Demitt yelled from somewhere behind and below him in his squeaky soprano voice. "Push him off!"

Easier said then done, Danny thought, amused by his manager's verbal barrage. If it were so easy, why didn't he climb in the ring a take this pummeling?

Danny bit down on his mouth guard and pushed Olivio off long enough to skip around him and get free. In the process he threw a quick left into the big man's ribs. No sense in wasting an open shot.

The bell rang, its steel ping loud and clear in the cavernous gym. Olivio and Danny stopped and nodded to each other.

"You got some nice moves there," Olivio said, spitting the

mouth guard into his glove. "Pretty soon you'll be as fast as Chip."

"Don't count on it," an all too familiar voice added from ringside.

Danny turned to see his older brother, Charles "Chip" Sinclair standing there with his latest tart, a blonde named Lisa Martel. She clung to his arm, mashing her oversized tits into him like a pond leech. Danny never understood Chip's taste in women. Then again, a lifetime of *Playboy* and *Penthouse* mags stuffed under their beds properly explained it all too well. After winning the middleweight crown eight months earlier, the brash, talented boxer had found he had his pick of the ladies. A temptation he gave into readily.

"Give me a few more matches," Danny warned as he climbed down out of the ring. "And who knows, I might just surprise you."

"Sorry, kid, but there's only one champeen belt, and it's all mine."

Standing so close together, it was physically obvious that these two young men were of the same bloodline. Each was six feet tall with a lean, hard body, their faces almost identical, except Chip's hair was dark and straight while his younger brother, by a year and a half, had light brown hair that curled when he sweated. But both had the same hard jaw, thin nose and lively brown eyes. Both were boxing junkies by the time they were in their teens. Father Conklin at Saint Martin's often likened them to the battling apostles, John and James, calling them the "The Fighting Sons of Thunder."

"Still, think of the purse, big brother," Danny grinned. "A Sinclair versus Sinclair match up would pack the house. We could clean up big, no matter who won."

A dark scowl descended over Chip's handsome face. "Sometimes kid, I wonder what happened to your brains. We're family. I don't fight family."

"Aw, come on, Chip, I was just pulling your leg. You know that."

"Right." The scowl dissipated slowly. "But some things just ain't funny, Danny."

Before either of them could continue their filial debate, one of the towel boys called over, "Hey, Chip, Mr. Gladman wants to see you up his office."

Bill Gladman owned the gym and contracts to ten of its finest pugilist, including the Sinclairs. When he said jump, they asked how high.

"Tell him I'm coming," Chip responded before asking his Danny, "I've got a table reserved at the Spaghetti Castle for dinner tonight. Maybe you and Pops can join us?"

"I'll ask him when I get home and give you a call." Danny still lived at home with their father, Paul Sinclair, a retired steel worker. Their mother had died of cancer when they were still in high school and it was "Pops" who had pulled them through those days of pain and loss. He was as devoted to his boys and they were to him.

"Great. I'll expect your call. Now hit the showers, you stink, little brother."

"You ain't no sweet petunia either," Danny wrinkled his nose. "What is that you got on, ode da skunk."

"It's French cologne," Chip held up his arms as if modeling. "At twenty bucks a bottle, drives the broads nuts. Ain't that so, sweetie."

"It certainly works for me," Lisa confirmed, reaching up to kiss his cheek. "Makes me want to eat you all up right here and now."

"See what I mean, kid?"

Danny thought he'd vomit. Lisa was a gold-digger of the first order. It amazed him Chip couldn't see that. Then again, maybe he did and just didn't care as long as the sex was good. Danny did have to admit, with her chassis, she was most likely very, very good at bed Olympics.

"Yeah, yeah. See yah later."

* * * * * * *

"So when's my next fight?" Chip asked Bill Gladman as the promoter poured himself a whiskey from his mini-bar to the right of his ornate, teak wood desk. The champ and his blonde were seated in the deep leather chairs facing it.

Gladman had the look of the classic fat man, short, rotund, decked out in fancy, tailor-made suits. His hair, what was left of it, was gray and his eyebrows looked like overgrown brushes shading his eye over the thick glasses he wore. It was the façade of the harmless soul who loved life and eating in equal parts. When Gladman had first entered into the fight business, he'd learned that people tended to underestimate his true business savvy because of his looks. It was a fact he cultivated to the max.

"What's the hurry, Chip?" Gladman put down his drink and poured a second for Lisa. Booze was off limits to the champ. "We've still got plenty of time before you need to get back into the ring."

"That ain't what you told me after I knocked out Meldoni. You said that I needed to stay out there so that the papers would keep playing things up."

"I know, Chip, but the truth is, I'm not at all happy with the lackluster crop of contenders out there right now." Gladman handed Lisa her drink and went around the desk to sit in his own chair.

"What's that suppose to mean?" Chip was easily confused by how the business end of the boxing game worked. All he cared about was climbing into that square arena and going at it with his next opponent.

"It means the only boxers with enough decent wins to qualify as real challengers are chumps and their records are weak. None of them could give you a real fight. And we certainly don't want to make you look bad now, do we?"

"Well, no, I suppose not." Chip scratched his chin. "So what then? I just sit around training all the time?"

Gladman's eyes blinked through his glasses as he swallowed the aged alcohol. He put his glass down and wiped his mouth with the back of his hand. He was clearly setting something up, that much the champ could see.

"Well, if you would reconsider the possibility of fighting Danny as we discussed last week."

"What, not you too! I just went over that with the kid not ten minutes ago down in the gym. Are you two in cahoots or something?"

"Only in that we both seem to have come to the same conclusion as the same time."

"I don't want to hear this, Gladman."

"You're being unreasonable, Chip. A bout between you and Danny would be big news. It would draw a packed house and most likely put you on national television. Think about that for a second."

Gladman was warming to his subject, his hands weaving through the air like a snake charmer. "Why we'd clean up on the licenses alone. And I'm talking millions here, champ, you understand that, millions."

"Because I beat up my own brother."

"I know, it's twisted, but you know as well as I do folks go for that kind of soap opera crap. Hell, it's even biblical. I mean, the first recorded crime was when Cain killed his own brother, Abel. Right?"

"Jesus, Gladman, that's sick. I ain't gonna kill Danny."

"You know what I meant. I was just speaking figuratively. Still a match like this could set you both up for life. Think about that. You and Danny would have more money then you'd know what to do with."

"No." The word came out of Chip's mouth like a lead weight and instantly stopped Gladman in mid spiel. The boxer's resolve was etched on his face. Gladman knew it all too well.

"Alright, have it your way, champ. Still, you're making a big mistake here."

"It's my call, Gladman. Are we through now? I want to get in some bag work this afternoon." Chip was already out of his chair.

"Yeah, sure. We're through. Go on."

Chip looked at Lisa and she held up her half empty drink. "Mind if I finish this first, sweetie. I'll be down in a minute."

"Suit yourself."

After the door closed behind Sinclair, Lisa took a sip from her drink and uncrossed her shapely legs, aware Gladman was leering at them.

"Chip can be very stubborn at times," she said coyly.

"Tell me about it. He's blowing one hell of a paycheck for all of us."

"Well, maybe I could help you out a little."

Gladman's attention sharpened instantly. He'd always suspected there was more to Lisa then her boobs and long legs. She too was good at wearing masks.

"How so?"

"You never mind that, Mr.Gladman. I just want to know how much it's worth to you?"

"What?"

"This fight between Chip and Danny. Would you pay ten grand to see it happen?"

"In a flash, lady. Are you telling me you can do that?"

"Yes, I can. You just get your big old check book ready."

When Lisa smiled, Gladman recalled another biblical figure, Delilah.

* * * * * * *

Danny had stayed in the shower a few minutes longer than usual, letting the warm spray ease the tension in his nerves. Chip was so bull-headed, it frustrated him. Still, he had always looked up to his older brother and it was a habit hard to break, no matter if he thought he was right.

In the locker room, he'd put on his socks and pants when he heard someone enter from the hall door. He assumed it was just another fighter and was buckling his belt when Lisa stepped around the row of lockers and surprised him.

"What are you doing back here? Dames aren't allowed in here."

"I just needed to talk to you, Danny," she said hesitantly, coming closer, her head bowed. "It will only take a minute."

"Talk about what?"

"About us." She kept getting closer. "I always get the feeling you don't like me, Danny."

"That's because I don't," he said bluntly. What the hell was she after?

"Why do you have to be like that? I've never done anything to you, have I?"

She was standing in front of him, her rose scented perfume filling the air. He was acutely aware he was bare-chested and it made him feel awkward.

"Look, Lisa, we both know you're only after Chip's money. He probably knows it too, though I'm thinking he really doesn't care one way or another."

"Then why do you?" She reached out her right hand and touched the muscles of his upper chest. "We're just having fun."

"There's more to life than just fun."

"My, my, you are such an uptight prick, aren't you?"

The words stung him and he grabbed her arms. "Get the hell out of here, now!"

"Oh, Danny, we could be good for each other."

"Right." He let her go only to have her throw her arms around his neck and pull his head down.

Then her mouth was on his and they were kissing. He was confused, caught totally by surprise. Her lips parted and her tongue was in his mouth. Danny's thoughts were spinning crazily.

He heard the footsteps at the last possible moment. Suddenly Lisa was pushing him away and yelling, "Stop it, Danny!"

Her hand shot out and slapped him across the face just as Chip and his trainer, Stan Beronski came around the corner. Dressed in a tee-shirt and sweat pants, Chip had been working on the speed bag and now had a towel draped around his neck.

"What dah...hell?" Chip was frozen in place trying to take the tableau of his brother and his girl breaking from a clinch.

Lisa looked like she was going to start crying. "He asked me to meet him here, Chip. Said he wanted to talk about something. Then he just grabbed me and started to put his hands all over me. I told him to stop, but he wouldn't listen. Oh, God."

Danny blinked. The words coming out of her mouth spewed forth like bullets from a machine gun with an even deadlier result.

"She's lying!" he blurted, realizing how lame he sounded, especially with the dame going into her hysterical act. "You can't believe her, Chip!"

"Why the hell not?" Chip snapped, moving towards him, his gloved hands swinging by his side. "Why shouldn't I believe her, little brother? You tell me."

"Because she's just a lying slut up to no go...."

Chip's punch caught him on the side of the head and Danny stumbled back almost tripping over the long, wooden dressing bench. For a second he was seeing stars as he tried to shake off the effects of the punch.

But Chip was enraged and came at him with another swing. This one Danny blocked and then jumped out of the way. "Stop it, Chip! I don't want to fight you!"

For his efforts he took another punch, this one on the shoulder which spun him around. Then instinct took over and Danny let fly with a left upper cut that nailed Chip across the right cheek and dazed him.

"Cut it out, you two!" Beronski yelled pushing himself past Lisa and getting in between the two brothers. Chip shoved past him and tried to take another punch only to have Danny deflect with an upper arm block.

Then several other fighters were charging into the room and several of them swarmed over the Champ and pulled him, away from the target of his rage.

"Knock it off," Beronski tried again, this time getting in Chip's face. "This ain't the place for a street brawl, Sinclair.

You want to do that, take it outside."

The words got to Chip and his anger abetted slowly. The men holding his arms released him and stepped back waiting to see if they would be needed again. The boxer glowered at his brother and pointed his gloved fist at him.

"Okay, then, you said you wanted a fight, we'll I'm gonna give you one. How's that grab you?"

"Fine by me," Danny shot back, brushing hair from his forehead.

"Good, then it's settled." Chip turned to Lisa and indicated the door. "Come on, Baby, let's go talk to Gladman. We got a match to set up."

As they marched out of the locker room, Beronski scratched the back of his head and looked at Danny, puzzlement written all over his face. "Now what the hell was that all about?"

"I wish the hell I knew, Stan. I got the feeling that little bitch just had the last laugh on all of us."

* * * * * * *

Brring!

"Sports desk, Brown speaking."

"Hey, Jimmy, Bill Gladman here. Have I got a scoop for you."

The veteran sports columnist made a face. Scoop? Where the hell did Gladman find his vocabulary, from old black and white movies?

"Really? What yah got?"

"Just the fight of decade, that's all."

"Between who?"

"The Sinclair boys."

Brown sat up in his chair, back straight, completely alert now. "No shit. The Champ going up against his kid brother."

"Exactly, gonna be a sell-out ticket. Believe it."

Brown had grabbed a pen and was adjusting his scratchpad on his desk. "Hey, this isn't some kind of joke is it?"

"All on the level, Jimmy boy. Gladman promotions is scheduling a fifteen round welter weight contest for the crown to take place at Sackman's Arena on the night of August the fifth."

Brown glanced at his desk calendar. "That's in two months. Kind of short notice isn't it?"

"Not really. Neither fighter has had a bout in six months. Both are in excellent physical shape. They really don't need any more time to get ready."

"Okay, I gotcha." Brown was scribbling quickly. This would make a great story indeed. Then his writer's curiosity kicked in. "One question, Gladman."

"Shoot."

"Why?"

"Why, what?"

"I thought those two were close. What the hell would make them want to climb into a ring and beat each other's brains out? And don't tell me it's the dough. It has to be something else."

"That's what I love about you, Jimmy, you're the best there is. And you're right, it's more than just dough. The whole thing is because of a dame."

"Ah, now that sounds like a juicy story. Fill me in."

* * * * * * *

When Chip and Lisa returned to his uptown apartment later that evening, he was in a surly mood and rebuffed any attempt she made at small talk. Finally she excused herself to go shower, leaving him alone in the living room. Once she was gone, he went to his well stocked bar and poured himself a bourbon.

Sitting back on one of the over stuffed sofas in the living room, he sipped his drink and tried to clear his thoughts. He couldn't fathom his brothers' actions no matter how he tried. Oh, he and Danny had often competed for the same girl back when they were kids in high school; there was nothing strange about that. But to actually put the moves on Lisa like he had, that was crossing the line.

What bothered Chip was the fact that Danny had never once shown any interest in her before. So why would he all of a sudden have the hots for her like that?

He sipped his drink and thought about how excited old Bill Gladman had been when he charged back into his office and told him to set up the fight. The guy all but jumped up and starting clapping his hands, he was so happy. He just kept rattling on about how they were all going to be rich. No doubt about it.

Right. So why was he still feeling so lousy? He'd barely touched his steak at the fancy place he and Lisa had stopped for dinner. So annoyed was he about the day's events, he'd even ignored the fans who were ogling them in the eatery, his only concern was to eat and get out of there.

"Chip, are you okay, baby?" Lisa had come out of the shower, a yellow terry bathrobe loosely tied around her body.

"Sure, I'm okay. I just need to get my head straight, is all."

Lisa came over to the couch and knelt down beside him, allowing him a very open view of her firm, large breasts hanging down as she leaned over to kiss him. "Here, baby, let me help you forget all about it."

She leaned over and they kissed. Her left hand dropped to his thigh and began to move up to his center. Chip's senses were getting lost in the soapy smell of her skin, the seeking heat from her lips and the pressure of her roaming hand.

Then the doorbell rang.

"Now who the hell is that?" Chip growled, pushing Lisa off.

"Whoever it is, send them away," she advised, also annoyed by the untimely interruption.

Chip pulled back the door and was surprised to see his father standing before him. "Pops?"

"Can I come in?" At sixty-eight, Paul Sinclair was still an impressive figure, standing just a few inches shorter than his son, his barrel chest and powerful arms had lost none of their vitality. Forty years handling molten steel had toughened him and although the years were slowly etching themselves on his face, the strength behind his gray eyes was still formidable.

"Yeah, yeah, sure thing, Pops. Come on in."

When Lisa saw who their visitor was, she pulled her robe

tight over her bosom and stepped off the couch. "I'll leave you two alone."

"No," the senior Sinclair said, "I'm not here to pull my punches. You should hear this too."

Lisa was clearly uncomfortable and Chip had an idea what was coming. "Okay, Pops, what do you want?"

"I want you to call off this insane fight with your brother, that's what I want."

"Well, I can't do that, Pops. He insulted Lisa and...."

"For heaven's sake, Chip, are you that dumb? Look at her, she's a tramp...."

"Whoa, hold on...."

"...whose only interested in whatever money she can steal from you."

Lisa started to walk away. "I don't need to listen to this crap...."

"Stop it, Pops," Chip ordered, anger coating his voice. "I should have figured you'd take Danny's side on this."

"I'm not taking anyone's side, boy. I just know a con when I see it. She and Gladman have been trying to get the two of you in the ring for months now."

"That ain't what this is about?"

"Isn't it?"

"No. Danny's been jealous of me and what I have ever since I won the title. His getting fresh with Lisa was the last straw, Pops. Period."

Paul Sinclair looked at his son desperately trying to find a way to reason with him. But all he saw was anger and doubt, all of which the bimbo had played on. He was simply wasting his breath.

"You're being played for a fool, Chip. But I suppose you'll figure that out in the end." He turned, grabbed the door and started to open it.

"Pops...." Chip's voice was pleading. "Don't...."

Paul Sinclair looked back over his shoulder, "I'm just glad your dear mother never lived to see this day."

Chip watched the door close and stood statue still. He felt like he'd walked into a pond of quicksand and was hopelessly sinking no matter how hard he struggled to stay afloat. How much more could he take?

"He had no right to say that," Lisa chirped, hands folded over her bosom. "You can't listen to him, Chip. He's clearly taking Danny's side."

"I don't know what to think any more?"

Lisa approached him. "What's wrong? You're not having second thoughts about the fight, are you?"

"What if I am? Shit, I'm just so bloody confused."

"Oh, baby, they're the ones confusing you." She reached up and touched his face. "And I hate that. But you can't back down now. If you do, everyone will say you're afraid of Danny."

"What? That's ridiculous."

"We know that, but the others won't. Chip, the papers will have a field day saying you chickened out. That you're scared of your own brother."

"I'm not afraid of anyone, let alone Danny."

Now Lisa was pressed up against him. She'd let the robe fall open and her naked breasts were up against his torso. "Oh, baby, you're the bravest man in the whole wide world." She pulled his head down and kissed him hard.

Slowly he responded, once again aroused by her body. Then his lips were working their way down to the nape of her neck, as his hands reached up to play with her breasts. The nipples were hard as marbles. With a shrug, Lisa's bathrobe fell to the floor as he scooped her up in his arms and carried her to the bedroom.

* * * * * * *

The noise in the arena was deafening as Danny Sinclair walked down the aisle followed by his trainer, Arnie Demitt and his father who was going to be his ringside second for the contest and his cutman, Joe Webster. He looked at a sea of faces to either side well aware the building was filled to its thirty thousand seat capacity. Even for a title fight this was unheard of. Of course every one of the folks now cheering him as he passed had all read Jimmy Brown's daily sports column concerning the "Blood Feud" match between the two Sinclair boys. In the remaining days of his training, he'd been unable to escape the circus atmosphere created by the papers and television and was hounded everywhere he went. So this is fame, he thought sourly. It felt more like an ancient gladiatorial event with those thousands of screaming faces only wanting one thing, blood.

Once inside the ring, his father peeled off his robe and Danny began to hop around the ring, one final opportunity to get loose, to relax his body before he had to demand everything from it.

The crowd had died down a little and then there it was roaring once again as Chip Sinclair and his entourage made their way into the stadium from the opposite entrance. Trying to see beyond the glaring florescent lights that hang from the ceiling, Danny could barely see his brother and his two ring men. As his glance turned downward, he spotted Lisa seated in the second row behind the judges touching her lipstick with the help of a compact mirror. She was wearing a tight red dress that looked as if it had been painted on her. Fat Bill Gladman had the seat beside her, looking as happy as old King Cole and was probably mentally envisioning the night's receipts.

Lisa closed her compact, saw Danny looking at her and smiled, blowing him a kiss. He shook his head and turned away, not letting her get a rise out of him this close to the coming folly she'd heartlessly orchestrated. He hated the bitch and swore to himself, regardless of the fight's outcome, he would see that she was dealt with once it was over. One way or another.

Chip was laughing as he reached the ring, greeting some of the notable celebrities seated in the front rows. He saw Lisa and waved to her before climbing onto the foot stool and through the ropes with his trainer's assistance.

Straightening up, he looked at Danny and the smile on his face evaporated. Both brothers turned their backs on each other and went to their respective corners to ready themselves.

The announcer, a flamboyant tuxedo character took hold of the boom mic as it descended from the ceiling and immediately went into his spiel announcing the evening's main event and introducing the combatants; first Danny as the challenger and finally Chip as the reigning Middleweight Champion. At the sound of his name, Chip had pranced around his half of the ring making sure to avoid any further eye contact with Danny or his father. Then it was time for both of them to meet at center ring for the referee's instructions.

Butch Calhoun was an ex-fighter who had won and lost more fights than anyone could remember. A balding fifty year old with a beer gut, he stood between the two silent brothers and let them know in no uncertain terms that he expected a good clean fight and he would not stand for any extensive clinching or foul strikes below the belt. With that he told them to shake and, at the bell, come out fighting.

Danny looked up at Chip and for the first time saw something other than hate. Chip merely nodded, slapped his glove against Danny's and returned to his corner. The waiting was over, the excuses and recriminations now mute.

Paul Sinclair patted his youngest boy on the shoulder. "Do what you have to do, Danny. You understand me?"

"Right, Pops. I understand." Danny took a deep breath and mentally prayed whatever God watched over fighters and fools would save him and Chip.

DING!

Chip came racing out of his corner like a thoroughbred out of the gate, his steps quick and light, his hands up and ready. Danny refused to be intimidated and stood his ground, his stance balanced and ready for the assault.

Chip threw a series of short punches to test his defenses, none of them packing any real strength. Danny spotted an opening and parried with his own jabs and they too were mostly ineffective. Opting to widen the ring, Danny slid away and began to dance around the ring, keeping his arms up and ready as Chip, less graceful, followed him, continuing to attack with various combinations, each driven with more and more force.

One cross-in right connected with Danny's chest and rocked him. He bobbed backwards, then suddenly moved in with a hard left that got past Chip's block and hit him in the shoulder hard. Both men moved away from each other for a second, now aware of the real threat each provided. Each had been trained to box, to leave the street fighting wildness out of their minds when in the ring. Now, more than ever, it was crucial that they adhere to that regiment as each was personally aware of the other's skills.

Almost evenly matched, Chip had the longer reach on Danny, who compensated for being quicker on this feet. When they traded blows, Chip had the clear advantage of being able to endure his brother's barrages as they rarely connected solidly enough to hurt him. Whereas Danny, after taking several hard punches to the torso and stomach, wisely moved out of Chip's reach and began circling him, hoping to land punches in and out before suffering any counter blows.

When the three minute bell rang, both boxers were surprised, so momentarily startled having become totally immersed in the fight itself. They retreated to their individual corners breathing heavily, each with respect for the other.

* * * * * * *

Round two was a virtual repeat of the second, except now Danny's confidence in his footwork encouraged him to throw more combinations when striking. One such left counter hit Chip on the chin and his head went back, eyes glazed for a second. The crowd erupted with yells and screams. It was the first time they had actually hurt the other.

But Chip gave as good as he got and he answered Danny's punch with two quick strikes, one to the ribs and the other to the side of the face. Dazed, Danny backed away fast, bringing his arms up in a peek-a-boo position. Chip came in and rained another half dozen blows at his body, only to have Danny stand his ground and withstand the assault.

By the time the bell rang, Chip could feel his arms getting heavier. Back on his stool, his trainer, Steve Nolan, sponged his sweating face and cautioned him not to go overboard too quickly and leave himself empty by the later rounds. "Don't let the kid out box you, Champ. Hit when you can, but stop chasing him. Let him come to you for a change."

Chip ignored Nolan's advice and when the bell rang for the third go-round, he came across the canvas like a freight train barreling at full steam. Danny had only a second to dodge a vicious right cross, followed by a power-house left upper cut. Chip was trying to end things quickly now aware that Danny posed a real threat in a long contest of weave and jab. It was time to use his superior reach and strength and beat him into submission.

He drove Danny back into the nearest neutral corner and his arms became jack-hammers, hitting his brother with all the force he could muster. Some of the blows broke through the kid's wall and his head rocked several times. He had to be seeing stars, Chip thought. Even as he continued to pummel Danny, a detached part of his mind was disgusted by it all. How the hell had he let it all come to this? Was he really such a puppet that others could so easily pull his strings and get him to do whatever they pleased?

For a split second, the champ's mental wandering caused him to drop his own guard. Like lightning zapping out of the sky, Danny's left fist came out of nowhere and plowed into his face. Chip went reeling backwards, stunned with pain and disorientated.

The crowd rose up out of their seats like a single organism, creating a fanatical demented choir seeing he'd been hurt. Danny, suddenly revitalized by that one punch, took the offensive. He moved in on Chip delivered several body shots before landing a second to his face, this one splitting the flesh over his brother's left eye.

Now it was Chip's turn to retreat and find a safe haven to regain his wits and equilibrium. Danny had used the same tactics earlier and continued to press his advantage. He herded the champ back into the ropes and started throwing more punches. Blood appeared over Chip's left eyebrow, a thick red stream oozing into his eye. He tried to blink it away, his vision marred by the blood.

The bell rang and Danny dropped his arms. He saw the bleeding wound on his brother and regret filled him as he returned to his corner and his crew. As he sat back on the wooden stool and spit out his mouth piece, he looked up at his father and said, "Pops, we have stop this."

"We can't, son. This is one game nobody folds on."

* * * * * * *

"Well, that's gonna be it for the champ," photographer Lenny Hale said adjusting his camera lens, as Jerry Brown continued to scribble short hand notes in his notepad. Sitting at ringside, they were by Chip Sinclair's corner and could see his cutman squeezing the abrasion of his left eye, pinching it close and apply the super strong septic ointment.

"Huh?" Brown replied flipping a page over. The notes would cue his memory when he was back at his desk in the city room writing up the fight's scenario blow by blow. "What are you mumbling about?"

"The cut, it's a bleeder," Hale added. "The kid's gonna be going after it like a starving rat on cheese."

"Nope, not going to happen," Brown disagreed.

"Really? Why the hell not?"

Brown looked up. "They're brothers, Lenny. That's why."

"If that means something, then why are they beating themselves up in there?"

"Look, I got no time to explain it to you. I'll bet you a twenty the kid leaves the cut alone."

"Twenty! Done, you're on."

Brown grinned and went back to scribbling just as the bell sounded for round four.

* * * * * * *

A few minutes later Lenny Hale realized he'd lost twenty dollars. Danny Sinclair continued to batter his older brother everywhere else but the left side of his face. They continued to trade punches but each was starting to slow down as the punishment they had already inflicted on each other began to take its toll on both.

Rounds four and five produced lackluster performances from both boxers and as the fifth ended several hecklers in the crowd began to boo.

"Something's wrong with Chip," Danny said between deep breaths as he was sponged off and offered the water bottle to wet his mouth.

"What is it?" Pops asked even though he'd come to suspect the same thing.

"He's going easy on me, Pops."

"Are you sure, Danny?"

"Pops, I know Chip. So do you."

Paul Sinclair nodded and knew what he had to do. Without another word, he turned and walked across the ring to Chip's corner. Calhoun was caught by surprise and started to cut him off but the old man was too fast for him.

Chip looked up past his trainer and his eyes widened. "Pops?"

Paul leaned over the trainer's shoulder and said in a low voice, "Knock it off, Chip. Do not disrespect your brother like this. You owe him a real fight."

Then he was gone, the referee accompanying him back to the other corner.

Twenty seconds into the sixth round, the champ drove a hard right into the challenger's jaw and dropped him.

Danny hit the canvas, his senses jumbled. The world had suddenly turned upside down. Wow, what a punch. He shook his head and tried to sit up. He reached up and grabbed the ropes. He could hear someone calling out numbers through the fog. With his last ounce of strength, he made it to his feet. The world righted itself and Calhoun's mug in his face; the referee taking a hold of his gloves.

"What's your name?"

"Danny Sinclair."

"Where are you right now?"

"Sackman's...getting whipped."

Butch Calhoun chuckled. "Ready for some more?"

Danny nodded and Calhoun moved aside to let the contest continue.

Danny did his best to hold off Chip, but his legs felt like rubber and he was immediately pushed back into a corner with no desire to leave it. Chip connected with one solid blow after another until Danny couldn't feel them.

Calhoun pulled Chip away, looked at the kid and held up his arms, "Fight's over!" he yelled.

The crowd went wild.

* * * * * * *

Danny sat on the massage table waiting for the buzzing in his head to go away. He hadn't been fully alert when Pops and Arnie helped him back to the change room, amidst the chaotic celebration of Chip's victory. Once safely in the dimly lit room, the ring doctor had stopped by to check on him, a precaution in case he had suffered a concussion. Fortunately he checked out fine, though the doctor suggested he take a couple of aspirins and get a good night's sleep before exiting the small, crowded room.

Arnie helped untie the kid's gloves while Pops slowly massaged his back. None of them was in a talking mood. They could all hear the clamor in the corridor beyond and knew Chip and his crew were being overwhelmed by the reporters and cameramen all trying to get a quote or a photo for their morning editions. Eventually the noise died away and the place grew quiet.

"You want to take a shower before we go?" Pops asked as

Danny stretched his fingers while Arnie peeled off the tape on each hand.

"Naw. I can do that at home. I just want to get dressed and get out of here."

"Okay. I'm cool with that."

"Maybe we can stop and get a few burgers on the way," Chip Sinclair suggested standing in the open door. He was still in his royal blue bathrobe.

"What are you doing here?" Danny wanted to know. "Come to gloat."

Chip touched the butterfly bandage over his head cut. "You really should have kept at this."

"Not the way I wanted to win."

Pops stepped between his boys. "What are you doing here, Chip? I thought you'd be out celebrating with your girl by now. Painting the town."

"Lisa's gone. I told her to take her a hike."

"Really?"

"Yeah, Pops. I was a dope and I should have known she was lying all along. When I told her to hit the road, she confessed Gladman paid her ten grand to make the fight happen."

Chip awkwardly shuffled his feet and looked at Danny. "I'm sorry, kid. For everything."

"You always were thick headed," Danny grinned unable to hold a grudge.

"I also told Gladman I was done fighting for him."

"You did what?"

"I made that fat hustler rich. Enough is enough. He whined like a baby, but I'm sure by tomorrow he'll find another green chump to manage."

"But what are you going to do now?" Pops' concern was obvious.

"Ah, don't worry about it, Pops. I'm the champ. There are dozen of managers I can sign with."

"True, but all of them don't own a gym like Gladman does."

"I know, but we'll work something out."

"Maybe we could buy our own place and go into business for ourselves."

"Pops, what are you talking about? You know how much dough it would cost to do something like that?" Chip wondered if the old man was starting to lose it.

"Oh, I do. The old Conklin gym on the south side has been on the market for a while. I think fifty grand would pay for the building with plenty left over to fix it up and buy some new equipment."

Chip began scratching his head. "Geez, Pops, my take for tonight is about eighty grand and I'd be willing to...."

"I'm not talking about your money, Chip, I'm talking about mine."

Danny slid off the table, now as confused as Chip. "Pops, you ain't got that kind money."

"I do now. I bet everything I had on the fight."

Both brothers were speechless. Arnie Demitt just shook his head, a knowing smile on his face.

"Of course it wasn't easy," Paul Sinclair went on. "The odds were on Chip's winning the fight, so I had to spread my bets across the city with six different bookies. But I got it done."

"Whoa, wait a second here," Danny piped up. "You bet against me?"

"Danny, I love you dearly, but there was no way you were going to beat Chip. I saw this as an opportunity for all of us to get out from under and start our own place.

"Think about it boys," Sinclair continued, putting an arm around each of them and drawing them close. "Sinclair's Boxing Gym, it has a nice ring to it, don't you think?"

"Damn it, Pops," Chip admitted, "it does at that."

Danny wanted to be sore at his father, but instead he just started laughing. Maybe Pops' dream was crazy enough to come true after all.

TANGO

BY ROBERT S. P. LEE

The Day Before

"Sooo, what do you think about this guy you're fighting tomorrow night, G? Is he a cream puff or does he get your undivided attention?" Weigh-in was done this morning, so Nat and me went down to Jerry's steak house, a block over from the Motel Super 8. I was starving!

"Meh, he don't look too good Nat," I said in-between bites of a medium-well done two-inch steak with large cut home fries and a stuffed red tomato. "I watched the tapes. Ain't nothing to get hot about. I can take him."

Nat slurped his vanilla shake; a sparkle in his eyes. "Well, do yo best, partner." His excitement was palatable.

"Thanks for the vote of confidence, man. Always good to know my Latin brother from another mother has all-ways got my back, really."

His hands went up, palms facing and his shoulders shrugged at the same time, "Hey, hey. Don't be that way, cousin. You know how you get. What about Billy 'First Among' Equals last month, huh? That guy had the worst technique I ever saw, I swear. Guy's record hit bottom when Trump was still building his towers. That fight, you were the favored 8-2, but what happens? Bum takes you the distance and wins by points! Now he has a title match and what have you got? Some jerk-off named Tippy, the hell man?!"

Mack trucks rumbled by outside behind the people coming in for the grand slam breakfast, ten a.m. to 12:30 p.m. In the fight world, I kinda developed an unpredictable streak. On the fights I was the favorite, I'd lose. Not throw the fight, but, I just got bored in the middle of it. Damn opponents had no style, so I lost interest. But on the fights where I was the underdog, oh, the fighters usually had a spark of skill that made me go for mine! Usually throwing the betting crowd for a loop, screwing up the curve.

"Yeah, yeah, but as I remember, you made out like a bandit because you bet against me. You have a very bad habit of that."

A Japanese child squealed with joy, as his Pops did an airplane with a spoonful of Farina. The child's arms flying up and down.

"C'mon man. How could I pass up a bet like that? You gave all the signs so I knew I'd make out if I pushed the odds in favor of you. Hey, I did split it with you."

"That's not the point, man. You know I was goin' through my blue period."

Nathane's head shook as usual. "There you go again, talkin' that Van Gogh shit. You ain't some crazy one-eared painter. This is boxing Gerard. It's about the money."

I pointed my fork at him, A-1 dripping from my steak, "That may be the idea *you* have, but to me, the ring's my canvas, my fists are the brushes. You just don't get it."

"Nah, G, I don't think you get it. We'll see when you dance with Tippy."

I shrugged, "At least I bet on me, always. 'Cause even I can't tell what's going to happen," biting into my stuffed tomato.

"Yo, G, I got something to show you. Check it out."

Nathane threw in the burned DVD into the Toshiba player in our motel room.

"I know you been kinda bored with the fights you've had lately, and showin' you this might give you a wake up call to the truth about boxing. I ain't seen it yet, but Toby passed this along to me. You seem to be 'ready' for Tippy, so I thought what-the-hell, right?"

The default screen came up, showing a simple menu. Nat hit play. "Toby said, 'You got to watch this. It's...insane.' Some new middle weight's debut or something. Can't see the big deal in some newb's first match though."

* * * * * * *

It was round two, last two minutes. Yunoshi Mitsushita in black trunks, Jerry Romaine in red.

Jerry rushed in after connecting with a right cross, and that was his mistake.

Mitsu blocked the follow-up left with his shoulder, ducking and stepping in with a left kidney shot. Jerry's body hunched, head drooped low. Most would have went for the uppercut and they would have been right, but Mitsu...didn't. His body language said something I hadn't seen in a long time.

He was gonna make an *example* out of Jerry for all to see.

I could feel the hairs on the back of my neck stand & my skin felt hot. He went for the body; left-side, right-side, left/pivot, right-pivot, left-side, right-side, left/pivot, right-pivot, then—when Jerry's legs could barely hold him, a left aimed down. His body crumbled...but not yet! I could feel Mitsushita's intent & my hands balled so tight my knuckles crackled!

Right uppercut, left uppercut, right uppercut; Jerry fell into the corner, arms hanging at his sides. I was there, in the fight. If I was in Mitsu's position and with his intent, everything would seem to be moving slow. The ref must have been too shocked to move any faster, because it was like he was in slow motion, trying to get in-between Mitsu and Jerry...but he was *just* too slow. Left uppercut, right uppercut, left uppercut, right uppercut and to end it, a full body right—down the pike!

The ref finally jumped in-between them like a father trying to save his son from a speeding semi.

If Nathane's never seen a broken fighter before, now he had.

The bell rang, the crowd was silent. The announcer was so shocked that he must've forgotten he was on air because there was dead sound coming from his mic.

Mitsushita turned, his hand raised, walking slowly back to his corner.

I was in his place, sitting in his corner. My thoughts were his. '*The crowd was silent, and I can feel the stare of the ref at my back. Smell the fear of his thoughts that his breathing translated through the silence, carried on the air-conditioned wind.*'

Jerry was my signature.

The ring cameraman zoomed in on Mitsushita's face. He turned, staring at the lens, a small smile played at the ends of his thin lips.

I shook Nathane by the shoulder, "W-when can I fight him, man? When, when, when!" It was the kind of fight that legends are born from, and a true artistic creation could be made. Nathane's mouth drooped, as I still shook him.

Now

Round 5. My mind was still thinking about the possibility of fighting Mitsu. When I got hit. Then...it was nothing but a Pollack.

My left hit his jaw, causing him to stop. His arms dropped—waiting for a solid right piston-fast uppercut charging up from the depths of hell, causing Tippy Harrison to freeze on the balls of his feet. Paused in a boxer's stance, Tippy stood: eyes rolling into the back of his head: a loud snoring buzzed—cradling inside my eardrum. The ring ref pushed me, yelling for me to 'return to my corner'. I turned. A single fist raised. The crowd was silent, waiting for the ref's confirmation of Tippy's condition. I rested in my corner against the buckle.

The ref examined Tippy, tilting his head, checking his eyes. The ref, holding Tippy in one arm, the other hand, swinging towards me, his open hand pointing my way. The announcer blared, "And the winna by *knockout*, Gerard 'Two-Touch' Moses!" Tippy's corner was climbing the ropes. The crowd;

some cheered, others cursed, throwing down their betting tickets. I jumped up, straddling the buckle, screaming, pumping my arms. I'd knocked out the twenty-to-two favorite. After I got done here, I had to go and collect my winnings.

My best friend, and worst cheerleader, Nathane, held his head in his hands, crunched up tickets huddled in between the gaps of his fists. He did not look happy.

Neither did the greasy haired olive-skin colored gents a few aisles down.

They were staring in Nathane's direction.

* * * * * * *

"You bet against me again, didn't you, Nathane?" I finished showering, drying off, and doing the basics before I was going out to celebrate my hard-earned victory.

Nathane never listened, still couldn't figure me out. Too damn bad. Fighting was an art form for me, speed, execution, style, a dance of pain that brought out my best, when the other guy had some ability. Like Rocky Marciano. The man was a poet with his fists.

When he stepped in, his fists wrote volumes on the other guy's face, especially when it came to adding the period! Ali, man, that kat could dance with the best of them, and the impact of his hits were jackhammers. Rope-a-dope style!

Oh, I'd be remiss if one of my favorites didn't come into my mind, Roberto Durán.

Barkley/Durán fight in '89 was what made me want to fight. I wasn't on either side, I just watched. I couldn't move from the thirteen-inch TV we had in the living room. It was, beautiful. A dance of destruction, a...will to power.

I wanted that to be in moments, with fighters who fought with more on the ends of their fists than the dollars they were makin'.

That-didn't sit well with Nathane. We'd been best friends since we were kids on Long Island. I was from Jersey first, then we moved into my mother's aunt's place in the Bronx. That lasted all of two weeks before my Mom got a job out on the Island. I was thirteen and he was eleven. Nathane was always lookin' for the big scam, the easy score, even at eleven. Nathane would run shell games on rich kids on the way to the Hamptons when we hopped the train to visit some girl he'd finessed.

He thought that my ideas towards boxing were bullshit, that art didn't pay the bills.

I got ten grand for the fight—plus another ten for the bet.

"Shit, man! Why'd you have to beat that white boy's ass to sleep? I had good money on him to win. You'd usually lose to a punching bag like him. What gives?"

I was in a pair of light brown trousers, dark brown loafers, white dress shirt, white gold chain with cross, and matching bracelet. "Because, during the fight, he did this move with his feet combined with his hip movement; you know, the left/right combo he caught me with in the fifth? That move got me excited. Showed me that this Kat might have a little something to make this fight worth me tryin'. So I turned it up. Not my fault his ass only had that one move. Shit! I was looking forward to a real fight this time." I was putting on my blazer. Nathane had his head buried in his hands.

"What's up with you, Nathane? Oh, wait, let me guess. How much do you owe to the bookies this time?"

"'Bout twenty grand."

"Jesus Christ, Nathane. So, do we have tickets on the last train?"

"Yeah, sorry, man."

I closed the locker—my gear was in a Nike duffle.

"In the alleyway, waiting for us, right?"

"....yeah, sorry, man."

Same shit, different town. "Hold my bag. Make sure the cab's out at the alley exit. Three, right?"

"There's three of 'em."

* * * * * * *

I was in the alley. Two of them had chains, one had brass knuckles.

Even a street alley can become a blank canvas.

Time to mix the paint!

BATTLING BENNY

BY G. D. McFETRIDGE

This story took place back in the old days, during the times when people rode passenger trains, the Dodgers played in Brooklyn and airplanes all had propellers. I was young and full of beans. I liked drinking and gambling, and I loved New Orleans because there was always plenty of action to bet on, plenty to drink and a good saloon to do it in. But these days everything's too regulated, politicians are as crooked as gangsters, although probably they always were—it's just nobody realized it.

I'd been working in the Gulf of Mexico on an oil platform, doing a thirty-four-day stretch, twelve-hours a day, six days a week. Sundays we rested, but there wasn't much to do. When I got ashore all the money I'd earned was burning holes in my pocket. Back in the day, in sweet and sweaty New Orleans, we called them pick-up fights. Some guys used the phrase warehouse rumbles. Here's how it worked: A promoter, applying the term loosely, would set things up in a location with enough room for a makeshift boxing ring and a couple hundred spectators—men who liked seeing blood and betting money on unregulated fights—then fighters showed up and beat each other's brains out. Usually it was six or eight rounds, sometimes ten or twelve. In the olden days, these fights were bare knuckle and savage, but by the time I was old enough to get involved, the laws had changed and the risk of bare-knuckle fighting was too high, so all the promoters and organizers kept gloves on their fighters. Although they'd cheat if they could. And of course New Orleans' finest were paid off from the captain down to the flatfoot walking the beat, but if word leaked out about bare-knuckle fights even the cops would stop looking the other way.

The fight was scheduled for Friday nine p.m. at a place the locals called the "Little Arena," which was really a rundown warehouse about nine blocks from the river. Two middleweights were headlining—a young Irishman down from Memphis, Terry O'Casey, and a local boy named Archie Thibodaux. I reckon you could say he was Cajun, or at least his daddy was, although by the look of him he had some Irish blood of his own. I paid my twenty bucks to an old bruiser outside the back door and went in about an hour before the main fight. After beers and socializing with a few roughnecks who worked for the same outfit as I did, I laid down a C-note at the betting window, at even money—there were no odds makers, it was bet to win or bet to lose. The promoter and his bankroller took ten percent skim off the betting pool—that was understood—plus whatever they made at the door. If the bets were running too hot on one fighter, then the big boys would cover the disparity. That was the only risk, but of course they knew what they were doing.

Two featherweights, both Mexicans boys—one of them a wetback someone sneaked in from Texas—put on a six round warm-up show, but the crowd was small until the last two rounds. Then seats filled up fast, I'm guessing something like a couple hundred men and a dozen or so women. Go figure. What kind of woman goes to a back-alley pick-up fight? Mistresses of the downtown business execs?

The majority of the crowd was working-class, some fisherman and shrimpers, but oil workers mostly with big paychecks in their pockets. The rest were three-piece suits from the uptown district, rich guys looking to slum it a little, and maybe an occasional politician pressing palms. It was an odd mix, and need-less-to-say, the suits had all the ringside seats.

Terry O'Casey, wearing green trunks, muscular and wiry, measured out at five-nine and 155 pounds; Archie Thibodaux,

5-8 and 160, wearing baggy orange trunks with blue stripes. I had my money on Thibodaux, figuring it would come down to the local boy's edge, plus I also figured it'd be a scuffle between a dancer with reach and a heavy-shouldered puncher, so unless the Irishman was real good, foot movement would only take him so far.

It was a ten-round fight and it went off on time. The first two rounds were close, a split as far as I could see, but then O'Casey, using a stick-and-move strategy, came on fast and strong in the third and fourth, a lot of footwork, in and out, with quick left jabs popping in Thibodaux's face. Thibodaux kept coming forward but he was paying the price, and O'Casey kept turning him left, left, then right. I was worried that Thibodaux might get cut around the eyes and start bleeding. In the fifth each man knocked the other one down, flash punches, but they were short counts in both cases and neither fighter could put the other away. It was pretty clear that O'Casey had planned to come at Thibodaux from the outside, to keep him away and at the end of his longer reach, side-stepping any time the heavier man tried to come inside. But Thibodaux was a dark-eyed pit bull with a hard head and thick brow ridge, and he shook off most the jabs, slowly yet relentlessly making O'Casey fight more on his terms.

The sixth round pace slowed, both fighters being careful not to make a mistake and get knocked down again. In the last thirty seconds O'Casey went out on a limb with a flurry of jabs, ducked a right hook and then caught Thibodaux with his own big right. Thibodaux's neck snapped back and a mist of sweat made an aura around his head in the pale smoky light, but he stayed on his feet and made it to the bell. When he got back to his corner I noticed the cut man moving fast with both hands to get a swab and adrenalin on Thibodaux's upper eyelid. "Shit," I mumbled.

The guy sitting next me glanced over, "He's cut, they'll bleed him to death."

Starting the seventh, O'Casey punched himself on the sides of his head and came fast out of the corner, although midway through the round it seemed like he was wearing thin, his feet weren't moving, damn near flatfooted. Then he tried stepping in and Thibodaux countered, hammering him with a one-two, one-two combo to the cheek and jawbone. The second right made a loud smacking-thud sound, after which O'Casey's knees almost buckled. I jumped to my feet thinking my money was good, but then O'Casey covered up, took a few hard shots to his ribs and liver, and started back peddling until the bell. The eighth was even for the first minute or two, Thibodaux hunching forward and looking to plant another big right. But O'Casey's trainer must have told him something smart because he feigned a couple weak moves, drew Thibodaux in and whacked him hard with a right to the eye. The cut on the upper eyelid split wide open, and flecks of blood splattered all over Thibodaux's chest and left shoulder. The ref called time and checked the cut, then signaled the boys to continue fighting. Thibodaux did his best to protect the cut, while O'Casey danced in and out throwing as many jabs as he could, putting twist on them to further tear open the cut. When the round ended, I watched Thibodaux's cut man working frantically with his swab, then gauze and thumb pressure, then some adrenalin-laced salve. The corner men were talking in both Thibodaux's ears at the same time and watering him, and to tell the truth, I didn't like the look of it. It was a bad cut. My money was slipping away.

The bell for the ninth sounded and the fighters went at it like a pair of mongooses, moving left and right, turning, blending, punch and duck, each one moving like shadows in bright light, neither slowing down, both wanting the winner's share of the purse. The cut reopened and they were half-saturated by Thibodaux's blood. Halfway into the round, his eyes clouded by the bleeding, Thibodaux caught a hard right that put him down on one knee, but he was up in two counts. He took the mandatory eight and kept his eyes fixed on O'Casey like a snake watching a mouse, his head down, jaw thrust forward, set not only to meet opposition but to seek it out. The ref waved the fighters back at it, and Thibodaux threw out a left-right-left, the second left a blur. O'Casey stumbled backwards and caught himself on the ropes. Thibodaux rolled forward like a Sherman tank, and while O'Casey covered up, he started on the ribs, heart and liver. Two of the punches were so hard they made O'Casey gasp, eyes rolling upwards, but he grabbed Thibodaux and held on for life. Thibodaux's cut man must have done a good job because the bleeding had all but stopped.

In the tenth, O'Casey looked like his legs had gone numb, and the best he could do for the first minute was cover up. Thibodaux had no quit in him, plus the crowd was in his corner, and he pounded on O'Casey's ribcage and heart. One blow landed on O'Casey's liver and froze him in his tracks. He back peddled then and lowered his hands, wincing from the pain. Before Thibodaux could take advantage of what he figured was an opening, O'Casey stepped forward with renewed speed and got in a sneaky right, hitting Thibodaux squarely on his chin. The punch had a slight downward angle and knocked open Thibodaux's mouth enough so that his mouthpiece flew out and bounced off the canvas. In that brief moment of distraction, O'Casey drop-twisted his right shoulder and caught Thibodaux with an uppercut that sent him down like the Titanic. The moment he hit the canvas I knew my money was gone up the chimney. Win some, lose some. But not to worry, I'd be back next time.

* * * * * * *

There was a fire on the oil platform in the middle of August, and although it wasn't too bad, as oil fires go, it put a couple contractors behind schedule. The union dispatched me and I was put on a crew working seven-tens until September, which was good money, but then I got laid off along with a couple dozen other guys who were low in the pecking order. So it was back to the union hall to sign the out-of-work list. I figured I'd be riding the list for two or three weeks, maybe a month. The downside was I'd have too much time on my hands and that generally meant more drinking and gambling, but I never apologize for the way I am.

It was a Saturday night at a joint called Red Birds, still early. I'd been drinking since four and had my eye on a skinny blonde who had parked her ass on a barstool, smoking cigarettes and talking with the bartender. He seemed bored. On the far side of the place there was a pool table, and four or five dockworkers playing eight ball. I thought about putting my coin on the table and having a go at it, but an old pal from the union hall named Frankie Lee showed up and we got to yakking about work. And from work, the conversation moved to the fights. "Anything good coming up?" he asked.

I shrugged. "I'm out of touch—I lost big money on that sonofabitch Thibodaux."

"Shit, I hear he's a bleeder."

"It wasn't the blood. He got his ass KOed in the tenth by an Irishman named O'Casey...out of Memphis."

"I hear O'Casey's back in town, set up for another fight at the Little Arena."

"Who's he fighting?"

"I was hoping you'd know."

"We need to talk to Louie and get the inside line on this."

"Yeah, let's go see Louie."

"We'll go see Louie...."

* * * * * *

Louie Fonseca was an old hustler, a half-black Puerto Rican who pimped and ran numbers in his younger days, and then moved up into bookmaking. He wasn't active anymore but he had a finger on just about every pulse in New Orleans when it came to any sort of action, including boxing to cock fights and most things in between. Frankie and me found him at a jazz club in the French Quarter, rubbing his big belly and laughing. I bought him a drink and made small talk, and eventually got around to the O'Casey fight. He grinned. "Benny Bodeen, middleweight out Mobile, Alabama...or so they say."

"What do you say, Louie?"

He gave me a sly look and tugged thoughtfully on his graying goatee. "I say nobody know much about this boy. I say maybe someone who lost a pile of green on the Thibodaux scrap is hungry to get his money back, reestablish his pride."

"Imported talent?" Frankie wanted to know. Louie made an upside down sort of grin. "It could be argued that with rare exception, when the money be right, all talent gets imported... and somebody always looking to put the fix in. Ain't that right?"

I nodded but didn't comment. The fix...the fix is like a ghost haunting your attic, because you know something's going on but you don't know what it is.

It was common knowledge that the mob had the lion's share of the action, or if they didn't have the inside, then it usually came down to some shady businessman or a local small-time hood. A big shot from Dallas or Houston might want to pit his best boy against some other crook's best boy out of Atlanta or maybe Miami. Back in the day, the promoters and grab-men had their own underground circuit, so to speak, and it covered much of the South. Most the fights in New Orleans were basic bush-league, but now and again something big got stirred up and the bosses and wise guys would try to sneak in a dark horse, which wasn't easy. Because to know for sure if you had yourself a real fighter, he had to be ring tested, and if he was getting tested and showing good stuff, word would get out. Then you have a hard time finding action. The fights themselves made money, but the big jackpots were the bets being made between the men who owned the fighters, and of course the inner circle of associates and wise guys.

I leaned closer to Louie and said, "So tell me something, Mr. Louis, all things being equal, between O'Casey and Bodeen, where would you put your money?"

Frankie leaned in too, his eyes wider than usual. Louie puffed himself up, like a rooster about ready to crow. "Well... now, you'd be wanting me to give away my secrets." He rubbed his belly and laughed. I slid a ten across the table. It disappeared under his large dark hand. "Do you expect me to whisper in your ear?" Louie said flatly.

I glanced at Frankie and raised my eyebrows. He fumbled for his wallet and pushed another ten toward Louie. "Alright now, here's my inside line. This Bodeen—they're calling him Battling Benny—truth is he's probably down from Chicago, or maybe Cincinnati, and that horseshit about Mobile, Alabama is just a fairytale. I can almost guarantee it, but who he really is, nobody seem to know. Maybe he fought under another name. The fight with O'Casey is a setup—mark my words—and he'll carry O'Casey on his back and then dump him in the late rounds. After this one's over, I hear tell his people are going after Bruno San Felipo, that Italian bastard who works for the Rosario brothers. They keep him on a leash up in Shreveport, but he does his fighting in Kansas City and St. Louis, sometimes Oklahoma City, once in a great while in Dallas. He's too good to get any action down here."

"Sounds like betting against O'Casey is money in the bank," I said, "if you got your information from reliable sources. What about Bruno San Felipo?"

"I got nothing to say about that fight, except I figure if it ever gets set, it's gonna be for real. There's a couple of big players who want bragging rights, or maybe they got a beef, but only one of them can have it his own way. Bet on Benny in the O'Casey fight. As for Bruno San Felipo, you're on your own." Louie laughed, rubbing his belly again.

Frankie and me thanked him and went on our way. Walking down the sidewalk Frankie said, "You think he knows what he's talking about?"

I chuckled, mostly for my own benefit. "He's been right before, but then again he ain't rich, if you get my point. I guess that's why we call it gambling. But I got a feeling about this one."

"About O'Casey?"

"He's no pushover, however, I'd say we're talking about the

size of the fish versus the size of the pond that the fish is in. Right?"

Frankie Lee grinned. "Sounds like Battling Benny might be a slippery crocodile dressed up to look like a fish."

I slapped Frankie on the back. "Guess maybe so, and in which case I'd say we're looking at a sweet payoff. Maybe two sweet payoffs if we play our cards right."

Not long after, I got my money down on Battling Benny—all four hundred of it. I'm talking a week's union pay plus lots of overtime. Frankie never showed up. I suspect his wife kept him in the house that weekend. The Little Arena was near capacity. I'm thinking damn near four hundred paying customers sitting in row after row of metal fold-up chairs with no padding.

The bottom line was simple: Old Louie couldn't have called this one better had he written the script. Benny Bodeen, the Battler, waltzed the Irishman for eight rounds and then quietly hammered him with a right hook that sent him to the canvas. Poor O'Casey was out for almost three minutes, and even after he got on his feet, he couldn't stand without one of his corner men propping him up. The crowd hissed and booed, but not enough to concern anybody. And like I said before, O'Casey wasn't without skill and good instincts, but the truth was Bodeen put on a show and then walked through him like he wasn't there. The fix was lurking in the shadows—so the trick was, get on the right side of the fix.

Now the question was whether Louie's mythical prediction would come true: Battling Benny the versus Bruno San Felipo. If it did, and word got around, and I wasn't stuck working at an oil refinery or out in the gulf, there'd be another big crowd and tons of money being bet. Flush with the money I'd collected off the O'Casey fight, I was thinking maybe I'd lay down five hundred on Battling Benny. After that, a vacation in the Florida Keys, or maybe Jamaica.

* * * * * *

In early October I got a short-call from the union to work the tail end of a shutdown at the Standard Oil refinery. Ten hours a day for four days, then I was back on the out-of-work list. Frankie Lee got word from his cousin's ex-husband that a fighter named Bruno San Felipo was working out at a private club, a place called the Eagle Street Gym on the north side of town. The ex-husband, Fritz, was a janitor and maintenance man for the gym, and he swore to Frankie that he could get him inside on the sly to watch Bruno work out. With the fight allegedly set for the last weekend in October, Frankie Lee and me were looking to get some kind of inside line before deciding on how to bet, or whether we should even bet at all. Plenty of high rollers would be looking for their own tickets, and so at the very least prices would be high and availability for guys like me, less than great. Nonetheless, I told Frankie I wanted go to the gym with him, if we could pull it off. He said he'd talk to Fritz.

Two days later my phone rang and Frankie said the union had called him and he was going to work, but Fritz assured him he'd sneak me in for ten bucks. Done and done, I said. I met Fritz at a café down the street. After I slipped him the money, he explained that if anyone asked, I was a steamfitter who was checking the old heating system. We'd go in through the back loading dock and mosey our way to a hallway leading to the training area and workout ring. Fifteen minutes later I was leaning on a lime-green wall watching San Felipo loosen up with leg exercises and stretches. He had dark oily hair combed straight back from his forehead, and eyes that were even darker. I figured he was about 5-9 and probably near the 160-pound limit, and he looked strong in the arms and shoulders. Not to mention his was a hairy sonofabitch. From certain angles, his back and shoulders looked like he was wearing a fucking fur coat, or to put it another way, he could have been mistaken for the missing link.

Then he got in the ring and hit the punch mitts with one of the trainers. What amazed me was his hand speed and the loud smacking sound every time he jabbed one of the mitts. After the mitts he did ten minutes with the big bag, practically ripping it off its chain, then ten more minutes on the speed bag followed by jumping rope. I swear the man's feet belonged Mercury, messenger of the gods—pure poetic motion, quick, rhythmic, agile.

Fritz tugged at my shirtsleeve. "We got to go," he said under his breath, and flicked his eyes toward the main door.

Two suits were walking in, both wearing fedoras and looking like they were auditioning for a second-rate gangster movie. They bee lined over to where Bruno was stretching out to do sit ups. It was the tone of voice that made me look over my shoulder as Fritz ushered me into the hallway. Bruno was on his feet and nose to nose, hollering at one of the mugs. "Who are they?" I asked Fritz.

"Handlers," he said, nervously. Two minutes later I was back on the sidewalk scratching my head and wondering who to bet on. Battling Benny was good, that much a blind man could see, but this San Felipo character looked like nothing but straight-up deadly business. Obviously, the big players were putting their best boys to work on this fight, for reasons only they knew, but whatever the case, the action would be red hot. And of course, where was the fix? Or was this one clean? That was the big question every gambler needed to know.

* * * * * * *

Word was leaking out all over the underbelly of New Orleans. "The Big Fight" was on everybody's lips. I was wondering how the organizers would even stage it, because it seemed like it was getting too big for its own good. The cops were bound to catch on and want more money. New Orleans, along with other big cities, had two different faces. One was above board, smiling for tourists and the press, while the other face was hidden in the shadows. But people liked it that way and nobody rocked the boat—at least not for long.

My problem was this: I'd blown some major money on dog races and a cockfight, and booze and women, so I needed to get back to work. But the fight was only ten days off and I had to put together a bank roll if I wanted to bet. Solution? Sold my Triumph motorcycle, then I put the money on some dog action and got lucky. Minus living expenses, I had a grand to gamble. The only thing left was to get inside on fight night, and that would be no easy task. In the eyes of the big players and organizers, I was a nobody, and I couldn't get anyone to pull a string to save my life. My only "in" was the fact that I'd been around a while and most the good old boys knew who I was, knew I was a betting man who usually laid down some serious green. And that was worth something.

To make a long story short, I greased a couple upturned palms and managed to reserve a seat at the Little Arena. When I walked through the door into that thick smoky haze, to the sight of that ring lit up like some sort of shimmering apparition, the hair on the back of my neck stood on end. A chill shot up my spine and hit my skull like the ringing of a brass fight bell.

Once I settled down with a beer, I noticed Louie chewing the fat with a couple jazz musicians I recognized from the French Quarter, so I invited myself into the conversation.

"So where's the smart money riding tonight?"

Louie shot me a look, one I couldn't make sense of. "What's the sound of one hand clapping in the forest when there ain't no one to hear it?" he said.

All three of them laughed and Louie rubbed his belly with big circular motions. I felt like the odd man out.

"Come on, Louie, talk to me," I said.

He gave me another look, and I thought I saw him wink, but I wasn't sure.

"Just flip a coin my man...or otherwise lay off this one and enjoy the fight for its own sake. Nobody in this whole place have any inside line, and if they say they do, they bullshitting."

I had the feeling Louie knew more than he was letting on. The taller of the two jazz musicians said, "Bodeen be in over his head." The other one grinned, showing gold teeth. "This ain't a fight for the benefit of little people," he said, as if from a superior understanding of the underworld, "it's about two big guys settling a score. Get it?"

"Sure," I said. "I get it." But maybe I did and maybe I didn't. What was there to get? I liked betting because it gave me a rush. So I put eight hundred bucks on Battling Benny. Why? Hell if I know. Maybe because I liked his name. Maybe the fix?

* * * * * * *

There was no warm-up fight. The big fight was set for eight p.m. and it went off right on time. The Little Arena had enough seating for four, maybe five hundred people, and there was at least another two hundred jakes standing three and four deep round the perimeter of the ring. I don't have a clue how or where they managed to park the cars that showed up, although most the street-wise gamblers and fight fans knew to take a bus to 42nd Street and walk the rest of the way. I had a seat, ten rows back, and a short fat man was in front of me. I had a decent view. And goddamn, what a spectacle it was. The bioelectrical tension in the air was so thick you could feel it expand in your lungs with every breath. The promoters and the mobsters and wise guys knew how to put on a show and jack up the atmosphere to a fever pitch. And I'll bet they were looking to make a fortune.

After the opening bell, the first round went off fast and furious. Battling Benny, his arms and shoulder muscles looking like they were cast from high-carbon steel, came in swinging. But Bruno wasn't there, in a manner of speaking, he was like fog disappearing in the hot rays of the morning sun. Benny glanced to his corner as if to get some sort of radar fix, and Bruno suddenly appeared out of thin air, hitting him in the ribs, left and right, right, left, left. The last two punches were power shots. The crowd buzzed and the high hissing sounds of whispering rose over the ring. Bruno, for a robustly built brick wall, was sticking and moving, with the kind of foot speed O'Casey had, only his punches were more punishing. Bodeen managed to clip Bruno a couple times with solid rights, but Bruno was head-bobbing side-to-side, back stepping, so most of Bodeen's shots were glancing blows with little effect.

The second round was nothing, mutual assessment and damage control, but near the end of the third, Battling Benny got off a seven-punch combination that put the crowd on its feet, me included. The barrage almost dropped the Italian, and for an instant he looked like a man who was second guessing himself. Between rounds, one corner man sopped Bruno with ice water squeezed out of a sponge, while the other hollered in his ear.

The bell sounded the fourth and the Italian came out leading with his right instead of his left. The real fight fans noticed immediately and a whispery buzz moved back through the rows of seats. I couldn't make sense of it, and it didn't seem to work. Battling Benny wasn't tricked or confused. He pivoted right and left, head bobbed, feigned a couple right-shoulder dips and then put several left jabs into Bruno's face. After Bruno tried to tie him up and muscle him into the ropes, Benny nailed him hard with a right hook that sent a pressure wave back through the crowd.

Bruno stumbled and the crowd was on its feet, pumping fists and yelling. I was yelling too and thinking my money was as good as gold. But he covered up and endured a flurry of body punches until the bell sent both fighters to their corners. The trainers on both sides were talking faster than Gatling guns, gesturing, sponging down their fighters with ice water. The crowd was creating a wall of sound that rose up like a tornado.

Waiting in anticipation for the fifth, I suddenly took notice of the air. Cigar and cigarette smoke was like thick fog, with the overhead lights making slanting vortexes and light patterns; and then the odor, the combined stench of tobacco smoke, sweat, and alcohol tainted breath, and all this made worse by the humid weather. Both fighters were dripping wet and taking extra water.

The fifth round started with the fighters circling each other, as if each was reconsidering his tactics, or the tactics of his opponent. The way I saw it, Battling Benny was holding a slight edge, although my gut told me that anything could happen, and I mean almost anything.

What I saw was Bruno hunching, bending his knees and trying to clip Benny below the belt, but I guess Benny saw it coming and twisted his hips and the blow landed on the inside of his thigh. Benny's corner men were howling at the ref to cite Bruno for a low blow, and then Benny aimed his own punch below Bruno's belt, but it was a grazing shot and the Italian remained unfazed. The crowd hissed and booed. After the bell, two older well-dressed men approach the side of the ring and one of them signaled the ref. He bent over and stuck his head between the ropes and listened, nodding several times as if they were giving him instructions. The crowd didn't like what they were seeing and a growing hum-buzz reverberated through the cavernous reaches of the old warehouse. I didn't like it either; it had a feel to it, like the insiders were rewriting the fight script. On the other hand, it didn't seem possible. I knew the big players always had their weasel fingers in more than one pie, and at any given time a fight might be fixed, or if not fixed, tampered with; although the general law of the jungle was this: The mob and their shady business associates knew better than to kill the goose who was laying golden eggs—if you can see my point.

The sixth and seventh rounds came and went like a goddamned church social. Battling Benny and San Felipo more or less tiptoed around each other throwing out jabs, bobbing and head faking, spending too much time clenching and rabbit punching each other's ribs. The crowd was booing again by the end of the seventh. I didn't know what the hell to think. After all the hype and underground back-alley promotion, it wasn't conceivable—at least not to me—that the promoters and bankrollers could even imagine they could pull off a scam. Not unless of course all the money that had been bet was one-sided. In street lingo we called it a "tilt." It's when by chance or some other quirky set of circumstances, gamblers are putting the lion's share of the money on one fighter. In good fights, when the opponents are both for real, chances of a tilt are small; however, if the wise guys start adding up their numbers and see that three quarters of the money's on one fighter, and depending on how they've backed the action, they could make a sudden decision to intervene on the outcome of the fight, rather than let it find its own natural conclusion.

I knew something was fishy when the eighth got rolling. Battling Benny was letting his hands down and turning Bruno consistently to his right. For a minute or so they went back to the same crap that they'd been doing in the previous two rounds. Then, while Benny's hands were too low, Bruno stepped in and there was a lot of movement, a lot of glove action, yet nothing seemed to really connect. But hell if Battling Benny didn't fold up like he'd been hit real hard and then dive to the canvas. He rolled on his back, whites of his eyes flashing, made spastic moves with his arms and legs, kicked his feet a couple times and lay still. The ref pointed Bruno to his corner and started the count. The crowd was on their feet booing and shouting. "Get on yer feet ya bum!" "Get up, get up!"

Eight counts later the fight was over and the place damn near exploded. A large portion of the crowd surged toward the area where the betting windows were located, me along with them. Although I don't know why, because I was holding a loser... maybe plain curiosity. And sure enough, two grease-ball thugs with violin cases were standing next to the first window. The message was clear. Those holding winning tickets, which didn't seem to be all that many, could line up politely and collect their winnings. Any losers with a beef had better think twice. But I couldn't believe it. I'd been in and out of the gambling scene for over ten years and never seen such a blatant rip-off fix. Couldn't believe the mobsters would shoot themselves in their own collective foot, but I guess they figured they could get away with it. Wait a month or two and all the gamers would be back. Mobsters and politicians, they think alike when it comes to pulling off fast ones. Do whatever you want, and then just wait long enough because it'll all blow over eventually.

Meanwhile, it was back to the oil platform and time to recover from my hefty losses. And I guess it's fair to say...probably I should give up gambling. And maybe my drinking? In any case, when all's said and done, the whole goddamned world's just one big fix—top to bottom.

Problem is, it's the only game in town.

BULLET FOR A BOXER

BY ARLETTE LEES

As I crossed the alley between the pawn shop and the Rescue Mission, a bullet slammed into my head and dropped me to my knees. It felt like a brick. falling from a great height, but there was no mistaking the tell-tale pop and the lingering smell of cordite. My hand flew to the long rip in my scalp, blood dribbling between my fingers. I struggled to retain consciousness.

It was too dark to see the shooter, but I heard the rapid retreat of shoes slapping against the wet asphalt, followed by a car squealing down the access alley behind the buildings on the main drag.

It was a moment before I realized that the bullet had sliced my scalp without penetrating the quivering grey jelly of my brain. I suppose that's lucky, if you want to look at it that way. The missile was probably lodged in the wall of the pawn shop, but I was more interested in reaching the safety of my flat above the bar than I was in collecting evidence.

Standing at the bathroom sink, I stemmed the bleeding, clipped away what little hair encroached on the wound, then did a piss-poor job of closing the gash with Band-aids. Tonight there was no time for doctors or cops.

I collapsed in the easy chair by the window overlooking Cork Street. Pink and purple neon from the movie theater across the street flickered through the rain. I downed a restorative shot of brandy and tapped a Lucky from the pack. With an unsteady hand, I lighted the tip with a silver Ronson that had outlasted my boxing career, my liver and Laura...beautiful Laura. Her smiling face met my gaze from a framed photo on the bookcase across the room.

Of course, there had been others since she'd walked out on me all those years ago, bleached blondes and redheads in war paint, who whispered little lies in my ear and saved the whoppers for their husbands. They meant about as much to me as I meant to them. That's the way it is when you're still in love with a ghost.

I took a long drag off of my cigarette, pulled the smoke down to my toes and exhaled toward the ceiling. I couldn't imagine who the hell would want to waste a bullet on a washed up boxer. I'd like to think it was a careless misfire, but the knot in my gut said otherwise.

"Michael, the musicians are here."

That would be Duffy calling up the staircase. He'd been tending bar at the Cork Street Bar and Grill long before my Dad had passed it on to me.

I could hear the drums and fiddles warming up for the St. Patrick's Day celebration. With my brain beginning to swell inside my skull like bread dough in a bowl too small for its contents. It was going to be a trying evening, indeed.

I reached for the doorknob and saw two. I'd been in the boxing game long enough to know the symptoms of concussion...the dizziness, the blurred vision, the nausea...but, my customers expected me to join them, so join them I would. I could sleep all day tomorrow. I took a deep breath, blinked to clear my vision, hid my wound beneath a driving cap and went on down.

I survived half an hour of drums and fiddles, dancing and the Irish whistle, but when Ben McCoy began torturing the bagpipes, my head began to spin. Why the English had once banned the pipes as instruments of war became acutely apparent.

"You're looking a bit green around the gills, me boyo." said Duffy, tufts of white hair poking from beneath his derby.

"Must be something I ate," I said.

"You go on up. Doyle can man the spigots."

The moment my head hit the pillow the room began to spin. I lit a Lucky, but it fell into the folds of the bedding. I was trying to find it when the nausea hit. I staggered toward the bathroom and things would have worked out fine if it had been where I'd left it just yesterday. My shoulder hit the wall and I dropped to my knees. When I looked down, a big black hole had opened beneath me and I tumbled downward.

* * * * * * *

When I hit bottom it was 1934. I knew because I'd been here before and recognized the poster tacked to the wall. It promoted tonight's heavyweight bout between me, MICHAEL "THE MICK" GANNON, and VITO "THE WOP" ANTONELLI.

My trainer. Jinx Riley, an energetic little leprechaun with a wild thicket of eyebrows, finished taping my hands and shoving on my gloves. He warned me once more about Vito's mean left hook, told me to keep by head tucked into my left shoulder and to keep my wits about me. Yeah, yeah, yeah, I was twenty. You couldn't tell me a damn thing I didn't already know.

My manager. Jerry Featherstone. leaned against the wall in his London-tailored suit and stylish fedora. I was the one done the fighting, so why was it he could always afford better clothes than me? But, I had to give it to him. He was good, really good, college-educated and all. He was an excellent negotiator, got me great bouts and kept us out of the breadlines.

Last year I'd been climbing the ladder toward a match with Ernie Schaaf, but when Primo Carnera killed him in the ring—he died a few days later of injuries from that bout—Jerry arranged a couple good bouts with up-and-comers like Vito. Tonight, we both went into the ring undefeated. By the end of the night one of our records would be broken.

Laura sat across the room in a tailored cream-colored suit, her dark hair cascading over her shoulders, her legs long and shapely in real silk stockings. You'd never know from looking at her that she was three months pregnant. She walked across the room and hugged me. I could smell the dab of Pavlova perfume behind her ears. She lived in constant fear for my safety, but, hell, she knew what I did for a living when she married me.

The first time I saw Laura she was performing with an Irish dance troupe at my Dad's bar. She was only sixteen. I turned to Dad and said, "Laura Kelly has eyes bluer than the sapphires in the jewelry store window." Dad looked at Duffy and Duffy looked at Dad and they laughed their asses off.

"The lad's got it bad," said Dad. Two years later we were married in St. Finbarr's Church.

I kissed Laura on the cheek and told her not to worry, I'd be fine. Then I handed her a dime and told her to go down the hall and get me a pack of smokes. I needed a private word with Jerry.

"I want you to send her home in a cab before the fight starts," I said.

"She's not cut out to be a fighter's wife," he said.

"Don't preach to me. Jerry. Just do what I say."

I could hear the crowd roaring and stomping their feet.

"The lions are restless," said Jinx. "Time to rumble."

* * * * * * *

There was a buzzing in my ears. Someone was slapping my face and calling my name. I didn't remember going down, but I had to be up by the count of ten.

"Michael, it's Dr. Weinburg. Can you open your eyes for me?"

I opened them half way but the light hurt my head. I saw Duffy across the room, but wondered where Jerry and Jinx had gone.

"It must have been the left hook," I said.

Duffy walked over. He and Weinburg exchanged a knowing glance.

"Michael," said Duffy, "you're in Santa Paulina General."

"What round did I go down in?"

"There was no fight," he said. "This is 1950. When Mrs.

Grady came in to do the cleaning yesterday, she found you on the floor. There was a hole burned in the blanket and a bullet hole in your head."

I reached up and felt a zipper of stitches on my crown. Dr. Weinburg bent over the bed and checked my pupils with a thin beam of light.

"Still mismatched," he said to Duffy. Then to me, "Michael, can you think of anyone who's out to get you?"

"Then or now?" I said.

"The lad's not thinking clearly. Doc," said Duffy.

"You have a concussion," said Weinburg. "We're going to keep you a few more days." He held something up between his fingers. "Do you know what this is?"

"It's a bullet, but I'm not that bad off. Doc." He seemed slightly amused.

"I picked it out of your skull. You're lucky you've got a thick one or it would have gone into your brain."

"No kidding," I said.

"Can you come up with an explanation?"

"Not really," I said. "Does it mean I lost the bout?"

* * * * * *

A few days later, when I was becoming myself again. Officer Pete Courneen came to the hospital to take my statement. The bullet was now in his possession.

"You got a beef with anyone?" he asked. "Maybe, a disgruntled customer down at The Cork?"

"Just Father Kilgore. He said I should be crucified, but he never said anything about a gun."

"And this would be in relation to what?"

"I told him to take his business on down the road, that we got no use for priests with a penchant for alter boys."

"Hmm," he said. "Anybody else on the short list?"

"None that I can think of."

Mrs. Grady had cleaned my room and thrown out the burned

bedding. She made me swear on the rosary not to smoke in bed. So as not to disappoint her, I waited until she was gone before I sank into the clean, white pillows and lit up. Women come and go. So does money and fame. But, even if you're broke, sick and lonely, there's always the cigarettes.

Around seven, Duffy brought up a corned beef sandwich and a pint of Guinness to wash down my pills. I drifted off to the tap of rain on the window and all the familiar sounds from the bar that I'd grown up listening to...the Wurlitzer bubbling red and blue...the clink of beer mugs...the dice cups thumping against the bar...the rattle and ding of the pinball machines. Between the drugs and a lingering fever I dreamt in color that night.

Deep in the silence of the night the phone rang. The wind was up and the rain came down in blustery swirls. I grappled for the phone.

"The bar's closed," I mumbled into the receiver. A branch of lightning flickered on the horizon and electrical wires along the street whipped like snakes in the wind.

"I know, Michael." A woman's voice. Low. Smoky.

I tried to shake off the effects of the sleeping pills, but couldn't quite clear my head. A draft leaked under the door. I smelled a faint hint of perfume.

"Laura, is that you?"

"I never should have left you the way I did."

"I'm dreaming," I said.

"I know, Michael, but you didn't dream the bullet." There was still a bit of the Irish in the cadence of her speech.

"No, I guess not."

"Look behind you, way back. Your life is an unwelcome chapter in someone else's script."

"What does that mean?"

A bomb of thunder trembled through the bones of the building and the phone went dead. When I woke in the morning, the receiver was lying on the floor beside the night stand. I put it back on the hook and reached for my Lucky's.

* * * * * * *

Duffy was serving scrambled eggs to a pair of pensioners playing checkers at the far end of the bar.

"Well, look at you all showered and shaved," he said. "You up for some breakfast?"

"Sure. How about a cup of black coffee and a Bloody Mary?"

After the early crowd moved on, Duffy joined me at the bar. He tossed a shot of Scotch into his coffee and buttered a piece of toast.

"So, what's up?" he said. "You supposed to be out of bed?"

I stirred my drink with a green and silver swizzle, then laid it on the paper napkin.

"Duff, have you kept in touch with any of the old crowd?"

He looked up from his cup. "You mean from the old fight days?" I nodded. "Not since you bowed out. You did the right thing. It's not a train you can ride into your golden years. You got out of it with all your marbles. That's more than a lot of them can say."

I rattled the ice cubes in my drink and squeezed the wedge of lemon.

"Laura's been on my mind," I said. Duff set down his cup and studied my profile.

"Why now? She's been gone since the mid-forties or thereabout. Drunk driver hit her car head on, remember?"

"In San Jose, right?" I turned to face him. "Don't you find it odd, that in the nine years before she died, she never filed for divorce?"

He shook his head and laughed. "Odd indeed: My three exes couldn't wait to drag me in front of the judge. What does it matter now?" I blew on my coffee and didn't answer. "You know," he said, "there is a name pops up now and again. Vito Antonelli. He's doing a long stretch in the state pen for second degree murder.

"No shit," I said. "Why am I not surprised?"

* * * * * * *

Antonelli and I sat on opposite sides of the glass partition with in-house receivers pressed to our ears. Since we'd last come face to face, my red hair had faded and thinned and Vito had become shrunken and stooped, his neck and arms black with prison graffiti. He proudly showed off the ink on his left arm.

"BORN TO LOSE," I said. "I admire a man who can predict his destiny with such clarity."

"But, I didn't lose that night, did I?" he said, with a smirk.

"You got me there," I conceded. "Put me in a two week coma. When I came out of it, the world I remembered wasn't there anymore."

He smiled, his teeth brown with cigarette stains, one incisor missing.

"You mean, Laura?" he said, leaning forward on his elbows. "You'd have lost her anyway. I heard she miscarried that night, all because you made her sit ringside and watch the bloodbath."

"That's a fucking lie," I said. The guard looked over and I lowered my voice, but not my intensity. "Who told you that?" I leaned into the glass and he instinctively pulled back like I might actually get at him.

He crossed his arms over his chest. "Who cares? It's ancient history. All I know is that Jinx moved on to train that Jew flyweight took the title, Jerry left for parts unknown and Laura just vanished. You want to know more than that I'll have to get me a crystal ball."

I took a deep breath and pulled away from the glass. "I lost my focus that night. Jinx warned me about your left hook."

If a rat could laugh, he'd look like Vito. "It wasn't the left hook cancelled your ticket that night, you chump. It was the 8 ounce lead sinker in my glove." He leaned forward in his chair. "It sure as hell sank your ship."

It all came back in a sickening rush...the blood on my brain, the jaw busted in two places, the shattered right eye socket and crushed cheekbone. I felt the color leak out of my skin.

Almost in a whisper, I said, "What, you couldn't take me like a man? Maybe, that's why I'm out here and guys like you are in there."

"Listen up, I wasn't there to take you. I was paid to kill you, you dumb mick."

I sat in stunned silence, my brain revving like a souped-up car.

"Are you telling me the Ganguzza's were behind that?" I said. "I always suspected you were mobbed up. Even with me out of the way, you never got a shot at Carnera, so what good did it do?"

"You ain't listening," he said, emphasizing every word. "That's the trouble with you potato-heads. The order wasn't coming from my end." He looked me hard in the eyes until the message sank in. I guess it was the head injury made me a little slow. When it clicked it took the wind right out of me.

"You can't be talking *my* end," I said. "Who? Who are we talking about here?"

"My trainer was too smart to let me in on that part of it. It was on a need-to-know basis. I just wanted the money. It was the Depression for crissake. Even FDR didn't know when things would get better."

"You must have some idea."

"You figure it out. Why don't you ask Jinx Riley?"

"Jinx? I didn't know he was still around."

"He won't be for long. Uncle Vin tells me he's in a care facility outside Stockton. He's hooked up to one of them machines with all the tubes. It breathes for you, feeds you, probably takes a crap on command."

"You know so fucking much, maybe you know who tried to blow my head off last week," and I lifted my cap so he could see Weinburg's handiwork.

He seemed to think that was very funny and gave a rat-laugh.

"You're a shit magnet, Mick, always have been. Sane people should stay away from you."

* * * * * * *

Driving back to Santa Paulina, the late afternoon sun lasering through my eyes, my head began to hammer. My liver was slightly distended below my right rib cage and I resolved to cut back on the booze. My mind wasn't on the road, and at a rural intersection I slammed into a skid and nearly rear-ended a truck carrying crates of live chickens. The driver jumped out of the cab and dressed me down in broken English, containing an impressive number of rolling R's and sharp fricatives.

* * * * * * *

It was dusk when I pulled onto Cork Street and saw the friendly green shamrock buzzing away in the front window of the bar. I pulled into the lot out back, looked around for any gun-toting bad guys, then walked up the outside staircase to my flat. Officer Coumeen had left a star-embellished card stuck in the crack of the door with his home phone scribbled on the back.

The day had taken a toll on me and I felt almost as bad as I had before I left the hospital. I dropped Pete's card on the end table, headed straight for the bathroom and downed a handful of various pills with a swig of mouthwash. I dropped my dead-weight on the bed and slept in my clothes, bright shards of broken glass exploding beneath my eyelids.

* * * * * * *

The next morning I felt surprisingly rested. I ate a real break-fast at the bar, washed it down with three cups of coffee and skipped the Bloody Mary. I turned to Duffy, who was scraping the griddle with something that made annoying noises.

"I want you to go somewhere with me," I said. "I almost cracked up the car yesterday."

He stopped scraping and turned around. "Sure, I can drive. What about the bar?"

"Call Doyle. He's always angling for extra hours."

"So, where to?"

"Stockton. To visit an old friend."

* * * * * * *

Duffy decided to remain in the waiting room while I walked to Room A-12. The place smelled like death and faded flowers and rubbing alcohol. Jinx scarcely made a ripple beneath the coverlet, machines clicking and beeping at his bedside. I touched the back of his hand. It was cold and speckled with age spots. His eyes were closed, his lips slightly blue.

"Jinx," I said. He opened his eyes. They were the color of faded denim. "It's Mike. Mike Cannon, you old cuss."

"Well, I'll be damned." His words came out in a dry croak. "Where's your hair? I thought I was looking at your old man." I smiled and pulled up a chair.

"Looks like you're not doing so good, partner."

"Doc says it's the cigarettes. What does he know? God, it's good to see one of the old crowd. You could punch a hole in a cinder block with that right cross of yours. Bet you thought I forgot about that."

"Those were the days, weren't they?"

"Yes, they were. When I was a kid, us micks owned the fight game, whole neighborhoods emptying into the gyms. That was before the Jews and Italians butted in. We were all going to get rich, buy our moms fancy hats and houses on the right side of the tracks. A few of us did."

Jinx was a talker. Hell, all of us Corky's were. Put us six feet under and we'd still be talking. We revisited all the great fights we'd seen, been part of, or heard of. When we got to the Antonelli bout, I told him about my conversation with Vito.

"That kid was a rotten apple," said Jinx. "He's where he belongs."

"You think he was bull-shitting me, or was there really a bowling ball in his glove? You know the guy's full of hot air."

"I always felt that win was bogus. Yes, he was good, but not that good. The velocity of his punch would have rocked you, maybe even decked you, but without the loaded glove you'd have been back on your feet."

"He said the fix came from our end. Do you believe that?"

A flame jumped in Jinx's eyes. I didn't know he had that much fire left in him.

"That's horse-pucky, boy. Doesn't make sense. You were our ticket to the big time. It had to be the Italians, the Zanferdino's or Ganguzza's. They always bet big on Antonelli."

"A TKO would have got them their money. No reason to kill me."

Jinx closed his eyes and tried to catch his breath. When I leaned over the bed and touched his arm, he opened his eyes. I decided to drop the subject. He noticed my row of horsehair stitches.

"One of your customers get fancy with a bottle?"

"Some things never change," I said, and let it go at that.

"Ain't it the truth," he said. He struggled for breath and coughed blood into a napkin.

When the lunch carts rattled down the hall, we said our good-byes. If it wasn't the Italians crossed me up, it had to be Jinx or Jerry and I didn't want to go there.

As Duffy and I headed for the exit, a nurse rushed over and handed me a cardboard box. "Mr. Riley wants you to have this," she said. "It's the sum of his worldly possessions. I'm glad you came. He doesn't get many visitors."

"Tell him I'll be back next week."

"Mr. Gannon, we'll be lucky if he makes it through the night"

* * * * * * *

When we got back to Santa Paulina, Duffy went home to get some shut-eye. Officer Courneen was sitting at the bar eating a hamburger and fries. I remembered with a jolt that I'd forgotten to call him.

"Bring the officer another beer, Doyle, and tear up his check. His money's no good here."

"You're a corrupting influence, just like your old man was," said Pete, wiping his mouth on a napkin and parking it on his plate. "Didn't you see my card?"

I motioned to a leather booth away from the crowd and we carried our beers over. I was decompressing from the drive and took a long pull from my glass.

"So what's up?"

"You and Duffy picked up a tail this morning, a guy in a black Buick sedan, the same creep I saw parked across from the bar yesterday."

"Did you I.D. him?"

"I tagged along for awhile, then pulled him over outside the city limits. His name is Paul Ratner."

"Never heard of him."

"Tall, bony, face like a death mask."

"You paint quite a picture. I'm sure I'd remember. You think he's the one who plugged me?"

"Can you think of any other reason he'd be interested in you?"

"No. I'm generally not this popular."

"He's about your age, rap sheet as long as a horse's dick. Mostly petty crap, but he could be matriculating to bigger shit. His driver's license puts him out of San Jose."

An invisible spider crawled up my neck and into my scalp.

"San Jose?"

"That mean something?"

"Probably not."

"He said he was a tourist."

I looked out the window at the cars hissing past on the wet street.

"Last time I looked, this wasn't exactly a tourist mecca. Was he carrying?"

"Nothing on him, but I wouldn't be surprised if he had something stashed in the vehicle. Problem was, I had no probable cause and that new rookie was riding along...."

"And you didn't want to set a bad example." We laughed over our beers.

"I did, however, manage to pull Ratner off to the side for a private chat. Told him if I ran into him again, I'd put a bullet in his back and The Chief wouldn't blink twice. Being a reasonable fellow, he turned around and went back the way he came."

We had time for another beer before Pete had to walk-the-locks off the alley. He stood, stretched and climbed into his slicker.

"So, what should I do now?" I asked.

"I'd suggest you look in your rear-view mirror more often."

* * * * * * *

That night my scalp itched fiercely in its healing. I took more pills than recommended and dropped down the dark vortex of sleep. I found myself fighting for my life in the sixth round of the Gannon-Antonelli bout, sweat pouring off my hide like a racehorse in the homestretch. Blood oozed from a cut above my right eye. I landed a glancing right cross and split Vito's upper lip, blood and sweat spraying into the ringside seats. The crowd rose to its feet with a deafening roar. The betting had been heavy, men putting their businesses, their houses, maybe even their marriages on the line.

From the corner of my eye I saw a figure pushing away from ringside into the main aisle...a tumble of long dark hair...a cream-colored suit sprayed with blood...a shimmer of silk stocking. Laura! Why was she here? What had happened to the cab?

My moment of distraction was the window of opportunity Vito had been waiting for. The last thing I remember was Jinx barking at me to keep my focus. I never felt the blow that ended my career, my marriage, and my dreams of climbing that golden ladder to the top.

I heard Laura calling my name and I rolled over in bed with a groan. I caught a wispy scent of perfume and heard the rustle of silk in the rising wind. I untangled myself from the damp sheets and walked to the window, sweat beading my forehead.

I leaned against the frame for ballast. The neon lights from the theater washed like bright paint across the wet asphalt. A homeless man pushed a shopping cart against the wind. A drunk slept in the doorway of the hotel. I walked to the bedside table, thumbed my Ronson and fired up a Lucky. I smoked until my hands stopped shaking, purple ribbons rising from the tip of my cigarette. It was then I had an epiphany.

* * * * * * *

I met Duffy at the door when he arrived for his shift the next morning. He yawned and set his car keys on the bar.

"Tell me something," I said. "Who told you about Laura dying in that car accident?"

"Michael, my eyes aren't even open yet."

"Please, Duff. It's important."

He walked behind the bar and poured an eye-opener. He tossed it back with a shudder.

"Okay, what do you want to know?"

"How did you hear about Laura's death? Who told you?"

"I think it started with a long distance call from Jerry to Danny Cooney down at Toony's Gym. Danny called my brother Tim, and Tim called me."

"Knowing word of her death would get to me, right?"

Duffy reached for the bottle again and pinned me with a strange look of inquiry.

"You gone back to Dr. Weinburg for that follow-up visit yet?"

* * * * * * *

I drove west. I suddenly knew that the answers I was looking for would be found in San Jose. In mid-afternoon I arrived at the Hall of Records in the San Jose Courthouse. An efficient-looking grey-haired woman behind the counter looked at me over her bifocals.

"How may I help you?" she asked.

"I need to locate a Death Certificate." She picked up her pen.

"I can help you with that. Name of the deceased?"

"Laura. Laura Gannon. G-A-N-N-0-N."

"Your relationship to the deceased?"

"Does it matter?"

"Only if you're requesting an official copy."

"My wife. She was my wife."

"Date of death?"

"I'm not certain."

"You don't know when your wife died?"

"The forty's. Yes, try the mid-forty's." It was a bit disconcerting the way she turned her eyebrows into little thin question marks.

"What?" I said, holding my hands palms up in a helpless gesture.

"I'll be right back," she said. After ten minutes she returned.

"I'm sorry, sir. I find nothing under that name."

"Try Kelly, then. Laura Kelly. It's her maiden name. If that doesn't work"...I was afraid to say it..."try Featherstone."

My heart thumped fast and hard until the woman returned, this time looking slightly bedraggled.

"I've tried everything you've suggested, sir. Are you sure you have the right county?" I put a stabilizing hand over my heart until it found its natural rhythm.

"Yes, I'm sure."

There was a painful uncertainty in the hope that swelled in my chest, because I knew how easily it could be dashed. In Laura's absence she may have assumed another name. Maybe, I did have the wrong county. Maybe, she was dead, but something was keeping that flicker of hope alive, because she'd reached out to me in my dreams. It took a moment before I realized the clerk was speaking to me. She was leaning forward on her elbows.

"Perhaps, we could try an alias, a stage name or a non de plume," she said, this time with a twinkle in her grey eyes.

"You're being facetious, right?" She tilted her head and smiled. I read her name tag, then leaned across the counter and gave her a noisy peck on the cheek. Her glasses went awry and she blushed.

"Thank you, Mrs. Popodopolous. You'll never know how helpful you've been."

Finding Laura's paper trail was worth one last shot. I walked to the window where marriage records were on file. Ten minutes later...for a small charge.... I walked out of the building with a document that confirmed my suspicions. In 1934, Laura Kelly Gannon, became Mrs. Jerold Featherstone.

In the phone booth at the curb I found no listing for Jerry Featherstone. I'd never known him to give his number to more than a few people, so I wasn't surprised. I did however, find a number for Paul A. Ratner. If I could lay my hands on Ratner, I knew he'd lead me to Jerry.

As I exited the booth, a poster tacked to a nearby telephone pole caught my eye. I walked over for a closer look and let out a low whistle. Councilman Jerold Featherstone, was in a mayoral runoff with City Supervisor, Rufus Kazner. One look at Jerry's smiling photo, with his perfect teeth, golf course tan and full-head of silver hair, told me he'd aged a hell of a lot better than I had.

I stood mulling things over until the tumblers fell into place. Jerry, had obviously gone into politics years ago and had been climbing the ladder ever since. Once he'd convinced people back in Santa Paulina that Laura was dead, he didn't have to worry about anyone coming to look for her. A charge of bigamy might not go over well with his constituents. Why Laura hadn't divorced me was anybody's guess, but the more I thought about it, the more I warmed to the idea. Our marriage was legal. Jerry's was not.

* * * * * * *

I drove into a rundown section of town not far from Civic

Center. Ratner lived in the once-elegant Princess Carlota Hotel. Today, it catered to a less affluent clientele. A sign painted on the outer brick wall advertised rooms for a dollar a day or five dollars by the week. Real classy digs. A black Buick sedan, patinaed in road dust, was parked in the back lot.

I bought a hot-dog from a street vendor for a dime and ate it behind the hotel as a light rain began to fall. Even a night crawler like Ratner had to slither from under his rock from time to time. I tossed my napkin in a garbage can and settled in against the wall by the back entrance.

Sheltering a Lucky in my cupped hand, I snapped a flame from my Ronson and smoked as I listened to water gurgling through the down spout. With Duffy and Doyle manning the bar, I had all the time in the world.

Half way through my third cigarette, the back door of the hotel burst open. A tall, bony fellow flew through the air and skidded across the wet concrete on his hands and knees, his cardboard suitcase landing nearby. The door slammed shut behind him, the lock sliding into place. I tossed my cigarette into the rain and it died with a sizzle.

Judging from Pete's description, this was Ratner. He had the gaunt face of a weasel and a pencil-thin mustache beneath a schnoz that was sharp enough to cut paper. His skinny frame resembled a metal hanger under his orange suit and purple tie. A real low-rent Romeo, this one.

"Let me give you a hand," I said, leaning down, keeping a lid on my anger. As I helped him to his feet, I relieved him of his wallet...which was empty...and his gun...which was not. He eyed me warily as I returned his wallet, like, where have I seen this guy before? When I removed my hat and showed him how close he'd come to blowing my head off, his hands flew up like they were capable of stopping a bullet. I calmly pocketed the tinny piece of shit he called a gun, then stepped forward and cuffed his ears, open-handed, as I would a rebellious teenager who'd used the F-word in front of a lady. He yelped and covered his head with his arms, but, I didn't stop until I had it out of my system.

"Shut the fuck up!" I said, giving him one final whack. "If I was going to kill you, you'd already be dead."

"Whatta ya want from me? I was just...."

"Following orders. I know. Judging from your unceremonious departure from The Carlota, I'd guess Featherstone stiffed you, otherwise you'd be rolling in dough."

"Don't go throwing that name around. You outta your mind?" Ratner was actually shaking, his face suddenly gone pale.

"Afraid of him, are you?"

"He'd kill me if he saw me talking to you. He's got eyes all over this goddamn town. He wouldn't even cover my expenses, but who can I complain to? He said he was paying for a hit, not a miss."

It didn't feel like a miss to me, but I let it pass.

"Whatta you want from me?" he said, looking at me like a whipped dog.

I removed two crisp fifties from my wallet and watched his eyes bug with imagined possibilities. The bills were so fresh you could smell them. The light faded from his eyes as I returned them to my wallet.

"You want to get back at Featherstone, now's your chance."

"Maybe," he said, brushing grit from the knees of his suit pants.

"What's in it for me?"

"Come on. We'll talk in my car."

We sat in the front seat of my Chevy, our faces rippling with rain shadows. I pulled out my Ronson and lit both of our cigarettes. He eyed my lighter, like it was a diamond broach from Tiffany's. I snapped it shut and slipped it back in my pocket.

"Before we begin, I want to know exactly how you and Jerry are connected."

"We were chummy in high school. He was the rich kid liked to hang with guys got an edge to them. When he came back to San Jose in '34, we hooked up, right off. I knew what ponies to bet, where the high stakes card games were, how to get dames to our hotel room for a midnight threesome. That I didn't get. Why go for ground chuck when his wife was prime cut?"

I opened the window a crack to let out some of the smoke and the sickening fumes from Ratner's cheap aftershave.

"Why put a hit on me now? Come on, enlighten me."

"What about them fifties you waved under my nose?" I ignored him.

"Okay, this much I've figured out," I said. "Stop me if I'm off base. If you're not straight with me, you'll be spending the next twenty years at Folsom. I've got the gun you used and the cops have the bullet."

"Okay, okay."

"Jerry fixed the fight back in '34. Made a bundle betting on Antonelli, but what he was really after was my wife, Laura. He's the one told her that I wanted her ringside that night. I can see why he wanted to bump me off back then, but why the hell now?"

"It's not all about you. He's been buying Vito's silence all these years. Not big bucks, just enough to keep Vito in cigarettes and dope smuggled in by a crooked guard. Now that Jerry's a shoe-in for mayor, he can no longer afford the unholy alliance. If he backs off on Vito, Vito's going to go public with the whole story. He's got a hit out on Vito too."

I was beginning to get the picture, but something was still a little off. "Who gives a shit what happened back then? After all this time, nothing is provable or prosecutable."

"It don't have to be. In politics, gossip can be as deadly to a career as evidence cast in stone. If Vito spills his guts, then the newspapers will be all over you for your side of the story."

The sky was darkening, the rain coming down harder. I worked on my cigarette and let my thoughts marinate until Ratner broke the silence.

"Every time I mention Laura's name...well...I think you still got feelings for her after all these years." He caught me off guard. The raw pain in my face made a response unnecessary.

"If my hunch is right, I got information for you that's worth a hell of a lot more than them measly fifties."

"I'm listening," I said, my stomach twisting into a knot.

"After Jerry brought Laura to San Jose, it didn't take long for her to see right through him, to see what a bag of shit be was under his fancy clothes. Truth is, I think she's been trying to work her way back to you for a long time, but Jerry had her convinced that you'd never take her back. When she overheard us planning your hit, Jerry caught her trying to warn you. He can't trust her no more, so he's got this ex-wrestler, Stig Overhalter, holding her hostage in the house."

I felt the same old spider crawl up my neck.

"Get on with it," I said, "and make it fast."

"Tonight Jerry's giving a fund-raiser at Veteran's Hall. While he has an air tight alibi, Stig is going to take Laura into the Santa Cruz Mountains. After a little sexual discipline, he's going to do her in."

"How much time we got? You lie to me, so help me, I'll kill you."

"How much money you got?" I wanted to backhand him, but resisted.

* * * * * * *

It was dark by the time my plan was in place. Ratner walked to his car with the first fifty warming his wallet. I stubbed out my fifth cigarette and spent the next fifteen minutes trying to cough up my lungs.

I located the address Ratner had given me on Blossom Hill Road. I put the car in low and climbed the steep, curved driveway, the rain hitting hard on the windshield. I parked the car in a grove of redwood trees and walked, hunched into my collar, the last hundred feet. A large Spanish house sat at the top of the hill. An ornate, tiled fountain in the center of the circular driveway overflowed with rainwater. A ratty convertible was parked out front. There was ornate wrought iron grillwork on all the windows.

I tried the front door and found it locked. No surprise. A light burned brightly in a downstairs window, so I eased through the dripping foliage and peered through the glass.

Laura was alone in the living room, her wrists bound to the arms of a chair. Her pink dress was torn open at the bodice, revealing something white and lacy. A cascade of dark hair fell over her shoulders. She was still as beautiful as the first night she danced at The Cork.

I reached through the grillwork and tapped lightly on the pane. She looked my way, but would only have seen her own image looking back at her. I knuckled out an S.O.S. hoping she'd realize that something was up.

A man the size of a hippo entered the room, his muscles bulging beneath his raincoat. He had a blond buzz cut and the kind of face nightmares are made of. I wanted to hang him from the rope he removed from Laura's wrists, except he had no neck to wrap it around.

When the hippo began dragging Laura from the room, I positioned myself on the stoop to the side of the front door, Ratner's gun hard and cold in my hand. As the door swung open an artery the size of a fire hose began pumping in my neck. Stig held Laura's hair close to the scalp and pushed her in front of him with his knee.

"Stig!" I shouted. He jolted like a startled animal and faced me. In that brief moment of distraction, she pulled free and ran through the rain toward the fountain. The sight of the gun in my hand...even though it wasn't much of a gun...should have given him pause, but the dumb shit went for me anyway.

The gun jumped in my hand and sent a bullet into his biceps. A normal man might have noticed he'd been shot. Stig just kept coming. This time I aimed for center mass, but the gun jammed like a cheap dime store toy. Then he was on me, his hands around my neck, his knuckles big and hard as walnuts.

Laura's screams were carried away on the wind.

I had to think fast. Stig was too close in for me to cock a fist. Desperate and oxygen-starved, I got creative and jammed the end of the gun barrel up his left nostril, a move that left him stunned and off balance. While he was still thinking about the pain, I delivered a crushing stomp to the instep of his foot. His hands dropped from my throat and he let out a tortured animal shriek. The gun skittered across the paving stones.

With distance between us, I was in my element, half boxer, half Corky street fighter. I flexed my fists, felt the steel harden in my bones. Stig came at me again with an enraged bellow. I danced away on the balls of my feet, not quite as buoyant as in the old days, but good enough for a fellow past his prime. I shifted my weight onto one leg, swiveled, and drove my shoe into his knee.

There was an audible crunch, the kind you hear when the ax man shouts 'timber.' With Jinx's words echoing in my ears, I cocked my fist and dropped the big ox with my signature blow. Didn't even need a glove filled with lead. 'You could punch a hole in a cinder block with that right cross.'

I looked down at Stig, crumpled on the ground like a pile of dirty laundry. A pulse still ticked in his throat, but he was down for the count.

Laura ran through the rain and collapsed in my arms.

"Oh, Michael:" she cried. "I was afraid they'd kill you."

I held her slender dancer's body close to mine. Her tears were warm on my neck. I took in the whisper of perfume in her hair, the same scent that had woven its magic through my dreams.

I took her by the shoulders and held her at arm's length. Raindrops jeweled her hair and her eyes were still as blue as the sapphires in a jewelry store window. A million emotions moved across her face...yearning and regret...sorrow and hope and love. She began to speak, but I touched her lips.

"You don't have to say anything, Laura. Just tell me I won't be driving back to Santa Paulina alone."

* * * * * * *

Jerry stood behind the podium at the front of the room at

the Veteran's Hall. He told a few obligatory jokes that were well-received, then took the usual questions from the audience regarding education, crime and taxes. Laura and I stood in the shadows at the back of the room. We didn't see Ratner, but when a reporter stood and identified himself as Ted Butler, from the *Sentinel*, I knew that Ratner had kept his end of the bargain.

"Yes, Mr. Butler," said Jerry, "what's your question?"

"Our newspaper ran a very flattering article about you in the Sunday section last weekend. It was called, COUNCILMAN JERRY FEATHERSTONE, SAN JOSE'S MOST ELIGIBLE BACHELOR. Do you recall being interviewed for that article?"

I could see Jerry wondering where this was leading, so he opted for a rather vague response.

"Not specifically. I've done a lot of interviews in the past few weeks."

"Councilman, I don't know if you had time to read the article, but it contained one major error." Jerry's wheels were turning. The color leaked from his face, but he plastered on a big, slightly shaky smile and went for laughs.

"I remember now. The *Sentinel* is the rag my illustrious opponent, Rufus Kazner, carries in his back pocket along with his bribes." The audience loved that. A few people clapped.

"The truth is. Councilman Featherstone, that you are so secretive about your personal life, that few of your constituents are aware that you are married, and have been for a long time, a fact you might have mentioned before we ran our article." A few whispers rippled through the room.

"I'm sorry for your embarrassment. Perhaps, you should be more attentive to your research in the future."

"A point well taken, sir." He held up the Marriage License I'd handed Ratner before he got out of my car. "I have a document here that records your marriage to a Laura Kelly, back in 1934, a woman we've never seen at your side in public. I find that odd." Everyone in the audience was suddenly on the edge of their seats.

"That document has been a matter of public record for sixteen years, sir. My wife is a very private person. Believe me, I do not keep her chained in the attic like Master Rochester's mad wife." This time the laughter was more subdued.

A lady in a feathered red hat stood. "Where do you keep her chained, Councilman Featherstone? Why didn't you publicly refute the bachelor article? You led us all to believe...." Now, everyone wanted answers. There was a look of panic on Jerry's face. Maybe, he hadn't chosen a good night for Laura to disappear, after all.

"If you'll please excuse me," he said. "I have an important call to make."

"Just one more question," said an elderly gentleman, rising to his feet with the help of a cane. "Back in '34, I remember a heavyweight boxer named Michael Gannon. His wife, Laura Kelly, vanished the night of his last fight. Is this mere coincidence or...?"

Laura and I stepped forward into the light, my arm around her shoulders. I thought Jerry would pass out. He turned and marched from the room, his political career sinking faster than the *Titanic*.

* * * * * * *

I met Ratner at the back door of the Carlota Hotel. He was fidgety, like he thought I'd stiff him, same as he probably stiffed everyone he'd ever met.

How did it go?" he asked.

"He's through," I said, and handed him the last fifty.

"I suppose you'll be leaving town now," I said.

"Not if Rufus Kazner is going to be our next mayor. You see, my sister has this boarding house down by the tracks. I know for a fact where Kazner spends those evenings when his wife thinks he's playing Bingo at the church." He wheezed a laugh. "I figure that's good for something."

Probably a bullet in the back, but I kept my mouth shut. He looked over at the car where Laura sat brushing her hair.

"I see you got the girl," he said. I nodded and tapped a Lucky from the pack. I pulled out my silver Ronson, flipped it open, then changed my mind. I snapped the lighter shut, handed Ratner the rest of my smokes, and with a twinge that caught me just below the heart, put the lighter in his hand. I didn't even know how to drink a cup of coffee without a cigarette, but maybe I'd figure it out. When it's my time to go, I don't want to go like Jinx. He looked like I'd given him the Hope Diamond. He mumbled a thanks.

"What now?" he asked

"Back to Santa Paulina. My stitches come out tomorrow."

"About my gun...," he began.

"Good-bye, Ratner. Have a good life."

I drove east into the deepening storm, Laura sleeping lightly against my shoulder. A couple hours out of San Jose found me patting my pocket for cigarettes. Pretty soon I was sifting through the butts in the ashtray. I emptied the contents out the window and watched the ashes blow away in the wind.

God, what I wouldn't give for a cigarette.

THE BLOODY MIRROR

BY TERENCE BUTLER

When Cole climbed out of the ditch he was confused. The gas tank lit off and he turned toward the light. He remembered reaching over the seat back and grabbing the wheel from the driver, fighting him for control, the car going off the road and down the embankment.

Cole sat down hard and watched. The flames wavered and danced, then steadied, then grew and lit the night. He could see Kiki in the passenger's seat, head down, burning. The driver was aflame too, caught in an attitude of attempting to get his door open. Cole's leather gym bag lay in the open near the car, but it was too hot there now.

The siren got him moving. Flickering red lights on the river road, coming fast. He tried to dash in and snatch the bag but the heat and toxic smoke held him off. He took a deep breath, dropped to his belly and crawled in. He'd end up with something like bad sunburn on his face and arms, but if it worked it was worth it.

Then he was splashing dirty ditch water on himself to cool his skin and running into the trees with the bag and a mission. It was simple enough. Get as far away from the burning guys' boss as possible.

* * * * * * *

In Grogan's Gym Cole was punishing the heavy bag and

wishing it was the champ. His training partner was keeping up a steady pattern too. "DIR-ty-MOTH-er-FUCK-ing-SON-of-a-BITCH! You hurt him now, Nate! His legs are going. He's dropping his arms." Archie Blalock was a second rate ex-pug who had a gift for teaching others things even though there was lots he'd never learned for himself. Like the fact that he'd never been as good as he thought he was. He had plenty of excuses for why he'd never had a real shot.

He was a great trainer and sparring partner though, and he taught survival tricks for the ring that take years to learn on your own. He would run lonely miles before dawn, stay up late watching fight film with Cole, and willingly live the Spartan life of boxing training. He'd jettisoned all his bad habits long ago, except the bitter anger.

Anger was one thing Cole needed in the ring. He'd heard the stories about Archie and his temper getting the best of him, losing his cool, forgetting his boxing skills and getting a beating. But he'd also heard that Archie had the killer instinct and he thought he could learn that from Archie too. Maybe now would be the time it would show up. He'd need it, along with the anger.

Archie was toweling him off, saying, "You could beat this bozo, Kid. He's the weakest champ in years, maybe ever. Twelve years you been thinking you was on the road to the belt, fighting good fighters and beating them all. But Ron Prince and them had you *stuck* in the damn road, eliminating contenders. You beat good fighters who might beat their boy if they got a straight up chance." Archie gave Cole a final rough rub of his head and pushed him away. He peered closely in at Cole under the towel. "They never gave you a chance because he beat you once 12 years ago. Those assholes think you're done, and now they're letting you have a shot. This is the best gate they could put together."

Cole raised his blond crew cut head, his blue-grey eyes looked up at Archie from under a worried brow. "I don't know if I can beat him, Archie. He has that devastating right. If he catches me with it I'm done. Just like before. I think I can keep him from knocking me out and I can win some early rounds, but it's in the middle rounds now when my legs start to feel numb."

"That's why we're training you the way we are! First you'll fight him in the middle of the ring, work on his body, let him get tired. He's got that standing up straight ahead punching style. You can slip his punches, pound his body, keep away from that right coming long distance. Stick your left in his face and tire him out. Then you can start to run." Archie was wheedling, talking himself into it as much as he was Cole. "He's the same age as you, Kid. Thirty and a birthday coming. He hasn't fought as many tough guys as you've fought, but you're smarter because of it. I'm telling you, you got this clown KO'd in seven!"

It was starting to sink in. In the back of his mind was still the dream he'd had years ago, a vision of himself in the bright lights, the crowd absolutely insane, the ref holding one hand high, Archie the other, the belt around his waist, the clanging bell sounding tiny in the roar. "Laay-dees and GENT-lemen! The new CHAMP-pion OF the World,.. Naate—'Kii-id'— Cooole!"

* * * * * * *

"That's right; they want you to take it easy. The champ is fixin' to retire after this and we want him to go out on a high note. You help him celebrate and we'll see you get enough for a nice vacation and as many more fights as you want. You can set yourself up if you play it right, Kid."

Akim "Kiki" Akbar spoke through a friendly smile full of gold teeth, a gold toothpick in the corner of his mouth. His voice was soft, his body language respectful and calm. He'd never be able to hide the malevolence in his dark eyes.

"Yeah, Kiki, but this is my shot and you know I...." Cole was sitting in a straight backed chair, his hair still wet, the towel Archie had used draped around his shoulders. Kiki sat behind Cole's manager's desk. He'd asked Grogan to leave and told

Archie to stay out. It was the quietest place in the gym.

"Kid! Kid! It ain't like you could beat him! Worse come to worse, the champ gon' take you out and you ain't getting no more fights." Kiki stood and walked around the desk while he let this sink in. He reached out and gently shook Cole by his slumped shoulders. "Go along, Kid. Get along. You had a nice career and you respected, man! Just let the champ have this las' fight and take the loser's share plus our offer. You can have a few more paydays and retire."

Kiki dropped his hands, turned to look at himself in the full length mirror. He straightened his tailored suit and brushed manicured fingers over his perfect cornrows. He liked what he saw, and his smile was even bigger when he turned back to Cole. "I went along with Mr. Prince and his associates when I was in your place, Kid. I'm doin' pretty good, ain't I?" Kiki shifted his big shoulders and gracefully slid his Italian loafers toward the office door. He opened it and stood for a moment, the smile gone now, dark eyes glowing in his skull. "I hate to think if you don't, Cole."

The fighter watched Kiki through the open door as he strolled through the noisy gym. He high-fived and hugged guys in sweaty workout clothes and shook hands and conferred with others in suits, scattering his blessings amongst the faithful like a Cardinal bringing blessings from their Pope; Ron Prince, the biggest promoter of fights the world had ever seen. Ron Prince; an ex-con, a thug many steps removed from the gang banging world he'd started in, but still as predatory as a hungry shark.

Cole watched him all the way through the turmoil and out the glass doors of the main entrance, watched him step into his Lexus and shoot from the curb into traffic. Watched him even when he was gone and even while Archie asked him what he'd said. He saw himself in that suit and in that car, thought of all the blows and humiliations he'd absorbed, the years of preparing for this one thing. He'd hate himself if he was Kiki.

"He said if I win I'm a dead man."

Archie swore softly and steadily, followed Cole's eyes to the street and stood staring that way himself for a minute. Then he burst into action, pacing around the office and shouting; "We'll call the commissioner's office! God damn it we'll call the god damn cops! We'll get Grogan's shyster on it. They can't do this!"

"I'm not calling anyone, Archie. All that would do is delay the inevitable. I'd never get another fight that would even pay my mortgage, and I'd be looking over my shoulder until someday, somewhere, they'd catch me out." Cole stood and walked through the office door, peeling off the robe and throwing it on a bench, getting up and bouncing on his toes, swinging his arms to get loose again.

"Whaddaya doin' Kid?"

Over his shoulder he said, "Training for my last fight, Archie. Whaddaya think?"

* * * * * * *

The big crowd had started to gather long before Cole and his five men had arrived. He was in the first car with Archie and Con Grogan, while Mario Solice, his other corner man, Wilson the freelance cut man, and Baggs the press guy came in another car right behind. They went through the dusk into the basement entrance and down the echoing concrete hallway to their dressing room. Across the hall two bruisers stood like library lions outside the champ's door. Nods, but no words passed from either camp.

In the dim, cool dressing room Archie was quiet, uttering only sounds that were questions about his fighter's wants and needs. The corner men got busy with their bags and tools and Cole stood waiting while Archie made sure the lockers were clean. Then he began to open the cases of gear. Grogan and the publicity man went out to the presser, blustering about sure outcomes and luck.

Cole's mind was empty of any thought but the devices he always used to get ready. This was the time when a fighter is most alone. Twelve years of it was still not enough to make professional boxing routine. A fighter needs to push away the urge to run and quit the game every time he fights, and the hour before the fight is a different, worse punishment than the fight itself.

The fighter went over the list of previous matches in his head; opponents name, date, place and outcome. A trip through things he'd done right and things he'd done wrong. He had a lot to be proud of, but he always got stuck on the sixth fight. It was the last time he'd met the champ, when both were heavily touted kids with plenty of style and stamina.

That Saturday night "Tree" Marshall brought his ghetto rage and Nate Cole brought his athletic ability. It was over in three. Cole lay on the canvas trying to rise, his brain wrapped in fog and a dull headache starting to spread. It was the first and ultimately the only time he'd been knocked out. He'd never seen the punch coming; a heavy right that arrived like an express subway train blasting into a station.

That punch still haunted Cole waking and dreaming. He watched film of it landing on other poor bastards, studying it to see if there was any way to avoid it, slip it, a way to minimize its crushing power. But it simply appeared somehow, like lightning does, startling you no matter how many times you saw it.

He shook that vision off and moved on to the seventh fight in memory. He'd surprised even himself with the ferocity of his attack that night, relentlessly pummeling his opponent from the start, the ref stopping the fight in the seventh. Anger was the fuel that had powered his blows that night. His career was on the line and it pissed him off. Tonight should be the same.

Cole took a mental image of Kiki and superimposed it on Tremaine Marshall's body. He powered that body with the engine of Prince's crooked puppeteering and derailment of his career, and the insulting offer to reward his willing disgrace. He thought of what his legacy would be if he took that offer, and the anger he needed began to build.

He moved rapidly around the room, punching the air and loosening himself, bringing a good sweat. This was the honest sweat of what he did for a living, his craft and art, and tonight he'd give it everything he had.

Archie steered him to the training table and began rubbing him vigorously, slapping the muscles and stinging him. "How you feeling, Kid?"

"Good. I'm good. As good as I ever felt, Archie."

"You're serious, ain't you?"

"Yeah man. I'm going for it," Cole said, pausing at each new thought. "Nothing else I can do. I worked too hard for this. Seems to me I deserve it. And fucking Ron Prince has all he needs in life, you know? Fuck him."

Archie came around in front. He lifted Cole's right arm and began pulling lengthwise on the muscles of it.

"They don't play, Nate."

"Neither do I."

The two locked eyes. Nothing was left unsaid.

* * * * * * *

Banging through the swinging doors to the auditorium, Cole's bunch following Marshall's, the difference in the heat and noise immediate and overwhelming. All the faces turned, mouths flapping or grinning, hands reaching to touch the meat of him, mouths ready to say they'd been there and touched him or the champ, the touch or the mere presence somehow becoming a high point of lives spent in despair of ever reaching childhood goals.

"Kill him, Kid!" "Kill 'em, Champ!" "Kill him!"

Up the steps and under the ropes, higher into the smoke and heat and roar, the ring a vortex of energy, of show business with blood, the booming, echoing PA introducing past champs and current favorites, an Irish cop to sing the anthem. Cole shutting it all out, staring across the ring at Marshall staring back, both in their bright robes, on their toes, taking vicious cuts at surrogate air, turning back to nod while seconds jabber at them, grabbing, rubbing, slapping like hyenas at a kill. Cole emptying his mind of everything but the mystery of what put him there. Staring across the ring at Kiki on the apron. Kiki smiling back at him, gold teeth and malevolent eyes flashing.

Now in the center, ignoring the ref's instructions for the hundredth time, nodding and seeing at the little roll of fat pooching out above the champ's trunks, looking up startled and seeing the uncertainty in the champ's eyes. Looking again to make sure, the champ looking away. Now the ref touching the fighter's gloves, reminding them to tap fists and come out fighting. Cole making a wide turn and looking at Kiki ringside, at Ron Prince belatedly taking his seat, Cole grinning at the two of them, grinning through his mouthpiece.

* * * * * * *

The early rounds were over and the butterflies were gone. The fighters had put away the film sessions and the strategy talks and moved on to muscle memory and trained second nature. Each had stung the other once and the crowd was into it. Cole was made to remember there was a reason Tree Marshall was champ, as Tree was now awakened to the prizefighter in front of him. Still Cole was sure he'd trained harder, sure the champ wasn't as fast as the film fighter and wasn't the machine he'd been. Cole knew he had a chance and that was how he'd proceed; as a fighter with a shot and therefore dangerous.

He took the fight to Tree as was demanded of a serious challenger, always jabbing with his left and moving forward to clinch and work the body, pulling the champ back to the center. The fighters weren't talking, neither being the type, but Cole listened to the pained sounds the champ made when his body blows landed. He heard the grunt of effort from Tree as he struck heavy blows to Cole's arms and sides. He listened to the champ's breathing and heard its raggedness and rasp. The Champ had not trained as he should have for a fighter like Cole.

In the corner he nodded to the words from Archie and heard noises coming from Grogan at the apron, but he was thinking only of how he would advance his strategy when the bell rang again. The momentum was swinging his way. The champ was truly defending his title and it was possible that Cole was ahead on points.

At a minute into the fourth, Tree Marshall tagged Cole with the big right hand and he went down. For an instant Cole's world went silent even as his body jumped back up. Things looked flat and strange, and for perhaps a millisecond Cole didn't know anything. The ref took hold of his wrists and wiped Cole's gloves on his shirt and peered into his eyes. "You OK, fighter?" he said. Cole jumped back on tiptoes, ready again. The champ was swarming, pressing, and the ref leapt away. Cole clinched and held onto the bigger man until the ref came back and pulled them apart. "Box now, gentlemen!" Cole covered and moved, slipping punches, not throwing any, absorbing punches. Before the bell rang though he was clear-headed again and ready for the one minute rest to revive him.

Archie was looking in his eyes, holding Cole's jaw in two hands. "That looked like his best, Kid! You OK with it?" He nodded vigorously, not wanting to waste breath. It hadn't been the same punch from twelve years before but it still was a punch many fighters simply couldn't withstand. He couldn't take more like it and knew he'd better stay away from it. He'd lost that round and probably the casual crowd. Time to backpedal and make like Ali until the champ was panting and frustrated.

Then came two rounds of bicycling backwards, stopping to jab and punch, hook to the body, cover and take, then get back on the bike. The crowd was unhappy and the champ was flailing at air and starting to shuffle. Nobody cared for Cole's strategy but Archie. He stretched on the stool while Archie sponged cool water over him. Wilson treated a tiny cut from an accidental head butt by the champ, but really used the time to check old wounds. He pronounced him fine; "He ain't been hardly touched but the once, Arch." Cole thought of his aching sides and chest, his forearms and shoulders throbbing, and knew that tomorrow he'd definitely know he'd been touched. But right now, right now was the tomorrow he'd always known would come. This day was his to never forget.

"I'm going after him, Archie. This round."

"You got him, Nate. He's shuffling and dragging his punches. He's an old man in there."

Cole looked across the ring and saw Kiki at the apron, not looking at his man but looking across to Cole, the threat telegraphed from twenty-five feet. Cole watched Tree Marshall move slowly up from his stool when the bell rang. He strode to the center and waited, not long, until the champ arrived.

This was a newly determined Tree Marshall. He started after Cole with a flurry of combinations, searching for a way to set up the right. Cole stood his ground and willingly traded hits for openings, still hooking crushing rights to the body and straight, twisting jabs to the chin. The fighters were in the center of the ring and their sweat flew several rows into the crowd, staining their finery, but going unnoticed.

They were on their feet and losing their collective mind, smelling blood. They yearned for a knockout—hopefully by the champ—but were willing to accept a new champ if the knockout came from Cole. The fighters were making them forget how much they'd paid to be there, making them forget their lousy jobs and endless debt. People hung on each other, pounded each other's backs, wielded programs like clubs and slapped them on seat backs. They grinned wild grins into wild eyes and shouted themselves dizzy. This is what it means to be a man. To watch as two fine examples of manhood pound at each other regardless of consequences. To be there as heroes battle for a symbolic crown and a gaudy belt, a shared-out purse of winnings and the fragile respect of raving, part time savages.

Tree was trying to knock Cole into the first row of seats. He couldn't become too cautious because he'd lose points, but he had to watch for the champ's big weapon, the ticket to sleepy time. As the champ expended effort in bringing punches, so Cole had to bob and weave, take punishing blows and still keep a clear head. He felt the first weakening in his legs as he missed with an uppercut, but it seemed that Tree was just as ready as he was for the clinch that followed. For the second time the ref had to separate the fighters.

When they joined again, Cole saw reluctance in the champ. Maybe he was wondering when the damn bell would ring, maybe he was hoping that Cole really was going to go along, maybe he just didn't care anymore. Cole's tiredness went away. He stepped inside a long distance right that would have been lights out if it connected, snapped Tree's head back with a strong jab and followed with a crushing right just beneath the heart. Tree's eyes went soft and he dropped his arms. Cole threw a combination to the head and stepped back as the champ fell prone. He knew the champ would not get up by the count of ten.

Cole leaned over and looked down. Time was crawling and the crowd noise was a backdrop like rushing water. "Twelve years," he said. The champ was twitching, gone somewhere out of town, and Cole went to his corner. He skipped backwards, watching the ref watch him, ready to count. He leaned on the ropes until Tree's people rushed into the ring, and then he let in the roar from the crowd.

It carried him to the center with Archie and Solice and Wilson lifting too. Cole let the crowd noise buffet him, turning and raising his arms until the announcer came in with the official result in his hands, and then he went back to his corner. He watched as people helped the champ to his feet, he shook hands with the exuberant Grogan, looked down on the scrambling photographers gathered at the apron, Kiki circling at the fringe, making his way through the crowd and keeping his eyes on Cole.

And then the gong was banging, demanding the attention of everyone lost in the moment. The official verdict would be read and a new champ announced and the cycle would begin again. Cole and Archie moved to the center and the announcer began his spiel. "Lay-dees and GENT-lemen...." The new champ didn't listen. He heard it, but he didn't follow it. Instead he moved his eyes around the building, seeing the blue pall of smoke and looking at the crowd, now seeming like figures in a painting or an old photo. There were individuals he recognized, ex-fighters, guys from the gym, old friends he'd come up with, even his brother. And Kiki, waiting near the aisle to the dressing rooms, eyes shadowed now, his mouth a taut line.

But Archie and Grogan were pulling him back to the center of the ring. There was more ceremony to complete. They put the belt around Cole's middle and for the first time the win seemed real and something like satisfaction crossed his mind. He crossed the ring to where Tree Marshall still sat on his stool, attended to now by the ring doctor.

"Can I say something to him?"

"Sure, Champ, that would be fine."

Tree was looking up at him as the crowd noise dropped a bit and a buzz ran through it. Cole put a glove out and Tree tapped it. They held there a moment and Cole said, "You were champ right up 'til the last, Tree."

"All yours, Kid." Sincerity and relief both were in his tired voice.

Then Archie was steering him to the ropes and through. "We gotta get the fuck outa here, Nate." Down the steps and past Kiki and up the aisle, through the gauntlet of well-wishers. Everything now was the first part of a new life of fear and flight.

When they got to the dressing room Archie told Solice and Wilson to stay there and wait for Grogan and Baggs, tell them he and Cole had gone to the gym, that Cole was too tired to talk to the press and he wanted to collect himself. Then he went to the door and told the already gathering press that the champ was somewhat emotional at the moment and asked them to be patient.

"You guys know this should have happened for him years ago, right? He just wants to be sure he has his head clear because he wants to make a statement."

An excited murmur went through the group. A post fight statement was an unusual thing for a new champ. Ron Prince's name was part of a shouted question. Archie said, "I'll let the champ do the talking," and closed the door. Then he and Cole changed clothes. Cole put on a hooded sweatshirt and a windbreaker and folded the belt into his leather gym bag. Archie put on his stadium coat and borrowed Solice's golf cap. He pulled the collar up and the hat down and looked at Cole. Cole was waiting with his hood around his head. They went out the window into the alley.

They crossed the street behind the auditorium and hurried into a perpendicular alley. They came out on a street of hotels, turned left, walked to a cab stand and got into the first one. "Grogan's gym," Archie said.

* * * * * * *

The forest ran back from the road a few hundred feet to the base of a bluff. Cole put his arms through the loops of the gym bag like a back pack and then scrambled up. Loose rocks and soil tumbled noisily down as he pulled himself from shrub to shrub to make the top. When he got there he rested, panting and blowing. Looking back down he could see that the light from the burning car was dimmer and the siren was howling nearby.

He considered just going back and letting the police take him. He could tell them what had happened from the beginning and take his chances that Prince wouldn't get to him.

He laughed bitterly, thinking of how at Grogan's, Kiki had walked in and shot Archie, pointed the gun at him then and said, "Le's go, motherfucker." No warning, almost as if he was invincible behind Prince's filthy, corrupted shield. Archie never had a chance and neither would he. Kiki had put him in the car and Cole knew that was to be a one way ride, so he took a desperate shot at freedom. But the cops would question him and he didn't want to think where those questions might lead.

There was no real proof that Prince had ever approached him. Kiki and Archie were both dead and it would be his word against Prince's. Prince could suggest that Cole had welched on a bet or failed to keep an agreement. He'd say that he had no knowledge of what had gone down, but that Cole surely must be a cold blooded individual if it was he who'd killed a fine old gladiator like Archie Blalock. Wasn't Archie supposed to be his best friend? And what about that suspicious accident that killed Akim Akbar and the other fellow? Was that just coincidence?

Cole knew that Prince would have a funeral for Kiki and he'd invite the press and he'd set the theme by whisper. Cole looking for a big payday, maybe he and Kiki approaching Tree without Prince's knowledge. Cole double-crossing everyone and taking the championship plus the funny money. Cole running out when it backfired somehow.

He looked desperately around at the forest. It thinned toward the west, away from the river and towards open fields. A single yellowish light flickered through the trees as they moved in the night's wind. Cole shivered and put the gym bag on his back and started toward the light. From somewhere inside came a primitive urge, a surge of fear. He broke into a run.

* * * * * * *

The light was further than it had seemed and he was staggering when he got close enough to recognize it. A yard light at Tree Marshall's rural training camp. Cole climbed a hummock and leaned and slid down the giant oak that surmounted it. Behind him the sky was brightening. He guessed the time at somewhere around five a.m. Several roosters clamored in the barnyard. The yard light stayed on, but no one moved. Cole stared at the old frame house, his mind a blank, hunger and thirst a dull need.

Then a light came on in the house, upstairs, in the back. Cole watched the light intensely, as if it might help him. It went out and moments later it was replaced by one in the room directly beneath it. In another moment the back door opened and Tree Marshall and a dog came out. The dog sniffed and marked its way around the yard while Marshall stood still gazing toward the sunrise. The dog sat and scratched a while then lay staring at his master, waiting. Cole watched until Tree began to rough-house with the dog.

"Tree! Tree Marshall, it's me, Cole!"

The dog immediately ran half the distance between the men, barking in full fury at Cole. Cole remained still while Tree called the dog and got it under control. Then he moved forward, hands open at his sides. Tree watched him advance, holding the dog by its collar while the dog wriggled and whined, yelping to get at the stranger.

"What you doing here, man?"

"Kiki killed Archie. I guess he was bringing me here to kill me. Maybe you want to kill me too, I don't know. I'm just running to stay alive."

"Kiki killed Archie? Why he do that?"

"I don't know. He didn't have to. He's dead now too and the other guy with him."

Tree yanked on the dog's collar, made him sit, looked back at Cole.

"You kill them?"

"I caused an accident that killed them."

Tree stared hard at Cole, then relaxed. "Ain't no big loss man," he said, turning toward the house. "Coffee?"

"Who else is here?"

"Just me, George, and the chickens."

"Who's George?"

Tree looked down, leaned to pat the dog's head. "This here ol' dog. I names all my dogs after George Foreman. He my main man comin' up."

Cole relaxed then too. "I know you punched like him comin' up."

Marshall smiled and went up the steps leading to the kitchen.

Cole had coffee and two bowls of cereal with sliced banana and then more coffee. Tree sat across the table, not talking, occasionally asking Cole if he wanted more of anything. When he pushed his bowl away Tree asked him what he had in mind to do next. Cole looked around the kitchen and then out the window and realized he didn't know.

"Keep running, I guess. Prince will still want to get me, and I'm sure he can anytime he wants. I have some money I can get at with my ATM card. I got my credit cards and stuff. I guess if you gave me a ride to town I could rent a car and head for the coast or someplace. My brother can sell my house and cars, send me the money. I'll be all right." He lightly kicked the gym bag. "I got the belt in here. At least I'll know I was champ."

"You could stay here and tell the truth."

"You know Tree, I thought about that, but I can't prove that he wanted me to lie down. I can't prove Kiki killed Archie, I can't prove I didn't cross somebody. It's a no win. Prince has lawyers in his office and politicians in his pocket. I got nothing."

"Me," Tree Marshall said, eyes downcast in his big, dark face.

"What?"

"You got me. I knew the fight was bad. I can tell the truth and you can enjoy your championship like you s'posed to. You done *earned it* ain't you?"

"Prince will kill you, man!"

"Not if I kill him firs'."

"Oh, man, don't even talk like that."

Marshall's big fist slammed down on the table, rattling the dishes and startling Cole. Tree leaned across and spoke to him in a low growl.

"Listen up, Kid. Mu'fucker think he *own* me like he own a slave, man. I been tryin' to get away from his ass for five years. Tryin' to retire. Come out here and raise my chickens. Prince? He want me to keep fightin, say he make fights with fools will lay down, say he need to make up what he spent to make me champ. Done tol' me I don't own this here property, he do. Mu'fucker say I *owe him* money! Say he gon' take my ass to court!"

Cole sat stunned, staring across at Tree's anger, at his eyes filling with tears of rage, at his huge fist picking up a coffee mug and crushing it into a dozen pieces before firing them across the room at the wall. Tree dropped his head to his chest and made an effort to control his breathing. Cole sat silently, waiting.

Tree said, "I got cancer, Kid. Only thing saved me from that mu'fucker is I got to die. Doctor done gave me a couple of years, say I should retire. I had to have the doctor tell Prince. Mu'fucker didn't believe me." A sardonic chuckle came from him as he shook his head and looked at Cole. "You believe that shit?"

"God damn, Tree. I don't...."

"Naw, it's cool. It is what it is. I agreed to one las' fight so he give me back this here farm. He comin' here tonight, sign it over."

"I guess I better move then, I don't want him to know a thing about where I am."

"Looka here, Kid. That press guy you got. He cool?"

"Baggs? Yeah, for sure. I've known Baggs for years. He's as honest as anybody can be in this game."

"Le's go find his ass. I'm fixin' to do some talkin'. I got years worth of stories to tell."

* * * * * * *

Cole looked down at Archie. Archie looked strange in a suit. He looked good, but strange. Grogan had bought him a suit for the funeral and paid for everything, and tomorrow they'd hold a wake and the next day they'd bury him. Grogan had asked Cole if he knew what Archie wanted for his final disposition but Cole couldn't recall ever talking to him about anything but fights, fighters and fighting. Their conversations might have been about other things but they were always couched in terms of the squared circle and its distorted reflection of the world outside.

"You'll find me at my desk in the foyer, gentlemen," the funeral director said. "You can be here when I close the coffin or simply leave. Either way, I'll be waiting in the foyer."

Grogan whispered something and went out with the funeral man. Baggs moved next to Cole and put his hand on his shoulder.

"Ready, Champ?" Without looking at him, Cole held up one finger and stooped to pick up the gym bag. "Hold this will you?" he asked Baggs. Baggs took it by the straps and held it out while Cole unzipped it. He took out the championship belt and held it in two hands, admiring it for a moment, and then he laid it gently over Archie's waist.

"Champ!" Baggs said, "Are you...?"

"Yeah, Baggs, I *am* sure. I wouldn't have it without him. And I had it long enough to know I won it fair and square." He turned and faced the press man, tapped him lightly on the shoulder. "Tell everybody goodbye for me, will you? I'm heading out tonight."

"Where you going, kid?"

"Oh hell, Baggsy, if I told you that you might come look me up. Just say I'm going somewhere I can raise some chickens."

A NICE JEWISH BOY

BY MARC SPITZER

You could never argue with pops even if he was dead wrong and I do mean dead wrong.

"A nice Jewish boy doesn't fight in the street," he would say when I came home with swollen knuckles and black eyes.

"Pops, I have to defend myself or they'll step on me out there. You don't see it. The anti-Semites don't understand us, but they do understand a punch in the mouth. That they get," I'd argue but pops would have none of it.

After I kicked Fontana's butt on the football field at school my reputation was made and no one would start with me.

I thought I'd have to retire my left hook and my overhand right. At least pops would be happy but little did I know at the time that I was just getting started.

* * * * * * *

Two days later my gym teacher Mr. Mishkin called me into his office.

"Sit down David," he said. "I was here dropping off some baseball bats on Saturday with my Uncle Moe. We saw you and Fontana through the window."

"Am I in trouble here Mr. Mishkin?" I interrupted.

"Hell no, kid. My uncle saw you drop Fontana with that left hook. Said it reminded him of Charley White. My uncle fought White in Toledo in 1919. He got KO'd in the fifth. Moe Mishkin.

My uncle wants to take you to the gym."

"A nice Jewish boy doesn't fight in the ring," was pops' response but I wore him down with promises of good grades in my senior year and temple on Shabbos and when I said, "Come on pops, Benny Leonard, Mendoza, Dutch Sam, Mitch Green, Charley White, Barney Aaron, Ross, Friedkin, Davis, Jews don't fight in the ring?"

Add David Weiss to that list but I make no claim of greatness like those guys.

I remember my first amateur bout in a high school gym in Queens. I was really nervous but Moe kept whispering in my ear to remember to set everything up with the jab. "You can do this kid."

I did do it.

My opponent was game but I walked through his punches and jabbed, hooked to the body, jab, jab, overhand right. Down, up at eight. Five seconds later he was down for the ten count and I was on my way.

That's how it went in the amateurs. I out boxed just about everyone I faced, took minimal punishment and lost only two decisions in thirty-five fights. One of those decisions was bull.

Pops was upset when I told him I was going pro but then I divulged that I had seen him at Gleason's Gym the night I took the city middleweight title. He didn't know that. He also didn't know I had seen the look of pride on his face or how I cried in the locker room thinking about that look. He still doesn't know that all these years later.

"A Jewish boy stays in school and meets a nice Jewish girl and gets a job and raises a family," said pops.

"I'm going to do all that pops. Aren't I taking courses at City College?"

"Part time."

"Part time's so bad pops?" I asked.

I was 10-0 with six KO's when Moe booked me in Atlantic City with George Bent, a trial horse who'd been in with two ex-champs and a bunch of contenders.

* * * * * *

Moe was talking to me in the dressing room, telling me Bent might be 21-16 with seventeen KO's but not to be fooled by the number of losses he had. "He's got a ton more experience than you and he's fought five game guys for every single one you've been in with but if you stick to the plan you'll be okay. Tonight's your toughest test kid. You get past Bent you're on your way, " he said.

"Who has or had the better shot? Me, or you back in Toledo against White?" I asked.

"About even kid."

I knew I was in for it but I had been in this game for a while now and I felt ready.

Then Bent's punches started coming at me from all directions and I wasn't so ready anymore. He seemed to be hitting me at will. Next thing I knew I had blood dripping down from a cut over my right eye. Moe was yelling at me to stay on the outside and box.

Jab, jab, my head snapped back and then his left hook to my ribs made me wince painfully so I tied up and the bell mercifully dinged and ended the first. Seven to go.

"The plan *boychik*. Jab. Stay on the outside and box. You can't slug with him," said Moe.

"He's rushing me Moe."

"Push off, back up at an angle, jab, body shots, come on David," he said working on the cut. "Do it." He put my mouthpiece in.

The second round was much like the first except I got lucky when Bent stepped into a blind rising left hook that bounced off his chin and put him on the canvas for a count of seven.

The bell rang as I moved in and he sneered at me. "Lucky bitch," he said, turning toward his corner, pretending not to hear my "up yours."

My left jab said "up yours" better than words could convey to open the third and when Bent dropped his arm for the body shot he expected next, I hooked upstairs and drove him into the ropes where he bear-hugged me. The referee separated us and I went for the overhand right but Bent danced away.

I saw how my right had just missed his chin and put that information in the bank and went back to the jab, jab, hook, connecting all three times and getting a rise out of a surprisingly good Wednesday night crowd.

Back in the corner Moe drenched me with cold water and raised his voice to get and keep my attention as I tried to catch my breath. "Keep boxing this guy David," he said. "Be patient. Feint with the hook. When his hands come down, bang with the right, then back to the outside. Stay on the outside."

I was patient for a little over two minutes of the next round when I thought I could sneak my right over his guard but instead walked into a left that dropped me and re-opened the cut over my eye.

I rose at five and thought I was okay but was glad to tie up with him when he moved in for the kill. Turned out I was still wobbly.

"You dancin' with me or fightin'?" he asked as we came together.

"Too damn ugly to dance with," I replied and was delighted when the bell rang shortly after that.

It came together for me in the fifth. My jab pelted his face time and time again and set up the right which I backed him up with and stunned him with at the bell. Lucky for me I had no problem with the eye.

I was winning the sixth round the same way I won the fifth when Bent got inside and hit me low. I was doubled up for just a second but managed to ward him off with the jab and stayed on the bicycle until those three minutes were up. Lucky me.

"You're doing great, boychik,' Moe said between rounds. "We're winning the damn fight and the crowd loves you. Remember what I've been saying about boxing this guy. He wants a street fight."

In went the mouthpiece. Up and at it at the bell. Ding.

If Bent thought the low blow was the end of me, he was dead wrong. I boxed him the entire time like Moe said and I out hit him three to one in the round with a combination of jabs, hooks, rights and an uppercut that sent him flying into the ropes. It should have been the second time in the fight that I scored a knock down because the ropes kept him up but the ref didn't see it that way despite Moe's protests.

"Come on Larry," he called to the official. "That was a knock down damn it!!!" To no avail.

We touched gloves and Bent came out with murder in his heart and in his gloves with wild swings but my jab started to reach and bounce off his chin and his rapidly swelling right eye. I kept him at a distance and landed all the telling blows in the round. He was completely flustered and seemed glad when the bell ended the fight.

We hugged each other in the middle of the ring. "Great fight kid," he said, looking me in the eye as we each pulled back from the embrace. "I never fought a tougher man than you," I said, returning the compliment.

Moe was in the ring to greet me when I came back to the corner. His smile was as wide as the arena. "You are something boychik," he said, taking me into his arms. "You are really something. That poor Fontana sum bitch never had a chance."

Moe's smile started to fade when he saw the ref's reaction to the two scorecards he collected from the judges. Neither man would look him in the eye.

Moe turned to me and whispered words that still tick me off all these years later. He said, "They're gonna steal it from us, kid."

And they did just that with only the ref scoring it for me five rounds to three on a split decision. I can still hear the crowd booing and the sound of the programs flapping into the ring, thrown from all heights and all directions.

* * * * * * *

A couple of hours later Moe and I were in the bar across the street from the arena drinking away our anger and frustration when pops walks in.

"A Jewish boy doesn't drink at the bar," he says, "but under the circumstances I'll have a shot of scotch and maybe two."

Then he looks me right in the eyes with that pride I saw that night a few years before and he says, "My son, you have nothing left to prove in the ring. Finish school. Find a nice Jewish girl. Raise a family. That's what a nice Jewish boy like yourself should do. That's what your dear departed mother would want you to do."

You can't argue with pops. Especially when he's right. Dead right.

My children, you should know, love their mother, father, grandfather and Uncle Moe. They all play tennis.

BET YOUR OWN MAN

BY C. J. HENDERSON

Kate's eyes opened wide, focusing tightly on her friend.

"You're going to fight who?" Andy kept skipping rope, not missing a beat.

"Why," he asked, "does everyone have that same reaction?"

"Because everyone else," replied Kate, "must have heard the same thing I did—that you're going up against Tiger Ortiz in the N.H.B. Anyone who hears that is pretty much guaranteed to have the same reaction."

Sweat dripped its way out of Andy's crewcut, streaking the hard lines of his face, neck, shoulders, back, chest. Drops of it flicked away from his body as he continued his routine. He'd worked out harder the night before when he'd learned he was paired off against Ortiz. Now, on the day of the match, he was taking it easy, sticking to the rope and the bag to keep loose.

"Glad to see everyone has such faith in me."

"It's not that, Andy...it's just, I mean...Tiger Ortiz?"

"Damn," he thought. "Damn it good."

Captain Andrew Turner, a.k.a. the Spider, was not happy. His mood went dark for a moment as he sighed to himself, silently cursing whoever had spilled the night's line-up early.

The No Holds Barred Competition was the one unofficial event that no upwardly mobile young officer ever missed. Declared whenever—happening as often as eight times in six months—the N.H.B. was a bag glove, any style, one-on-one. If the generals perceived the post needed some excitement, or were just bored themselves, or the promotion list needed a few names to round out its feel for one reason or another, word would spread, and the notice for 'Special Duty Volunteers' would go up. Those who wanted to impress the upper echelon signed it as often as they could. After a half hour the list would come down—opportunity time kept short—letting the brass see which ones were keeping their eyes open, eager to please, and which ones were lucky; they like both kinds.

After that, all the names on the list went in a hat. Two would be picked out. Those two individuals were notified and, the next night, those lucky soldiers would get to N.H.B.

"Ortiz is a monster. The man is three hundred pounds, and the majority of it is muscle. He's got over a hundred pounds on you. He could easily be a Golden Gloves contender in his weight division—and he's just as good with his feet. On top of that, he's NHBed six times. Three of his five knockouts left his opponents crippled in one fashion or another. The last one simply ran out of the ring.

"He's not stand-up. He'll kick you while you're down just for fun. He's out to grab rank, and he knows there are enough guys at the top who think someone who stomps his enemy is a clever and wise kind of tactician. He'll hurt you, Andy...just for the fun of it."

Kate clearly did not like this N.H.B. She and Andy had played at romance when they'd first met in boot camp, but had never become lovers. They had remained friends, however, and as his friend, she was extremely worried. Understanding where her concern came from, Andy didn't allow Kate's seeming lack of faith in his abilities to upset him overly. But, slacking his rope and catching his breath, he did ask her;

"Kate, was your name on the list?"

"Yes. I made it in time, but...."

"And," he cut her off, "if it had been you and Ortiz, would you have backed out of the ring?"

Kate bit at her lip. Half-American and half-Chinese, she had been raised from birth to be a fighter, trained by her police captain father and former Olympic boxing coach grandfather. Kate and Andy were both members of the code-named Suiciders team, a covert operations squad that tackled the worst assignments. Kate was acknowledged as their most dangerous member by everyone else in the team. She knew Andy was really asking her how much better than him she thought she was.

"Andy...that's not the point."

"Yeah," he answered sourly, walking back toward the showers, "that's what I thought."

"But, he'll get murdered."

"Anything is possible."

Kate fumed silently, staring at Rice. She had gone to the major in charge of their squad in the hopes he would order Andy not to fight. Rice agreed with her that Andy was overmatched by Ortiz, but disagreed with her on whether or not the fight should take place.

"You're looking at this thing far too emotionally. Mr. Ortiz is a fairly deadly individual in the ring and Andrew will certainly have to keep his wits about him, but that is no reason to stop the fight." Kate started an interruption, but Rice waved it off and kept talking.

"You have to remember, the N.H.B. is an unofficial thing. I can't very well order a man not to partake in something which officially never happens. Also, it's quite a personal thing. Tell a man to drop out of the N.H.B., and you're telling him you don't think he can pass the muster. No...better to re-evaluate your self-esteem a bit after a thrashing than to lose your spirit altogether because you think you backed out of a tight situation.

"If you want to help Andrew, stop tearing his confidence down. He's going to fight Ortiz whether or not you and the rest of the squad are on his side but, he might do a better job of it if he believed he had a chance—and, if he thought those around him believed he had a chance."

As Kate left Rice's office, thinking about what he had said, the major quickly filed away the report he had been finishing and then pulled on his cap. Checking the perfection of its placement in the mirror, he thought;

"Well, it's about time someone stopped Ortiz's little climb to glory, and I think it would certainly be a good thing if it were someone from our team." Heading out the door, he said aloud, to no one in particular;

"Yes; a very good thing, indeed."

* * * * * * *

Anytime people discovered Tiger Ortiz was NHBing, the post gym was packed to overflowing. That night was no exception. By 7:30, hundreds of seats were already taken. By 8:00, dozens were still waiting to place their bets. The fighters remained in their dressing areas. Their 'handlers' would let them know when to make their entrances. Kate waited with Andy, trying to reverse anything negative she might have added to his mood. She told him;

"They ought to be giving us the high sign any time now."

"Yeah. Then I can go out and get put in the hospital for you."

"Oh, come on." Kate snapped a towel at Andy, telling him, "You know I was just worried about you. Besides, are you saying you wouldn't have tried just as hard to talk me out of fighting Ortiz if I was the one going out there against him tonight?" Before he could answer, though, the door burst open. Psycho Red, another member of Kate and Andy's team, came in, shouting;

"I don't believe it. No one believes it! You're sure as hell not going to believe it!"

"Believe what?"

"Rice! He's bet five grand on you!" Andy stared dumbly for a second before asking;

"On me?" Psycho nodded his head, grinning wide. "Rice? Bet five thousand...'bleed-every-penny' Rice? Bet five thousand American dollars—on me?"

"Yeah. He did—he did indeed." Andy sat down—clumsily—stunned at the news. "Odds were six-to-one against you. That dropped them to three-to-one—boom—crash. Of course, by this time, Ortiz hears what's happening and comes out to see what's goin' on. So—so—" Psycho laughed loud, throwing his head back in a jerking motion.

"So—then, right? Then, the old man goes over and thanks Ortiz for financing his next vacation."

While Psycho Red continued to howl, Kate put her arms around Andy and gave him a hug and kiss for luck. Smiling, she sat back and asked;

"Now how do you feel?"

"Ohhh," drawled Andy, smiling back at her, "like I better win."

Psycho continued to howl until Kate threw a bar of soap at him. It bounced off his head and rebounded into the sink. Psycho yelled;

"Bank shot. Our team wins!"

Kate rolled her eyes. Andy and Psycho leaped to their feet and broke into a short spate of shadow boxing until the door opened—another of their team coming to announce ring time. Psycho Red grabbed up Andy in a bear hug—squeezed—and then dropped him back on the floor, saying;

"Kill him, Spider. Wipe up the floor with him." Grinning, Andy shot Psycho a mock salute, answering simply;

"Okay."

Then he left for the ring.

* * * * * * *

The noise of the crowd rippled, sections of it leaping from high noise to silence to frenzied whispering as each person caught the look on Andy's face. He was smiling. Out of all the emotional options open to Roger Ortiz's opponents, smiling was not thought to be one of them. That confused many in the crowd—excited others.

As the officiating non-com rehashed the N.H.B.'s bare skeleton of rules, Andy and the Tiger looked each other over. Ortiz up close was even larger than Andy had imagined—solid, scarred and massive. As they approached each other for the glove tap that would begin their match, Ortiz growled;

"I'm gonna mess you up, pretty boy. Bad." Andy laughed. Ortiz howled, spit flying from his mouthpiece;

"You're dead. You're dead meat. Dead meat!"

Andy shook his head, smiling sadly, as if correcting a grade school student. Ortiz snorted. The referee called for combat. The N.H.B. began.

Ortiz bulled past the ref, faster than he might usually, eager to get at Andy. He swung wide, forcing Andy into a backward/sideways step which put him behind his opponent. As Ortiz wheeled to face him, Andy got off two quick jabs, catching the bigger man on the shoulder and the chin. He jumped away instantly then, easily dodging the murderous right he'd been expecting.

Ortiz was so solid, whenever someone landed their first clean punch on him, its lack of effect usually stunned them for a second, giving him the chance to connect with a crippler. Having picked up on that trick from watching Ortiz's previous bouts, though, Andy not only wasn't waiting for the right, but was in position to deliver his own blows to the off balance fighter.

He slammed the Tiger with everything he had—one, two, three, four crunching hits. He worked Ortiz's side savagely and then danced back before a ham-sized left cut the air between them. Ortiz nearly overstepped, but didn't. Catching his footing, he moved after Andy quickly, trying to force the smaller man into the corner. His longer reach allowed him to keep Andy hemmed in, constantly backstepping. The crowd screamed, searching for blood. The Tiger grinned. He'd made a bad start, but things had finally started moving the way everyone expected.

But then, suddenly, Andy dropped to the floor, rolled, and then came up within Ortiz's swing radius, plowing into him. He shot hard and fast, delivering two sharp jabs to the side and then danced away again, listening to the wind gasping in Ortiz's throat. The larger man swung again, wildly, following with a surprise left, both of which Andy was able to dodge. Stepping behind Ortiz, Andy kicked at his left leg, hoping to send him down. The move staggered the larger man, almost to the ropes, but didn't topple him. As nicely cut a move as it was, the Tiger hadn't been off balance enough, or light enough, to topple. Turning with a sneer, Ortiz came back to the fight.

The pair danced around each other, neither of them landing any blows for the rest of the round. Ortiz was not a slow fighter. He was fast for a man his size. He was fast—period. But he wasn't as fast as Andy.

By the end of the first round, though, both fighters were glad for the respite. Andy took his corner, Kate and Psycho waiting. While Kate sponged his head and shoulders, Psycho squirted him a swallow of water, saying;

"Hey, nice stuff, Spider. You're still alive. Very entertaining."

"I'll see if I can keep it up for you."

"You do that."

The trio laughed for a moment and then, the fight was back. Ortiz came out fast, rushing the opposite corner, hoping to get in the opening shot. Expecting the move, though, Andy was up and away before the Tiger could get to him. He chopped away at Ortiz's side again, one-two, one-two, taking only a glancing blow on the arm in return. As the round continued, Ortiz slowed down, trying to analyze what was happening. He'd had opponents who had made it to the second round before, and long beyond...but this was different. Andy didn't seem to be afraid of the Tiger's reputation, or of the possibly bone-breaking reality of being within the ring with him.

Andy watched his opponent's eyes, waiting for a glimmer of anything that might signal him to advance the battle. The Tiger wasn't used to real competition—not any more. It was the one thing Andy was counting on to get him over the top.

The second and third, fourth, fifth and sixth rounds passed in a similar haze to the first—Andy dodging and weaving, staying a bare fraction of an inch away from Ortiz's devastating fists, waiting for his chance, and Ortiz absorbing but shrugging off the majority of Andy's stinging blows.

The crowd remained in constant turmoil, cheering and booing, throwing popcorn, beer cans, clothing, crumpled paper, and food at the ring, those immediately outside of it, and each other. Screams and curses flew indiscriminately, the din of it creating a deafening silence. By halfway through the seventh round, Andy and Ortiz were circling each other slowly, ignoring the taunts and flying debris, concentrating on each other's eyes, watching.

Then, suddenly, a paper cup of ice hit Andy in the side of the head. Cubes flew across the ring, filling the air. Ortiz, seizing the moment, broke forward and slammed Andy across the chin—hard—sending him flying into the ropes. Following up his advantage, the first for either fighter in the entire match, he worked Andy's left side over viciously. Andy's defense crumpled. He pulled himself into a protecting ball, trying to take as much punishment on his arms as he could. Then, seeing an opening, he butted up with his head, catching Ortiz on the chin.

The Tiger staggered back. Andy reeled from the ropes, following him across the canvas. Although he was able to pace Ortiz, he couldn't clear his head fast enough to press him. By the time he was solidly on his feet again, the larger man was also. Knowing Ortiz realized there was nothing for his opponent to gain by attacking, the smaller man did the only thing he could. He attacked.

The crowd rose as a single animal, roaring at the sight. Leaping into Ortiz's attack radius so unexpectedly, he caught the Tiger off guard, getting the chance to do some damage. He pistoned Ortiz's jaw twice, making contact with the same spot where he had just landed his head-butt. Ortiz staggered but then whirled, coming up with a roundhouse kick as Andy came in again, sending him sprawling across the canvas. Blood exploded forth as Andy's nose cracked, splattering those at ringside as he bounced off the ropes. Ortiz was right behind the blow, ready to give another, but the bell cut him off. Both men went to their corners, each beginning to wonder seriously who was going to win.

Andy flopped onto his stool with all the strength of a wet rag. Seven rounds of trying to stay out of Ortiz's reach was beginning to take its toll. He was losing too much water, and too much steam. He knew Ortiz was beginning to crack as well, but he had no way of knowing if the larger man was anywhere near ready to go down. At first, Andy had gone into the ring believing he had a serious chance. Doubt was starting to work its way through the cracks, though, the gasping pain of his side reminding him he might possibly lose more than just the fight.

While Kate and Psycho administered to him, Rice walked up to the corner. Ignoring the now continual wave of screams pouring out of the crowd, he hoisted himself up to Andy's corner and said;

"Good show so far, Andrew. How are you feeling?" Coughing up a huge phlegm ball, Andy spit it out and then answered;

"Like I'm going to be a big disappointment to you, sir."

"Rubbish." Rice stroked his moustache, continuing, "You've done us proud so far, lad. I don't see you stopping any time soon." Gasping to suck down oxygen, smarting from the pain of doing so, Andy leaned forward as close as he could and asked Rice;

"Why, sir? Why'd you do it?"

"I assume you mean my bet?" As Andy nodded, Rice explained, "A bet is a gamble. I looked at the odds, at you, and at the opposition, and then I did what any gambler does—paid my money and took my chances. After all, when you're part of a team, you stick together, you bet your own man.

"Do remember, though...I could have shown my support for you with a hundred dollar wager. I bet as I did because I think you can win." The bell rang, calling for the eighth round. As Andy rose, Rice yelled, "So go do it!"

Andy turned, his jaw set, eyes narrowed. As Ortiz moved across the canvas, Andy waited for him, stepping only a few feet out of his corner. The larger man hesitated, wondering what new strategy he was facing. Andy called out through his mouth-piece;

"Come on, kitty cat. Time for beddie-bye."

Ortiz's eyes became slits. Hunched behind his fists, he crossed the middle of the ring. He moved forward slowly, saying slightly off center, maneuvering to come in on the left, hoping for another shot at Andy's ribs. As he closed in, Andy stepped out of the corner trap and then back pedaled quickly, seemingly running from Ortiz. The Tiger followed him, cutting across the center of the ring, blocking any possible retreat. Andy, however, had cut back as soon as Ortiz had moved, placing himself where the larger man had been.

"Now," he thought, "let's try this my way."

Throwing himself forward, he took a hasty defensive block on the shoulder to put himself up next to Ortiz. Then he dropped to the floor, his left leg between Ortiz's. As the larger man tried to step back and away, Andy kicked out at the leg still planted. Ortiz managed to lift it just in time. As his other came down, however, Andy rolled to the attack once more, sending Ortiz leaping to keep from having that leg knocked out from under him.

The Tiger was quick enough again, but suddenly found his back against the ropes. His hesitation was only that of a second, but it was all Andy needed. Unlike his first two bluffing attacks, this time Andy put everything he had into a two-legged swing, one strong enough to topple Ortiz. The larger man crashed to the canvas, the mad babble of the crowd around them somehow impossibly doubling in volume.

Quickly abandoning his crab-style attack, Andy threw himself up and forward, coming down on top of Ortiz. The Tiger caught him in the side of the head with a solid left, but his awkward position kept him from putting enough power in the blow to shake Andy loose. Kneeling on Ortiz's chest, Andy pulled back and slammed him across the jaw, bouncing his head off the floor. Ortiz spit out a tooth and a large splash of blood. He brought up his arms, grabbing at Andy, but his opponent was already gone, on his feet, laughing at Ortiz as he staggered upright.

And then, something snapped within the Tiger. As the crowd shrieked, screaming for an end to things, Ortiz bellowed and charged, coming at Andy with no style or form, attacking with size and weight and fury. Dragging himself out of the way with the last of his energy, Andy avoided Ortiz's rush, somehow managing to throw his arm out in the way, straight and stiff, clotheslining the larger man.

The Tiger went down again—hard—crashing into the canvas. As he made to stand, dragging himself upward, Andy crossed to Ortiz's side and brought his doubled fists down on the man's head with a brutal chop. Down went Ortiz again, blood from his face splashing the ring with an ugly circle. Again Ortiz struggled to regain his feet and again Andy cold-conked him. And then again. And then again.

Andy held his sides, the air in his throat pulling razor blades across his lungs. He was out of energy, out of tricks, out of steam. His brain told him he was finished, that he had nothing left to give, that he'd thrown everything he had at the man laying on the canvas and there was nothing left in the register.

And then, Ortiz began to rise again.

His head came up like a wrecking ball slowly being reeled back into place. Andy stared, trying to will himself forward, unable to move. Ortiz made it to his knees, then to one knee. His hands pushed slowly, struggling his body upward. Screams rocked the ring from all directions. Ortiz's right hand left the ground, grabbing at air, struggling to balance his body. Andy took a step, knowing he had nothing left to give, and then, suddenly, it was over.

The Tiger fell back to the canvas, too tired, too spent. Not knowing how much more punishment was waiting for him, he collapsed for lack of will. On the second the referee finished the ten count, Kate and Psycho and a dozen others were in the ring, hoisting their man onto their shoulders. Ortiz's people fought through the confusion, helping their man off as best they could, forced to battle their way to his side through the ever-increasing throng around them.

While the crowd swept the victor and the vanquished out of the gym, Rice joined the tiny group of gamblers who had wagered on Andy. As he waited for his winnings, he reflected on the caliber of those in his team, prouder than ever to be commanding such a force. Finally, as he made his way to the head of the line, the unfortunate bookmaker who had taken his bet paid him off, sourly, telling him;

"You're one lucky bastard, Rice."

The major agreed—not letting the man know their reasons for agreement were miles apart.

BOXING, BABES, & BULLETS

BY GARY LOVISI

The big fist hit Bobby hard, a hammer to the kisser. His nose spouted blood. Damnit, he was leading with his face again. Joe always warned him about that—but the bait had worked, it lead Killer Kowsalski to come in close, just where Bobby wanted him. Now 'Battling Bobby' Rizzo let loose with that vicious left that was his pride: boom, boom, boom! The jabs were hard and the Killer was surprised, stunned. Then out of nowhere Bobby shot a swift right uppercut that slammed into the Killer's chin like a freight train and knocked the big Pole's lights out. Killer Kowsalski went down like a felled tree and Bobby Rizzo won the first fight since he'd been back. Won by a knockout. It was sweet.

It was June, 1946, and Bobby Rizzo was finally home where he belonged, in Brooklyn, New York. He was home from the Pacific Theatre of war and back in the ring again. The former Marine had recovered from a wound compliments of the Japanese on *Iwo Jima* and had built himself up, ready to take some bouts.

Thank God, Big Joe Jackson was still around. Big Joe had managed Bobby before the war—had billed the kid then as "Battling Bobby Rizzo the Brawlin' Eye-talian "—and they had even won a few fights before Uncle Sam sent for the young boxer. Bobby knew they was mostly brawls, but they were still wins. He was no finesse type boxer and that was okay with him too.

Joe didn't see things quite that way but he didn't complain when they won. Nevertheless, he always tried to get Bobby to be more of a thinking fighter than just a toe-to-toe slugger.

"You lead with your face you're asking for trouble, I told you that a hundred times, Bobby," Joe said after the fight. It was their first fight together since the ex-Marine had returned to the ring.

"We won, didn't we?" Bobby laughed, wincing at the bandage on his nose. It wasn't broken, not this time.

"Yeah, we won, Bobby. Bottom line, that's what matters in this game."

Joe was a good egg. He stood six feet two and was as dark as night. He would have made a hell of a champ himself, but a bad ticker caused him to quit the game before he'd even got started. It was sure ironic, for in those days not much was open to a Black man except boxing, and here was Joe—a natural who couldn't compete—but not because of race but because of his bum heart. Thing of it was, Joe had more 'heart' than any ten boxers combined. Joe would have kept fighting 'til he died in the ring if it hadn't been for Alicia, his daughter. She was the apple of his eye and all that was left in his life after his wife, Samantha, passed years back.

"I don't cry over spilled milk," Joe told Bobby when they talked about it that first day after he'd come home.

Bobby wanted to fight again and he wanted Joe to be his manager.

Joe told the kid, "If you fight again, I'll manage you again. It'll be just like the old days. You got real heart, who knows where it can lead."

"Okay, then we're a team, you and me straight to the big time!"

Joe began training his young fighter and built him up to become what he called a 'formidable pugilist'.

"You got a hard head, Bobby," Joe told him one day when

they were sparring at the gym, "and a right that's as hard as a brick. You can take punishment and dish it out, that's good, but you have to watch out for that finesse fighter who is also a smart fighter. That combo could do you in. Hurt you. You have to stay away from him, don't go for the bait, stay back and tire him out, wear 'im down with jabs and body blows. Then when the time's right you can draw him in and brawl. Duke him with your hard left, then put 'im away with that mighty right. Then it's lights out. Like what I want you to do with that Jim Day fellow tonight."

Bobby nodded, he always listened to Joe. In the months before the war he'd won half a dozen fights, two by knockouts. It was mostly against bums or has-beens, but Jim Day was a contender, he'd even fought the great Tammy Moriello, who had himself fought the great Joe Louis and almost knocked down the champ! But Bobby was to find that Day had powerful friends. Joe and he learned that just before the fight when Albert Giacomo himself paid them a visit.

Joe was taping his fighter up and the ex-Marine's girl, Veronica, was also there that night. She came in late as usual. She'd been giving Bobby the brush all day then had come to see the fight, but now that Giacomo and his goons arrived she lit out fast. Bobby couldn't blame her.

Albert Giacomo never went anywhere without his two goons, Mutt and Jeff, or whatever their names were. They were each bigger than Bobby, bigger even than Joe, and they never talked. They did all their communicating with fists, saps—or guns.

"What you want here?" Joe asked Giacomo none too politely, not happy to see the gangster at all. A visit from a guy like him was like death darkening your door.

"Shut up, you!" the gangster boss barked, then looking over to Bobby, "You've got a good right, kid, you're hard and fast, but tonight you're going down. Got that, Rizzo?"

Bobby shook his head, "I don't think so, Mr. Giacomo."

"Albert, call me Albert, we're partners now," the mobster said confidently, his goons smiling. "Bobby, you go down by the third round, or you go down after the fight with a bullet. Do I make myself clear?" He didn't wait for an answer, he walked off with his goons trailing behind him to leave Joe and Bobby alone with the cold sweats on a very hot summer evening.

"Well, that's that," Joe said sadly.

"What do you mean?"

"What do I mean?" the manager looked at his young fighter like the boy was crazy, and maybe he was, because what Giacomo had said got Bobby's blood to boiling now that he thought about it.

"You gotta go down." Joe said.

"Like hell I will!"

"You crazy, Bobby," Joe shouted in exasperation. "You know what they'll do if you cross them?"

"This is my one chance, Joe, *our* one chance!" Day is a contender, if I beat him—*and I know I can*—I move up on the bill, maybe even into the big time. It's what we always wanted."

"If you don't do like you been told, you'll never live to see the big time."

Bobby glared at Joe defiantly but he knew his manager was right. That had been a reality of the fight game before he'd gone away to war and it was worse now.

"Look, Bobby, I'm behind you one hundred per-cent, you know that. I just want you to realize what you're getting your-self into by bucking these guys. This is the mob, they don't ask twice."

"I know. Look, Joe, maybe you should leave now, go home. I don't want you involved in this."

Joe just shook his head but Bobby could see the man wasn't going anywhere. Joe's loyalty touched the kid and made him smile.

Just then the door flew open and Sammy, a lackey from the arena stuck his head inside, "Hey, Rizzo, you're up next. Two minutes!"

He nodded, got ready.

Joe put his big paw of a hand on Bobby's head and rubbed his hair for good luck.

"You never had no sense. Hard-headed even for an eye-talian."

"Sicilian," Bobby corrected.

"That's even worse!"

They both laughed. Then Joe helped his fighter with his robe and lead him out of the room, down the hall, and into the arena where a cheering crowd awaited the arrival of the formidable Jim Day.

The crowd was large and vocal, looking for a good fight and Bobby wanted to give them one. Day was tough and fast but the ex-Marine knew that he could take him. Bobby was supposed to go down by the third round, but he put down Day in the second when the boxer gave him an opening he just couldn't pass up. Then Bobby connected with a pile driver to the guy's left temple. Day saw stars and went down. Bobby won by a knockout and the crowd went wild.

When the ref raised Bobby's hand in victory over Jim Day's prone form, he noticed Albert Giacomo and his boys glare at him from their front row seats.

* * * * * * *

The next morning Bobby was at Junior's Restaurant on Flatbush Avenue with his babe, Veronica. They'd been sweethearts before he'd gone away but today she was giving him his marching orders.

"We're through, Bobby," she said sharply, no *ifs*, *ands* or *buts* about it. "I wanted to wait until after the fight to tell you."

"Yeah, I figured." For weeks now something always seemed to come up when he wanted to see Veronica. When he phoned her, she was never home. When he made a date she was always busy or stood him up. How can an unmarried girl who doesn't work and doesn't go to school, never be home?

"I'm sorry," she said as if that made it all square. She sipped her milk shake like she didn't have a care in the world now.

Bobby couldn't even touch his cheesecake.

Veronica shrugged, "That's just the way it goes, Bobby. While you were away, things changed."

"Yeah, a lot changed. You changed."

"I did, I wised up. You should too. You're a loser, Bobby. I don't hitch my star to no losers. Goodbye."

Veronica got up and left and the fighter sat there alone dumbfounded, fuming at her insults and at how his life had seemed to hit rock bottom. Then he saw Albert Giacomo and his two goons come into the restaurant and walk over to his table and Bobby realized his troubles hadn't even begun.

Giacomo glared at the young boxer, "You cost me some money the other night, but we'll make it back, and a lot more."

Bobby swallowed hard, waiting for the other foot to drop, probably on his face. Was Giacomo going to have his goons rough him up, or even shoot him now, right there in Junior's?

"Look, Albert...," Bobby stammered.

"No, *you* look! I'm a generous guy, you can ask the boys here," he said nodding at Mutt and Jeff who absolutely agreed with him, their heads bobbing in perfect symmetry. "I ain't gonna kill you, won't even hurt you. Not yet. I ain't even gonna hurt your buddy, Joe. Not yet. You know he has a daughter? Sweet young thing I hear tell, the apple of old Joe's eye."

"You wouldn't!"

"No, I wouldn't, if you do as you're told."

So that was it. Not him any longer, but Joe, and his daughter too. Bobby sighed, all the wind had gone out of his sails.

"What do you want?"

"Now that's what I like to hear," the gangster said with a confident smile. He pinched the fighter's cheek like he was his grandson. Then he looked over at his goons, "See boys, a nice conversation and common sense can go a long way. There's no need for violence. Not yet."

Mutt just shrugged unconvinced but he made sure the fighter saw the holstered .38 under his arm when he opened his jacket. The other guy, Jeff, just sat looking at Bobby meaningfully, cracking his knuckles.

Bobby waited silently.

"You got a fight next weekend. You take a dive in the fourth round, understand?"

"Yeah."

"No more games, I'm out of patience with you."

"Alright, by the fourth."

"That's nice, Bobby, be a good boy and you'll make out okay. Now finish your cheesecake, and be happy...that you're still alive and can eat it. Come on, boys."

Bobby ignored the cheesecake. He sat there alone thinking about Veronica having dumped him and the threats against Joe and his daughter. Albert Giacomo didn't scare him—well not too much—but no way he would put Joe and his family in peril. He owed Joe, the old guy had been like a father to him. Bobby was in a hell of a spot.

The young boxer jumped when he felt the tap on his shoulder. He thought it must be Giacomo or one of his goons returned to put some physical emphasis to their words but when he turned around all he saw was a beautiful raven-haired young woman. She sat alone at the next table and had leaned over to get his attention. She sure was a dish! She had his attention now for sure.

"I hope you don't mind," she said softly.

Bobby looked her over, unable to speak for a moment. She was lovely. Dark eyes, red lips, dressed like a secretary or maybe even a model.

"I'm sorry, but I couldn't help overhearing," she continued, explaining, "I heard what those men said. I think it was disgusting."

"Yeah," he said with a smirk, confused, wondering who she was and what her game was. "Disgusting is one word for it, sure."

"What I mean is...." She got up from her table and came to sit at his table. "I hope you don't mind?"

Bobby shrugged, he didn't mind much of anything right now,

"Nah...take a seat."

"My name is Susan Goldman, I work in the Williamsburg Savings Bank Building over at One Hanson Place...in the offices of the New York State Criminal Task Force...."

She kinda let that last part drop in his lap and it took him a moment to get the meaning of what she'd said.

"Whoa, you're a state agent?" he asked immediately suspicious but also curious.

"No, silly, I'm a secretary, but I work in the Brooklyn office. My brother, George, is an agent and I think you should talk to him about what's going on."

Bobby just laughed, "Look sister, I don't know who you are or what you want. For all I know you might be a plant sent by Albert and the boys. Even if you're on the level, no one can get me outta the fix I'm in."

"You'd be surprised, Bobby," she said and flashed him a little smile that caused him to smile back.

"Yeah, well.... Wait a minute! How do you know my name?" he blurted suddenly suspicious. Then he realized that since she'd heard his conversation, she must have heard his name too.

The girl smiled sweetly, "You're 'Battling Bobby', I know you."

He took another look at her then, "You know I'm a fighter?"

"I saw you fight, Bobby," she explained. "Last night against Jim Day. You were terrific!"

Bobby gulped hard. She sure was a dish! Was she into the fights too?

"You've got a good left hook," she added with a light grin, "but not a long reach, which means you have to get in close to make your play with your powerful right. That's also where it could be dangerous for you."

"You sound like my manager."

She laughed sweetly," I know a little bit about the sport."

Bobby let out a deep breath. She was sure right about his fighting but he wasn't so sure she was talking entirely about boxing, or was it something else?

"What's your game, sister?" he asked sharply, serious now, wary but intrigued as well.

"No game, Bobby," she said demurely. "I saw you fight last night because my brother George fights golden gloves and I went there to watch him in an earlier bout. When I came into Junior's I noticed you and your girl right off. I didn't expect to see her...well...dump you. Then when those three mobsters came in to brace you.... Well, it just didn't seem right. I guess I want you to know that not everyone in this town is against you."

Bobby nodded slowly, then smiled at her, she was sure a vision to look at. As she smiled back at him her deep red lips and warm mouth were as inviting as any he'd ever seen. Bobby let out a deep sigh. What could he say...?

"So how's the cheesecake?" she asked.

"The cheese...? I don't know, I haven't tried it yet."

"You should, Junior's makes the best cheesecake in the city, it's world famous," then she took his fork, cut off a small piece and brought it up to his mouth.

"Open up."

He did as ordered, and she fed him that piece of cake like he was a child. He didn't know what that meant, or what she figured to prove, but Bobby suddenly forgot all about Veronica and Albert Giacomo. She said her name was Susan. He kind of liked that name.

Then he took the fork from her and cut off a piece of the delicious creamy cheesecake and fed it to her. She took a bite, smiled, laughed, wiped the corners of her mouth.

"Tell me why you like to box, Bobby?"

He looked at her closely, not knowing where to start. It was his life, simple as that. It was all he'd ever known and all he'd ever wanted to do. It was all he ever thought a poor Sicilian kid could do growing up in Brooklyn without family or connections. Boxing was like magic—like being one of the gods—being in the ring made him feel immortal, untouchable—at least until another boxer touched him! Bobby told her all this and more and she listened avidly until he finished. He was a little embarrassed afterward by his unnatural long-windedness.

Susan just laughed pleasantly and then he did also.

They left Junior's and walked down Flatbush Avenue looking in all the store windows, talking about their lives.

"You were in the war?" she asked.

"Yeah, in the Pacific. I was wounded at *Iwo Jima*."

"Oh!" she said and he saw a sudden sadness come into her face.

"What is it?" Bobby asked. They had stopped walking now. She was silent for a long moment.

"Your ex, Veronica," Susan said softly, "she doesn't know how lucky she is. My future husband, Tom, was killed in the war. He died on *Iwo*."

Bobby didn't know what to say. "I'm...sorry...Susan."

She gave him a sad little smile, slipped her arm into his arm. He hesitantly moved his hand over her own and held it tightly. They moved closer together, then began walking again.

Finally she added, "We were to be married once he returned."

"He must have been a great guy."

"He was, Bobby, you would have liked him." Then after a few moments, "You know, he was a lot like you."

"Like me?"

"Yes, he was a boxer too, though strictly amateur. See, Tom and my brother George, grew up together. They fought golden gloves before the war. I met Tom through my brother and through boxing. I guess I've just got boxing in the blood."

They continued walking together, the talk finally petering out but that didn't matter by then, they just liked the feeling of holding hands as they walked. It was a warm summer morning, the streets were busy but not crowded. Life was going on all around them but it seemed Susan and Bobby only had eyes for each other.

He walked Susan to her office at the Williamsburg Saving Bank building.

"So what are you going to do about that fight next week?" she asked finally.

Bobby shrugged, "I don't have much choice."

He'd told her about Joe and his daughter and what his old friend and manager meant to him.

"It's a tight spot to be in I guess," Susan sympathized.

"Yeah."

"Why don't you come in and talk to George about it?"

He shook his head, "I ain't no rat."

"You wouldn't be a rat, Bobby, you'd be standing up for yourself, and for Joe and his daughter."

He thought about that for a minute. The way Susan said it, it almost seemed to make sense but he just couldn't squawk no matter what—especially to the cops or the state police.

"I can handle it my own way," he said finally.

Susan shook her head in disagreement, "No you can't, you need help."

"Maybe, but it's something I gotta do on my own."

They left it at that. He took Susan's number and told her he'd call her before the fight. Then she went into the bank building and her state police job and he slow-walked it back to the gym farther down Flatbush Avenue.

When Bobby got to the gym Joe met him at the door.

"I just had a visit from Albert Giacomo and his thugs," Joe said. His black face couldn't hide the fact that he had a nice new shiner underneath his right eye.

"You okay? What happened?"

"I'm okay, a 'love tap' they called it, just to get my attention. They want me to make sure you throw that fight next week."

"What about your daughter?"

"So far she's okay, they're just spouting hot air, unless we cross them again. Just to be sure I sent Alicia to my sister's place in East New York. I don't want none of this coming down on her."

"Good," Bobby said, relieved Joe's daughter would be out of the line of fire.

"Now, I ask you, what we gonna do?"

"I don't know, but I ain't going down in the fourth."

"I can help you, if you like. Maybe we can take 'em out?"

"Yeah, that'll surely do it, one ex-gyrine slugger and an old pro with a bum ticker. What kinda chance we got?"

"We can take 'em!"

"Are you serious! They're mob men, Joe. Connected."

"We could make 'em disappear. Happens all the time in their line of work, people would assume it was just another mob hit. There is a mob war going on."

"I don't know, what if we screw up? We're not killers."

"Then we're dead, but you don't throw the fight, we're dead anyway," Joe said simply.

"Well, that's sure great!" Bobby laughed harshly. This was getting more complicated. He was an ex-Marine and a boxer, not a cold-blooded killer, and getting involved in mob violence was just suicide.

"Hell, Bobby, we're dead anyway, because I know you and I know there's no way you're going down in the fourth. I know my boy—you got the ring in your blood and you'd never throw a fight."

Bobby shook his head, "We're really in a fix, Joe."

"You can say that again."

They fell silent for a while thinking it through.

"Say we were to do this crazy plan of yours," Bobby offered slowly. "How would we do it? It would mean killing them all— all three of them—then hiding the bodies. No one could ever find them."

"I got some friends up in Harlem, might give me a hand," Joe said carefully.

"Black gangsters?" Bobby asked just as carefully now.

"Well, they ain't eye-talians."

"I don't know, Joe. Maybe I should just go to that state task force."

"What do you mean?" Joe asked.

Then he told his manager all about meeting Susan Goldman at Junior's that morning and how her brother was an agent on the New York State Criminal Task Force.

"They're not Feds but they got major juice," Joe said slowly, "it might just work."

"Yeah, but I don't wanna rat."

"Rat-*smhat*, who cares, you don't owe them bums nothing," Joe offered. "Look, what you told me that new girl of yours said, it makes real sense."

"She's not my girl!"

"Not yet, my boy, but I see it in your eyes."

"Veronica...." He was going to update Joe....

"Forget her, she was never any good anyway."

Bobby shook his head in exasperation, but he had to admit that he liked the sound of Joe's words, about Susan maybe being his girl someday. He sure liked the look of her too. He was also surprised that she made him forget all about Veronica.

"State agents, huh?" he mused.

"They ain't Feds, but baby they got the kinda juice we need," Joe said, watching as the young boxer thought it over.

* * * * * * *

Each day that passed that week Bobby wanted to call Susan and talk, but all he could think about was what to do about the fight that weekend. That week was one of the longest and hardest for Bobby and for Joe. They went over what to do from all angles and it always seemed there was only one course of action. Bobby didn't like it but he knew he had no choice.

* * * * * * *

Susan Goldman picked up the phone expecting anyone but the person who was at the other end of the receiver.

"Bobby? Is that you?"

"I told you I'd call," he said, his happiness at hearing her voice again evident to her.

"It's good to hear from you, Bobby," she replied, not afraid to let her own joy show either. "I was wondering how you were doing."

"I'm okay," Bobby said, then nervously getting down to it, he added, "Look, Susan, I been thinking about what you said; coming in to talk with your brother and his state cops about the fights."

"You have?"

"Yeah, I been talking it over with Joe. Tell them I'll come in whenever they want."

"Oh, Bobby, that's great, I'm so happy for you. I'll tell George and I know he'll want to see you right away."

* * * * * * *

The fight was due to begin at nine that night, and 'Battling Bobby' Rizzo's bout was slated for an hour later at ten o'clock. They still had plenty of time. Joe had just finished wrapping Bobby's hands in tape and then put on his gloves. Joe was tying the laces when Albert Giacomo and his two goons walked into the arena dressing room. Everyone looked at everyone. Hard glares all around.

"Just so you don't get any stupid ideas," the mobster said. "Remember, we'll be right outside."

Bobby nodded. Joe continued tying laces.

Everyone looked behind them when the locker room doors suddenly flew open and three well-dressed men in three-piece suits entered. The man in the lead showed a badge, "I'm Detective George Goldman, State Task Force, who's Bobby Rizzo?"

"Jeese, Feds!" one of Giacomo's goons muttered.

Albert Giacomo looked at the newcomers without worry. "Not Feds, boys, they're just state cops bought and paid for," he said boldly as he drew a pistol and his goons did likewise. He pointed the weapon at the cops and barked, "Get the hell outta here before I fill you full of hot lead!"

"You got the wrong boys, Albert," George Goldman barked back as he and his men went for their own guns. Suddenly bullets began to fly.

Bobby and Joe dived under the table, being unarmed they were ignored as the three hoods shot it out with the three state cops. Bullets were flying everywhere. When one of the state cops went down after being hit in the arm, Bobby flew out of his place of concealment enraged. He ran up to Giacomo's goon before the mobster could execute the cop, giving him a hard one-two punch combo—chin and breadbasket shots—that put the thug down. More guns blazed and Bobby had to move off. The mob men gathered their fallen comrade and quickly ducked out a back door. They ran down a hallway and were soon gone.

Agent George Goldman came over and said, "They won't get away, we have the arena closed off, city cops outside stationed at all the exits. So you're Bobby Rizzo."

"Yes, sir," Bobby nodded.

"Well, that was a brave thing you did, you saved Agent Jones' life."

"Is he all right?"

Jones smiled, nodded, nursing a shoulder wound as his fellow agent bandaged him up. That agent said, "He'll be as good as new in a while, thanks to you."

George Goldman looked back at the young boxer, "I hear you have a fight later?"

"Yeah, ten o'clock."

"Well, you don't have much time. Get ready and don't mind us. Look for us at ringside, we'll make sure you're safe," Goldman said. "And Bobby, you don't have to go down in the fourth now."

"Yeah, thanks."

"Don't thank me, thank Susan."

"Yeah, I will," he replied as Joe finished up with the laces on his gloves.

* * * * * * *

'Battling Bobby' Rizzo was going up against Jesse Quinn, a

hard punk hitter from steeltown who didn't know the meaning of the word 'stop'. The two bruisers were pretty evenly matched and went at each other blow for blow with a relish that had the crowd screaming with delight. It was nasty and bloody, just what the crowd had paid their hard-earned money for.

Bobby saw Susan Goldman at ringside with her brother. His heart skipped a beat when he saw she was openly cheering him on. It made him feel good to see her there and have her rooting for him. She made him want to fight like a real champ and win.

Then he spied Veronica at the opposite end of the ring and Albert Giacomo was with her. The two looked more than friendly. That's when Rizzo understood some things about a girl like Veronica, that's also when Jesse Quinn connected with a hard right to Bobby's head because his attention on the fight had been diverted.

Bobby hadn't even seen the blow coming. He was stunned and fell back, Quinn followed up with another hard shot to the left temple and a low blow to the gut. Bobby was reeling now and in trouble. He was dizzy; the ring, Quinn, the crowd all seemed to be floating around him in some kind of bizarre kaleidoscope of sight and sound. He thought he heard Joe shout a warning. He couldn't make it out. He saw Susan shouting something at him too; she looked scared, panicky. He turned and saw Veronica smiling, her arms around Giacomo, then he saw the gangster pull out something from his jacket.

It was a gun and Bobby's eyes went wide. He heard Joe shout something in warning. Was it *'Get down!'*?

Then Jesse Quinn rammed another hard shot forward, a brutal uppercut that knocked Bobby back reeling. Quinn came forward for the *coup de grâce* when suddenly a loud sound shattered the raucous cheering in the hall. Quinn stopped in mid-step, frozen, confused, then fell down, blood pouring from his chest. The arena was in sudden pandemonium, panic and chaos triumphed as more shots were fired.

Bobby tried to rise, felt Joe at his side grabbing him, telling him to stay down.

A woman screamed. Bobby looked up and saw that it was Veronica. She stood holding up Albert Giacomo, trying to get him out of the row of seats and over the body of one of his goons who was slumped down dead blocking their escape. The other goon fired his gun at the cops and was soon shot dead where he stood. Then Bobby saw Goldman and his agents, augmented with city police, take Albert and Veronica into custody.

Bobby Rizzo looked at his manager with confusion.

"What happened, Joe?" he said, his senses returning as he started putting it all together. "How's Quinn?"

Joe shook his head as Quinn's men came to the boxer's aid, "He don't look so good."

Then the boxer suddenly heard his name shouted out by a frantic female voice.

"Oh, Bobby! *Bobby*!"

As Joe helped him to his feet they saw Susan Goldman rushing towards them. She was red-faced, crying, but her fear turned to joy once she saw he was all right.

He smiled when he saw Susan. She sure was a sight for sore eyes.

"Bobby! You're okay?"

"Sure, I'm fine," he said softly. She was so close to him now, he wanted to reach out and fold her into his arms, into his body, into his very soul. Suddenly she enfolded her arms around him and their lips met in a long passionate kiss.

Joe just shook his head at all that had happened, "Boxing and bullets just don't mix."

'Battling Bobby' Rizzo smiled at his friend's words, then drew Susan back down to him and planted another big wet kiss on her parted red lips. Susan melted into his arms as if they were two peas from the same pod. At that moment everything was right in Bobby and Susan's world.

"Hey! What's this?" Agent Goldman said now on the scene and sounding all brotherly and protective of his sister. "Come on, break it up!"

"He's right, we should save it for the wedding night!" Bobby said with a smile.

"Do you mean that you want to marry me?" Susan egged him on, the sweet smile on her face never wavered. Things were moving pretty fast—just the way she liked them.

Bobby didn't know what to say so he didn't say another word. They both watched as the city police had Veronica and Albert in handcuffs and were now leading them out of the hall. The mob man's two goons lay dead where they had fallen, the bodies now being bagged by men from the city morgue. An ambulance had already taken Jesse Quinn to the hospital.

"Well, Bobby?" Susan asked the boxer as the two stood together. "You have anything you want to ask me?"

"Yeah well, Susan...ah...I do have one little question to ask you."

Susan smiled sweetly, "Then I guess you'd better ask it."

Bobby nodded nervously, said, "Susan Goldman...will you... marry me?"

She looked up into his eyes, smiling sweetly she replied, "Why Bobby Rizzo, this is all so very sudden, but I will surely think seriously about it."

Bobby laughed and so did Susan.

"All right now, let's get outta here!" Agent Goldman said feigning exasperation though he couldn't help but allow a smile when he noticed his sister wink at Bobby, and Bobby wink back at her.

Joe saw it too and just shook his head at the entire crazy business, telling his young friend, "Babes and boxing don't mix either."

"Yeah, Joe, but what the hell can a guy do about it when love scores a knockout!"

FIRST MAN FALLING

BY GARNETT ELLIOTT

Ángel pounded the heavy bag. It had been wound with duct tape so many times it looked like a giant silver cocoon. *Whap.* A hard left sent the thing swaying.

"Keep it up," whispered Márquez, his oft-time trainer. "Scout's comin' this way."

Ángel shot a glance around the gym. The place was packed with sweating hopefuls. Would-be champions skipped rope, hauled weights, did crunches, and sparred inside the tiny ring with its sagging posts. The air smelled like the interior of an athletic shoe. About as hot, too. Somewhere among the crowd wandered a *Telemundo* cameraman, trailing two dark-suited scouts in his wake.

"Back at it, asshole," said Márquez. "Busy now."

Someone squeezed towards them. Ángel caught a flash of dark fabric. He fired off his best combination: a triple jab, three lefts landing *pop pop pop* against the bag, finishing with a right cross.

"*Que bueno.*" He felt a hand on his shoulder.

Ángel turned to a smiling, well-tanned face. One of the scouts. He wore a black blazer with a worn notebook tucked under his arm.

"Don't tell me," the scout said. "Ángel Martín, right?" He pronounced it An-*hel* Mar-*tine*, despite being an Anglo. "I already know your record. Eight and one, six by technical knock out. You're a heavy hitter for a semi-pro."

"We call him the King of Combos," Márquez said.

"I like that." The scout made a notation in his book. He flicked a card from his blazer pocket and handed it to Ángel. "Call me about arranging a preliminary bout. I assume you're interested."

"Very much, sir," Ángel said.

He would've said more, maybe bragged a little bit, but the scout was already walking away, waving at someone far off.

Márquez slapped his back. "Good job, man. You okay?"

"My heart's pounding."

"That's what fame feels like. You're taking me with you, right? I'll be your corner man. Márquez and Martín, headed for—oh, crap."

Fear flashed across Márquez's broad face. Ángel followed his gaze to a six-foot-four heavy with prison tats scrolling down both arms. The *hombre duro* lumbered towards them, shoving boxers out of his way. When he got within spitting distance he lowered his hands to his hips and locked eyes with Ángel. "Papa Reynoso wants to see you."

"What about my friend?" Ángel said, nodding to his side.

"What friend?"

Márquez had already vanished.

Ángel followed the heavy to a short hallway. Just outside, the *Telemundo* cameraman and a pretty female reporter were interviewing El Mudo. The deaf boxer squinted to read her lips and signed his answers to his trainer, who translated. His hooded eyes made contact with Ángel and he scowled.

* * * * * * *

"I told you not to come to my gym. Not today."

Papa Reynoso sat bolt upright behind his desk. He wore a white guayabera unbuttoned over a bulging, anger-reddened neck.

"I pay my fees," Ángel said. "Good money to use your shitty equipment. And the contest's open to everyone, not just your favorites."

The sounds of the gym and the crowd outside carried through the office's thin walls. "You," Reynoso said finally, rubbing at his temples, "you think talent gives you the right to talk like that. To me? You're not that talented, boy."

Ángel opened his mouth. Reynoso raised a finger. "No. You speak again and I'll call Chuy back in here. Give you a beating you won't forget. Out of respect for your father, I hold back. You understand?"

Ángel glared. But he kept silent.

"People from all over the Imperial Valley come to train here. Papa Reynoso's *Casa de Dolor*. Alright, so the equipment's a little old. So what? This place has soul." Reynoso made a wrinkled fist. "I train fighters, not yuppies. And yes, El Mudo's one of my favorites, as you say. The man's got real spirit. Determination. He's going places."

Unlike you.

Ángel stirred in his seat.

Reynoso chuckled. "You should see yourself right now. Like a dog that's been muzzled, but dying to bark. Go ahead, speak."

"I'm as good as El Mudo. Better."

"Ha."

"He's famous because he's handicapped. People feel sorry for him. It's a gimmick."

"How do you explain his record, then? How do you explain his beating *you*?"

"That was a three-round exhibition, not a real match. I wasn't trying."

"Excuses. Mediocrity is always making excuses. Mudo's one in a million. This contest, this 'Battle of the Barrios,' is his chance to break into the pro circuit. Once he's there, he'll skyrocket. You'll see."

"Then why can't I compete? If he's as great as everybody says, then I couldn't be a threat, right?"

Reynoso leaned back in his seat. He patted his hands together. "Ángel, Ángel. You understand the limits of your talent? You can hit hard, yes. And you've landed some lucky punches, won when by all rights you should've lost."

"That was skill—"

"So what would happen if you got lucky again, fighting El Mudo? Knocked him out, say? You'd advance, but your luck wouldn't hold in the professional leagues. Meanwhile, the better boxer, the *consistent* boxer, is denied his shot." Reynoso shook his head. "It wouldn't be fair."

"None of this is fair. Keeping me out of the contest, is that fair?"

Reynoso held out his hand. "Give me the business card that agent gave you. Chuy saw you take it."

"You can't—"

"Yes, I can. I could make you a cripple if I wanted. That'd keep you from competing, wouldn't it? Now hand over the card."

Ángel made a show of indecision. He huffed. He cursed in Spanish. Finally, he reached into his pocket and threw the card at the desk. It landed with a flutter.

He'd already memorized the number.

* * * * * * *

Noonday sun scorched the rough dirt and broken glass behind Ángel's parents' tract house. One hundred and seven degrees in the shade. Even the lizards skittered with purpose.

One and two and three and....

Ángel did push-ups with his knuckles straining against stacked cinder blocks. Sweat dripped off him in rivulets. He worked slow, feeling the resistance as his chest dipped close to the ground.

"Stop that and come back to the house. Lunch's ready."

Ángel squinted up. A corona of sunlight shone around his mother's dark hair. "Almost done...."

"I made a pot of *cocido*."

He let himself collapse face-first. The breath groaned out of him. "I'll pass."

"There's nothing fattening in my soup."

"Got to lose another two pounds."

"Looks like you've sweated it off already. *Ándele pues.*"

She marched him to the porch. A towel lay slung over one of the lawn chairs, and she wiped him down while he chugged lukewarm water from a plastic bottle. The smell of *cocido* drifted through the kitchen window. Goddamn Latinas, he thought. They used food to make their men fat and dependent, until their wills weren't their own.

His father bore testament. Ángel Sr. sat at the small table off the kitchen, hands folded over his swollen stomach. Waiting for his dose. He nodded to Ángel as he sat down.

Mama Martín hustled over two steaming bowls. Ángel folded a tortilla and used it like a spoon, shoveling pieces of tender ox tail, squash, and potato into his mouth.

She waited until he was scraping the bowl. "You shouldn't fight."

"Reynoso's just trying to scare me."

"He's a member of *La Familia.*"

"He won't do anything."

She nodded towards the living room, where the TV glowed and chattered in Spanish. Ángel's girlfriend, Mónica, lay slumped on the couch, watching her stupid *telenovelas*. She had a swollen belly, too.

"What about her?" his mother said. "Your child? You don't want to worry about safety for your own sake, what about them?"

"Mónica believes in what I'm doing."

"Ha. All she cares about is getting a bigger TV."

"I heard that," Mónica said in a loud voice, not taking her eyes off the screen.

"You talk to him," his mother said to his father. "He doesn't listen to me."

Ángel Sr. set his spoon down. "He's a grown man."

"You want him to get his head pounded in?"

"Ángel's a good worker. I told him if he wants to stay with the family business, he can. He'll take it over someday. If the housing market doesn't collapse."

"There you go," his mother said, rounding on Ángel again. "You can run the business. That should be enough for anyone."

"Mother—"

"But you want to be some kind of star."

"Mom—"

"Get your head bashed in."

Ángel stood up. His father's 'business' was three men and a hot-tar machine. They woke before dawn to spread the black gunk over rooftops. At the end of shift, Ángel could wring a cup of sweat from his coveralls. He smelled tar in his dreams.

"I'm gone," he said.

He headed back outside for more push-ups.

* * * * * * *

Much later, the whole house dark, everyone asleep, Ángel lay on the couch. Mónica curled beside him, snoring in breathy gasps.

He tried reaching Márquez on the cell phone. His fifth try.

A *reggaeton* beat played in the receiver, then Márquez's voice saying to leave a message. Ángel could picture him on the other end, staring at the caller ID.

Fucking coward.

He could do this without a corner man.

He shuffled through TV channels and stopped on the local news. They were running a piece about the Battle of the Barrios. Some footage of Reynoso's gym. He watched close, hoping for a glimpse of himself. Instead, they switched to a story about El Mudo from a year ago, how he'd refused money for cochlear implants after a benefit thrown in his honor. The money went to a women's shelter instead. El Mudo had won national attention from the deaf community.

"Gimmick," Ángel said, and shut off the TV.

* * * * * * *

A '73 Impala with tinted windows cruised slow past the Martín house the next evening.

Ángel got the message.

He told Mónica he had to split for awhile and stole off to his cousin Raúl's place, out in the country. There wasn't much room. Ángel decided to bed down in the pigeon coop thirty feet from the house. Lying among the feathers and bird shit, he told himself it was better than sleeping outside.

The day of the contest, Raúl dropped him off at the fairgrounds.

Ángel wore a pulled-up hoody, despite the heat, and the biggest pair of sunglasses he had. His gloves, hand wraps, and shorts all went into a plastic shopping bag.

He slipped into the crowd. Families from El Centro, Mexicali, Brawley, and Calexico milled around the regulation-sized ring. The Tecate booths sold beer at a buck a cup. Ángel pushed past a *churro* vendor and a knot of Latina models in bikinis. He sensed eyes on him and glanced sidelong to see Chuy standing less than five feet away.

The big man gnawed on an ear of roast corn. But he wasn't looking at him. He was scrutinizing one of the girls.

Ángel ducked back and made for the tent marked COMPETITORS.

* * * * * * *

The Battle of the Barrios was set up like a typical smoker: four preliminary bouts at three rounds apiece, with the winners advancing to the main event of eight rounds, all in the same afternoon. The pace and the outside ring made endurance a key factor.

That was good. Ángel had endurance.

His preliminary opponent was a lanky jabber named Castaneda. El Mudo had been paired with Ortiz, an ex-gangster who threw looping rights and cheated whenever possible. Ángel figured it wasn't a coincidence he and El Mudo weren't matched first. The organizers wanted to build towards a finale.

During the weigh-in, none of the fighters looked at each other. El Mudo's eyes stared straight ahead, blank, his fingers rolling into fists and unrolling again.

* * * * * * *

Ángel took his man easy.

The first round Castaneda fired jab after jab, trying to build up points. Ángel moved and covered. He wanted to get a feel for the ring, the way his feet rebounded from the canvas after each step. Castaneda was almost an afterthought.

Second round Ángel jolted him with a straight right, just to show the crowd he was paying attention.

Third round Castaneda looked tired. Sweat plastered his hair flat against his temples, and his footwork slowed. Ángel allowed a jab to slide off the top of his head in order to close. He chopped a short right to the body. Castaneda's hands dropped reflexively, and Ángel's left sailed over his guard, catching the outthrust jaw. The taller man spun and fell.

Breathing easy, Ángel danced over to his empty corner while the referee finished the count. He saw Reynoso's head bobbing in the crowd.

"How's that for *luck*, old man?" he shouted, pride giving his voice wings.

* * * * * * *

By six-thirty the preliminaries were finished and the ring mopped clean of sweat and blood. The huge sodium lights hovering over the back half of the fairgrounds had flickered on.

Ángel sat in his corner, shirtless, watching the entourage surrounding El Mudo. His mother and stepfather, his uncles, his trainer, and Reynoso himself, all reaching over to slap the boxer's shoulders, massage the muscles along his arms.

Ángel had no one. As a rule, his parents never watched his

fights. Mónica was supposed to have shown for his first match, but called later to say it was too hot out. She didn't want to strain the baby.

His one consolation: El Mudo's bout hadn't gone so easy. Ortiz had caught him with an elbow the second round, and now a good-sized mouse swelled the flesh above his right eye. Mudo's cutman had done what he could, but the wound called out to Ángel from across the ring. Hit me, it said.

The announcer slithered in between the ropes. Ángel's heart lurched. He felt the cool panic start at his neck and radiate outwards, but a deep breath kept his head clear. Once he started hitting, he'd be fine. The audience seemed all nerves, too. They coughed and shifted, eyes shining. It'd been a good spectacle so far.

El Mudo's introduction drew thunder and shrill *gritos* from the crowd. Ángel wondered if the deaf fighter felt the energy he couldn't hear.

His own introduction was met with mild ripples of applause. Someone yelling his name in a bass voice. That was it.

He sucked in what inspiration he could and rose to meet his opponent.

* * * * * * *

The first punch landed fourteen seconds later.

El Mudo threw it. Ángel had a couple inches on him, but Mudo's arms were longer. He fought from an exaggerated crouch, like an orangutan who'd learned to box. But the man could hit. The hard muscle sheathing Ángel's stomach puckered.

He danced backwards. Adrenalin soaked most of the shock. Instead of pursuing, El Mudo's hands snapped back to shield both sides of his head. His eyes seemed blank as ever. Total concentration, Ángel realized. The man came by it easy, without sound to distract him.

Ángel feinted with a left jab, tried to hook off it and hit the swelling. Mudo blocked. He answered with a hard right that rattled Ángel's mouth guard.

The crowd howled.

Step closer, said the trainer in Ángel's head. Backing away from someone gave them more leverage. He slipped in and pounded a tattoo at Mudo's concave stomach. Left, right, left. Only the right connected, the other two being flicked away by Mudo's gloves. Ángel clinched him before he could counter, and the ref had to lean in to separate them.

First round went pretty much like that. The ref tapped El Mudo on the shoulder at ten seconds before the bell and again at the end of the round. Ángel wobbled back to his corner. Someone he'd never seen before rubbed Vaseline on his face and inspected him for cuts. A bored-looking card girl thrust a water bottle at his mouth.

He tried to imagine what a trainer would tell him. He'd lost the round; the stiffening muscles along his abdomen told him that. He needed a strategy. Across the ring, El Mudo's trainer signed at a furious pace, gesturing towards Ángel.

The bell rang.

* * * * * * *

Second, third, and fourth rounds all went to El Mudo. No question about it. Ángel lost count after that. Reality blurred and fell away at the edges of the ring. Ángel thanked his mother's saints for all his practice out in the heat. The air between him and Mudo had turned thick as bathwater. They both floated through the stuff.

A missed punch brought him back, a left hook that grazed his temple. El Mudo's features snapped into sudden clarity. The swelling above his right eye had gotten worse. Not that Ángel had been able to hit it much. Still, the flesh puffed down over his eyelid, and sweat dripped there, too. A blind spot. Ángel stepped left. El Mudo's guard instinctively covered the swelling. Ángel threw a right shovel-hook to the unprotected body. He thought about a lifetime of spreading hot tar and put his hips into it.

The punch landed flush. El Mudo's lips pursed into an 'O.' Despite the pain, he kept the right side of his head covered. Ángel cocked back and threw a haymaker at the left side. An undisciplined swing.

It connected.

Mudo reeled. The crowd let out a collective groan and Ángel became aware of them again, like someone had just turned up the volume. His hands felt feather-light. He drove a one-two and the right pulped Mudo's nose.

This was it. This was the kill. He sensed the rubber in his opponent's legs. He saw over Mudo's shoulders, at his corner man. Screaming useless commands his fighter couldn't hear.

Ángel shifted all his weight to his front foot. Chambered his left for a world-killing hook.

El Mudo's good eye gleamed. He looked at Ángel for what seemed the first time.

* * * * * * *

Of course, it wasn't the first time.

Ángel had known him since grade school. Back then El Mudo was just Manuel Esparza, a chubby-faced kid who couldn't talk.

They had lots of other names for him, though.

Ángel had been something of a bully. A ringleader. He'd gather the other boys and they'd wing dirt clods at little Manny as he scuttled home.

The look in his eyes. The emptiness. It must've started then.

* * * * * * *

He never saw the punch. He'd been ready to finish the fight one moment. The next, he was doubled over and his guts coursed with molten metal.

His liver. El Mudo had pounded him in the liver. Something more than muscle and skill had guided the blow.

Vengeance himself couldn't have hit harder.

El Mudo followed with punches to the solar plexus. Ángel felt a rib crack. He dropped. *He* was deaf now, from the crowd's noise.

He saw the ref stoop to look down at him, eyes wide with concern. The ten count began.

He wasn't unconscious. He just couldn't breathe.

* * * * * * *

When it was over, he sat on a folding chair in the competitor's tent, a towel covering his head. His ribs had been taped and it hurt to draw breath.

A hand snatched the towel away.

"Damn good thing you didn't win," Papa Reynosa said. Chuy hovered beside him, his dark eyes lowered in what could have been sympathy. "I was going to have you beat on general principles anyway, but I see El Mudo's done a thorough job. No need to skin any more knuckles."

He laughed and pitched the towel as they walked away.

Watching them go, Ángel realized he didn't have a ride home.

Someone laid a fresh towel across his shoulders. He turned to see the familiar dark blazer. "That was the best match in this whole series, by far," the scout said. "You guys had everyone on their feet."

"I lost."

"Well, yeah. Someone was going to. But you had major disadvantages. No corner man, for one thing. Plus what looks like outside pressures." He glanced in the direction Reynoso and Chuy had left. "I can't help wondering, with proper training, what you might turn into."

"I don't have money for proper training."

The scout stroked his chin. "There's a gym in San Diego, top-ranked. They're always looking for hungry talent. I could put a word in, maybe get you a position sparring. It'd be a start."

"San Diego, huh?" Ángel wondered what an apartment there went for.

"Think about it."

The next couple days, that's all he did.

PITY MADE ME MARRY

BY PENELOPE STANHOPE

I've been reading a book, *The World's Greatest Love Stories*. About the great lovers of history—Antony and Cleopatra, Dante and Beatrice, Lancelot and Guinevere—those romances that people still read about, though the lovers are long since dead and gone.

It made me think of my own love story. Maybe it is too ordinary to be compared with Cleopatra's romance—maybe not! But you can judge for yourself....

My wife is sitting on the rug as I write this, head on my lap. She'd been knitting things for the baby—they're lying beside her.

It was she who suggested that I write this, so I rose and came indoors to find pen and paper. Crazy, it may be, but I just felt I had to set down what happened to me... not that it can compare with the loves of Cleopatra and Antony—but, well, I just had the hunch I'd like to set down what love can mean to an ordinary bloke like me. I'm ordinary enough. Chuck Steven, that's me; and I drive the local baker's van.

But I'll begin at the beginning, when I was just Len Steven's kid, running around in ragged pants and a torn jersey. My old man didn't work steady, just picked up a living where he could find it. Mum was dead, and we lived in a dilapidated shack down by the shore.

I ran wild. Seems I was always in scraps, those days. And I sure knew how to use my mitts. I got into arguments with older, bigger lads, just for the joy of getting a scrap. I'd mix in with anybody—even if they were double my poundage. I Sometimes won, often I took a licking—It was all the same...I was learning, learning fast.

My old man taught me all the tricks there was to know. I tried 'em out in those rough-and-tumble fights. Dad taught me well. Somewhere in his varied past he'd traveled through the States with a boxing booth.

"Could have been a champ, Chuck...," he d tell me, with that wry grin twisting his lean, haggard face. " Only the booze spoilt my chance. But you got all it takes, kid."

Sure 1 had. 1 knew it. There was nothing to stop me.

Then the old man broke a piece of news to me, about the time I lost my job in the local steel mills through getting involved in a scrap with another fellow...yes, I was growing up then, big and husky...and tough, mighty tough.

"You're fighting at the Sportsdrome tonight, Chuck" Dad told me. " I got you lined up for a supporting bout. Do what I tell you, and you'll be okay....

I'll never forget that first night. The naked, glaring lights, a mob howling for

blood, the taut canvas of the ring—and the huge, hairy brute of a guy who was matched against me....

In the five-dollar seats at the ringside—well, I saw a smashing blonde, looking out of place amongst the fight fans all around.

A bent, wrinkled second told me she was Smarty Smith's daughter, and I pulled in my breath some at that. Smith was well known in the town. He'd a finger in a lot of pies—he ran a line of freight trucks, was. partner with Lee Cohen in a dance hall, and I'd heard he was going in for boxing promotions in a big way.

And I saw Rita Smith...that was her name...saw her smile at me, encouraging like, just as the bell clanged for the first round.

That smile did things to me, somehow. I tore into the other guy like I was a tiger, and nothing could stop mc. I wanted to show Rita Smith I was tough—and I did, knocking out the other fellow in the third round.

Afterwards, in the bare cubicle that did duty as a dressing-room, I was talking to Dad and a local sports writer, when a knock came to the door. Then the place seemed to overflow with men—stout, flashy men. who smoked big cigars. It took me a moment or two before I recognized Smith, Cohen and another guy I learnt later was their manager.

"I'm putting on a big fight at the Embassy next month." Smarty Smith looked at me, shrewdly. "Want you on the bill. Okay?"

I looked past the fight promoter's bulky figure, and saw Rita hovering in the doorway, looking one hundred per cent lovely in a fur coat that hung open so none of her classy curves would be hidden. She nodded, and smiled, so I told Smith that sure I'd fight at the Embassy. I'd the feeling Rita was behind the invitation—and I was right there, as I learnt later.

That's when we got to know each other really well. I'd shifted training quarters to a gym down-town, where her dad was bringing on promising fighters. That meant I saw a lot of Rita. In more ways than one.

Gosh, these days, I couldn't think of anything except her. She was so lovely, the sort of girl I'd dreamed about having one day. Yes it had all seemed so remote, when I was just Lee Steven's brat, living in an old shack on the wrong side of the railroad tracks....

Now we roomed in a classy apartment house, for I was really in the money. Those mitts of mine seemed golden, for they brought me plenty dough, as I was matched for more and more fights. I was climbing the ladder fast, getting in amongst the big shots.

"You're swell, darling...," Rita whispered in my ear, as we danced in her father's joint one night after I'd halted a promising scrapper from Boston in the fifth round. "Everybody says you are going places. Daddy is mighty pleased you're under contract to him...and me, I'm proud of you, Kid....

That's what they called me—Kid Steven. The sporting papers

were giving me swell write-ups. But the idea of Rita being proud of me—it bowled me over, so I felt I was in a sort of daze. A smashing dame like her, proud of me! She was so lovely, with blonde hair and the bluest of blue eyes. There wasn't a girl in the hall to touch her for looks...and the soft curves of her perfect body were. suggestively revealed by the tightness of a sheer silk frock, that was cut daringly low.

"A few more scraps," I boasted, "then I'll have real dough—enough for us to get married on, Rita. You'll marry me, won't you, darling?"

I saw her face cloud over. She gave a nervous little laugh.

"I don't know, Chuck. Marrying seems so final and lasting. Guess I'm scared...."

I looked at her, steadily. "Don't you love me enough to risk it?"

She smiled, faintly. I thought of all the times she had lain in my arms, sworn she loved me, promising nothing would ever part us...yet she said she was scared to marry me....

"I'm only kidding" she said, squeezing my arm. "Anyway, time enough for us getting married...."

I had to be content with that. Yet I was determined she would marry me—some day! I loved her so much....

* * * * * * *

It was the old man who warned me first. After I'd lost on points to a mauler from the South.

I saw Dad's face was worried, bending over me as I lay on the table in my dressing room.

"You'll have to cut out the gay times," he frowned. "You ain't in training, Chuck...that's the truth! Them late nights are telling. Why, you should have chopped that dope into little bits—but you couldn't! The first coupla rounds you was all over him...but you couldn't last the pace. I'm warning you, Chuck, you gotta stick to the training."

Flat out on the table, I lay blinking up into the unshaded electric light above my head. The old man was right, I granted him that. Yet his words didn't make any deep impression on me, not even when I lost the next two fights. Because there was Rita... who came first with me, always.

Other people told me I was slipping. A sports writer made some cutting comments in his column. I just laughed. For wasn't I right on top of the world?

Until that day....

A warm, sunny day, with a blue sky and only a drift of high white clouds. Rita and I lay on the grassy slope near the shore.... We'd been swimming, and relaxed now, feeling the sun's warmth dry our damp costumes.

I leaned over Rita, and caught her hand in a strong grip.

"See here, Rita." I knew my voice shook a trifle, but I couldn't help that. "How about us marrying? I got it arranged, Rita. Why put it off any longer?"

She looked at me with those blue eyes—can I ever forget that look? There was contempt in it...maybe some pity, too.

"Marry you?" Her voice was high. "Don't be crazy, Chuck. I wouldn't marry you, ever...."

That was a blow to me. I loved Rita so much, you understand? I'd always thought we'd be married, some day.

Infatuated, I didn't pause to remember that I was only Len Steven's youngster, who used to run around in ragged pants.... At best, I was a boxer...a guy who'd enjoyed the breaks, at first, but was slipping down the ladder faster than he'd climbed it in the first place.

And Rita Smith was somebody—her dad one of the wealthiest and most important people in the town.

"Marry you?" she repeated, and her voice cut into my heart, tearing out huge chunks. "You were all right to have around, Chuck but I'm not tying myself to you, see? For one thing, you're only a second-rate boxer—and what'll happen when your fighting days are over? No, Chuck, I'm being frank with you. Marriage is out, so far as we're concerned...."

Well, that was plain enough. Rita had been stringing me

along, all the time. It tickled her sense of humor to more or less tell me so to my face—I guess she enjoyed watching how I took it, seeing me crumple up, like I'd taken a jab in the middle....

I didn't know quite what happened next. Somehow, I managed to laugh, not a nice sort of laugh, but there it was—utterly mirthless, with a high pitch to it. I sensed the amusement in Rita's blue eyes.... Could guess she was enjoying this. And I felt I hated her, in that moment.

Getting to my feet, I looked down at her, agony in my gaze. She said something as I turned away...but I was past hearing or caring what she said.

To me, this was the end of everything. The end of life itself....

* * * * * * *

Funny how a disappointment in love reacts on a guy. Some take to drink, others kick over the traces altogether. Me, I just wanted to cut myself adrift from everything that would remind me of Rita.

I threw up the boxing game and traveled to a city about a hundred miles away, where I landed a job in a big auto factory. Hard work—but I loved it. Getting somewhere to live was my biggest headache.

Finally I got a back room off a widow, Mrs. Clancy. She'd a stepdaughter, Molly, who was around nineteen, small and shy, with big, wide, brown eyes. Always, she seemed sort of scared, like she was afraid of something—or mebbe of her stepmother, for a blind man could have seen that Mrs. Clancy didn't treat Molly very kindly.

My room wasn't great shakes, with big, damp splotches on the walls, and only an iron bedstead, a shaky chair and a broken dressing chest. A tattered rug covered the rough floorboards.

Not much, but all I could get. The food was plain awful, except when Molly cooked it. And she could cook.

Things continued on. I tried to forget about Rita—with little success!

I was lying on top of my unmade bed, smoking, and trying to read a magazine, when I heard sobbing in the other room. Brows furrowed, I swung my feet to the floor, tossing aside the magazine.

I thrust through to the Clancys' kitchen, and saw Molly slumped in a chair, crying her eyes out. Her dress was torn, and I saw red weals on her white flesh. That made me wonder if Mrs. Clancy had been ill-treating the girl while I was at work.

"What's wrong, Molly?" I crossed and touched her shoulder, so she shrank away from me, fear flaming into her brown eyes. When she saw who it was, something of the fear vanished.

She couldn't speak, not for a moment. I sensed she was trembling, and tried to soothe her.

Brokenly, she sobbed out the nasty story. "It's—it's Bart Cassidy...you know who I mean?" She looked at me with her wide eyes, and I nodded.

Cassidy was a bad lot; a widower, who lived further down the street. I'd heard plenty about him, and he'd a prison record for offences against girls.

"Bart Cassidy...wants me to go and stay with him—as his housekeeper...," Molly sobbed out. "Ma is trying to make me go—but I won't! Won't...."

My teeth clicked together. Molly—and that brute! I knew what it meant...his housekeeper! And Ma Clancy was trying to force Molly into going.... I could guess why, knowing Cassidy had been winning on the gee-gees, for he'd been drinking all the past week; he'd pay Ma Clancy well for making Molly go to him....

I smothered an impulse to break things.

"Ma—she's gone round to fetch Bart Cassidy right now...." Molly sobbed, and I put an arm around her shaking shoulders.

"You'll be all right," I assured her, for pity surged over in my heart, and I was determined that I'd see Molly was all right. My mind sought a way of escape for her—then I had a breathtaking idea.

Neither Molly nor I had much to live for in this crazy old

world. Our stake didn't amount to much. In a sense, our positions were similar.

"Get your things packed," I told her, with a smile. "They won't do this to you, Molly. I'll take you away. Listen, kid—we'll be married, see? Then everything will be okay."

She looked at me, Just as if she couldn't believe it was true.

"Married—Chuck...you'd marry me?" "Sure! Anything to say against it?" I joked.

Molly shook her head. Love was in her eyes, now; I saw it there, crystal clear. Gosh, the girl was head over heels in love with me! Crazy me—I might have noticed it before, only I was so worried about Rita that I never could get around to thinking of anything else....

I waited while Molly threw her pitifully few belongings into a battered case. A check skirt, two faded print frocks, a box that once held candles, scraps of ribbon, various odds and ends.... We were just leaving when Ma Clancy returned, and close behind her was Cassidy, an ugly, bloated mountain of a man, unshaven, his piggy eyes peering from behind puffed cheeks.

Mrs. Clancy gave me a nasty look, then her eyes traveled beyond me to Molly, who was hugging her case.

She called the girl a vile name, demanding to know where she was going.

"Molly's going with me," I grunted. "We're to be married, see? And just you try to stop us...."

Bart Cassidy started forward, his hairy fists twitching, mouthing threats to batter me to pulp.

For once, Bart had picked a loser. I hadn't his brute strength, but too much drink had bloated him. Besides, I knew how to use my mitts. Dodging the clumsy pass he made, I weaved in, landing successive short-arm jabs that battered his ugly face to bleeding pulp. A crashing uppercut slammed against his chin, sending him sprawling across a table, which broke beneath his weight, and he pitched to the floor, where he lay still.

Then I took Molly's arm, picking up my own case, which was already packed. We walked out then.

Guess it was like a dream to Molly, us being married by a preacher in his front room. She clung to me, eyes starry, and I could feel the thudding of her heart.

Poor kid. She looked up into my face, after the ceremony, and her eyes were brimming over with tears.

"Wh-what've I done to deserve this?" she stammered. "Oh, Chuck, I can't thank you enough, ever...."

"Forget it," I said, uneasily, for I hated having folks thank me. "It was just, oh heck...just time I was wed an' settled down! And you happened to be on the spot...."

A strange thing to say on my wedding day...but I said it! Guess it was a strange wedding, too, come to think of it.

* * * * * * *

We were lucky, and got a coupla furnished rooms off a bloke who worked alongside me in the auto factory; his house was too big for his wife to keep, with her working, too. So we moved in there. Reckon Molly was the happiest girl in the city when she had two rooms of her own...and, gosh, the furniture was shifted around, every time I came home....

Not long afterwards, the clerk at the window of the factory time office said there was a telegram for me. Taking it, I walked through the gates, slitting open the envelope.

When I saw the message...gosh, you can imagine the tumult I felt.... "DARLING...," ran the message, " I LOVE YOU. SORRY FOR EVERYTHING. WILL MARRY YOU, SWEETHEART. ALL LOVE.—RITA."

Yeah, that's what it was—from Rita, the girl who'd turned me down! And now she had changed her mind...too late! She wanted to marry me—when I was married already to another girl!

Course Rita didn't know that...she'd got the factory address from Dad, but I hadn't yet written to tell him I was married, so Rita didn't know that I already had a wife!

* * * * * *

What a position to be in! I still loved Rita—I always would, I reckoned—yet here I was tied to another woman! A woman who had first claim on me, by law.

A bitterness welled up inside me—bitterness against Molly, whom I unreasonably blamed for this awful mess I found myself in! Poor Molly, the little friendless kid, whom I had married out of pity, thinking the only woman in my life didn't want me....

I blamed Molly for it all. That night—well, I went drinking... had to do something to try and drown the misery in my heart.

When at last I got back to the rooms we rented, I'm afraid I... but I'll skip that. It isn't nice to think about even.

How I must have hurt small, sensitive Molly, telling her I wished I hadn't married her, that I'd be getting a divorce soon as I could....

Sometimes, even yet, I see her pale, stricken face, and seems I'll never shut it but, the agony in her eyes as she stared at me, clasping both hands against a heart that must have been broken.

"Chuck...you're drunk! Don't know what you're saying...," she gasped out.

I swayed on my feet, eyes red-rimmed and cruel—I could see my reflection in the mirror opposite, and it wasn't nice to see. Then I flung the telegram form in her face.

"Sure...I mean it," I told her, thickly. "I just married you... from pity! Nothing else! I love somebody else...and she wants to marry me. Yet I'm tied to you...."

She didn't say any more. Just gave a gasp and turned to run through to the bedroom. I heard the bed-springs creak, as she flung herself down, headlong, then awful sobs, hard and dry, like they were tearing Molly's slender body to bits.

And I slumped into a fireside chair. Guess I slept, for it was the middle of the night when my eyes blinked open. I was cold and stiff—from the other room came Molly's sobs, for she hadn't stopped.... I swore, vividly, thinking this was one heckuva mess I was in....

* * * * * * *

Weeks followed that weren't happy ones. They could not be anything else, with Molly a pale ghost of herself, and me going around like a bear with a sore head. I'd better skip the details of those awful weeks.... They weren't nice, not for either Molly or me. Especially for Molly—I guess, most nights, she cried herself to sleep.

I hadn't answered Rita's message. A letter came: it said she wanted me to marry her, right away, for she'd discovered that she loved me above everything else. I was all that mattered in her life.

But I didn't answer that, either. How could I? There was nothing to say. I couldn't explain about Molly—all I could do was rave and curse at the poor kid, making her life a misery.

Once she even said she wished she'd gone to Cassidy; even that did not sober me, but I flung back in her teeth that I wished to heck she had....

God, those were awful days, for her. Me, I was past caring. All I could think of was Rita, who loved me so much—and I couldn't reply to her letter....

Rita, who would have made me the happiest man in the world. And now....

My frustrated love for Rita spilled over, gnawing at me, nagging into my mind that I'd got a raw deal from life, marrying Molly out of pity.

I'd thought of a divorce, but that seemed out, for Molly wouldn't give me one. Besides, it would take time—I couldn't ask Rita to wait that long....

Then my father died. Suddenly, so I never got a chance to be with him at the end. All I could do was travel through to arrange the funeral. I was glad I'd made his last few years happy, for I'd kept on sending him money, so he could stay on in the rooming house, where he'd be well fed and looked after.

The funeral was simple, touching. When it was over, I went round to the rooming house with Bill Sorby, a cousin, for we'd have to go through Dad's belongings. Checking through drawers, Bill began to chat about the latest tidbits of gossip. I hardly listened, not until he mentioned a particular name.

"Hear about Rita Smith?" he said, and my heart sort of stood still. "Used to be the girl-friend, didn't she?"

I nodded, a sick ache in my heart. Deliberately, I held away my head, so Bill wouldn't see the light flickering in my eyes.

"You are sure well quit of her," he went on, surprisingly. "She was a bad lot, was Rita...."

That rocked me back on my heels, sending my head snapping round to stare blankly at my cousin.

"What d'you mean?" I demanded.

Bill shrugged his broad shoulders. He gave a low laugh— uneasily, sort of.

"Oh, she came a cropper. Got tied up with a married man. There was a baby coming—the guy skinned out, see? Soon as he knew what was to happen. Rita went crazy, kinda...tried to get some other sucker to marry her. Everything was fixed for her marrying Jed Skinner, only he got told 'bout the married guy, so he sheered off...."

My heart gave a sudden leap. Rita in trouble! A married was responsible...her desperately trying to hook some poor fish who'd be had for a sucker....

"When—when did this happen?" I demanded.

Bill thought a moment, scratching his mop of reddish hair.

"Aw, a while back. Let me think...." Then he named a date.

Yes—approximately the date that had been on the letter she wrote me! That letter saying she still loved me—that she'd marry me, right away!

I'll say she would! To hide her own shame!

That's the sort of girl Rita had been...selfish, out for her own ends, all the time!

I'd have fallen for her wiles, too.... If I'd been still single! Wouldn't have known about the baby—not until it was too late. I Wouldn't have known I was marrying a girl soon to bear another guy's child....

What would our marriage have been—in those circumstances?

I shuddered to think of it.

And this selfish, worthless woman.... She was coming between Molly and I! Poor, sweet, gentle Molly...the suffering I had caused her; in my madness....

That's what it amounted to...madness, all of it!

Poor Molly—her love was the real thing, something fragile and precious, that I'd done my best to kill....

Oh, I realized all that, now. It made me feel lower than a snake's belly. Molly's love was so good and pure, rising above self, a love that would last for always, growing richer and more wonderful with the passing of the years....

That was Molly's love—the love I had so nearly destroyed in my utter foolishness....

Trains could not take me back quickly enough to Molly. I went down on my knees to her, begged to be forgiven, as I stammered out some sort of explanation, praying she would understand and forgive....

For I knew now I loved Molly, loved her just as surely as she loved me.

She forgave me...simply, without questions or reproach. Because she loved me.

So...that's our love story—mine and Molly's. A love, story that wouldn't have had a happy ending, if the scales hadn't been lifted from my eyes in the nick of time. But they were, thank God.... And now we have found a perfect happiness and contentment in a love that is—to us—the most wonderful thing in the world.

I said at the beginning that Molly was busy knitting tiny garments as I started to write this. Yes, there'll be another chapter starting to our particular love story, mighty soon. A wonderfully exciting chapter, this. Molly, she hopes it will be a boy. Me...I'm not caring—so long as Molly is happy, then I'll be contented....

LOST ROUNDS

BY MICHAEL A. BLACK

The big man paused before entering the bar, partially silhouetted by the ambient light from the parking lot. His head bobbled around quickly, letting his eyes adjust to the soft glow of the subdued interior lighting of the tavern. Soft glowing globular lights hung suspended under slow turning ceiling fans which kept the boozy smelling, hazy air circulating lazily. The long bar was to the right of the door. Three men sat on the round stools at the far end, near the spigots of draft beer, with a couple of half-empty steins, greasy plates, silverware and a smoldering ashtray on the surface in front of them. Beyond the long polished counter the room expanded into a restaurant area, where some more people, mostly blue collar workers who'd gotten off late, drank beer and ate pizza in the dimly lighted room. A hooded video game and a jukebox sat in steadfast silence across from the bar. Hardly anyone in the place took very much notice of the new customer as he stood there.

Larry, the bartender, nodded as the big man approached, noticing that he moved with an almost incongruous grace for his size. As he passed under the first ceiling light, his reflection seemed to fill the mirror behind the bar and loom over the row of darkly colored bottles. He wasn't a young man, nor a really old one either, but he looked rather shop-worn. Thick ridges of scar tissue ran in a ragged perpendicular line over a huge nose, misshapen but more than just a few breaks. His light blue eyes scanned the bar as he tugged off his black, unmarked baseball cap and set in on the bar revealing a crop of thinning brown hair, sheared so short it almost resembled a Marine Corps boot camp style. Or perhaps a prison cut.

Yet it wasn't his face or his hair that attracted the bartender's attention as much as the man's hands. They dangled from thick corded wrists like two quart milk cartons, the knuckles above the first two digits as prominent as walnut shells. The guys at the far end glanced momentarily into the mirror. One guy slapped one of the others and pointed to the big man's reflection and smirked. They resumed their raucous conversation. The big man sat at the opposite end, near the TV, which was mounted on a bracket above the bar so that the screen faced the interior, showing the color images of a pitcher as he wound up to deliver a fast ball. The batter held firm as the ball sailed across the plate in the strike zone.

"What'll it be?" Larry asked. He was a white guy in his late thirties, going soft in the middle and losing hair at the crown.

"Gimme a beer," the big man said. His voice was a husky rasp, the words barely understandable. Like someone drawing a dull saw across tough wood.

"What kind?"

"Huh?"

"I said, what kind of beer you want?"

The big man shrugged. "Don't matter."

Larry shrugged and filled up a stein. He walked over and set it down in front of the big man who reached in his pocket and took out a folded bill.

Larry looked at it and shook his head. "That's not enough, sir."

The big man gazed at him slowly, as if the guy'd been speaking a foreign language, and leaned forward. "Whatchasay?"

"I said, that ain't enough. You got money to pay for the beer, or what?" The irritation in Larry's voice was obvious. He tapped the bill with his finger. "That's only a one."

The big man's eye's held a perplexed expression for a few moments, then he reached into his pocket again, withdrawing another bill. "How's this?"

It was a ten. Larry nodded and took it. As he started to move away the big man called to him.

"Hey, buddy."

Larry paused, looking back over his shoulder.

"What day is it today?"

Larry looked at the guy, then said, "It's Thursday. Why?"

"Thursday, huh?" The big man licked his lips. "Hey, how about turning on *Thursday Night Fights*?"

Larry shrugged and grabbed the remote, flipping through the channels until he found the right one. The image of two boxers, one black and one Hispanic, throwing punches in the middle of a ring came on. The big man smiled and followed their movements.

After a few moments one of the patrons at the far end glanced over at the TV and registered an exaggerated shock. He slapped the shoulder of the center guy, the largest of the three, and pointed. "Hey, Norm, take a look at that." Norm looked to be in his early thirties with massive shoulders and arms. His dust stained t-shirt and blue jeans had the look of construction worker.

"Hey, Larry," he yelled. "What happened to the ball game?"

The other two guys wore similar outfits. They hooted in agreement.

"Take it easy, Norm," Larry said. "This gentleman wanted to watch the fights, that's all."

"Oh yeah? Well, turn the fucking ball game back on."

"You guys weren't even watching it."

"That ain't the fucking point," Norm said. "Now turn the fucking ball game back on."

Larry glanced at the big guy who was seemingly oblivious to the conversation. Either that or he was just ignoring it. He sat transfixed, watching the figures on the screen as they darted in and out, throwing punches in combinations. Occasionally the big man's head would jerk to the side, as if he too was slipping a punch.

"Hey, Larry," one of the other construction workers yelled, "there's three of us and we all want to watch the ball game."

Larry frowned and grabbed the remote, switching it back to the baseball game. This whole thing was starting to take on an all too familiar feeling. In fact, he would wager it was going to turn out like all the other ones had. Norm and his buddies were predictable, if nothing else.

The big guy blinked several times, then slowly twisted his head toward the bartender.

After seeming to do some sort of mental calculations in his head, he asked, "Hey, buddy, what day is this?"

Larry looked at him slowly to see if he was joking. Seeing that he wasn't, he said, "I told you already, it's Thursday."

The big man nodded. "How about turning on *Thursday Night Fights*?"

At first Larry thought the guy was joking or something, but when he grinned, the big guy didn't. His face remained placid, blank, just like the first time he'd asked to have the channel switched.

"Ah, those gents down there want to watch the ball game," Larry said.

The big guy looked down the bar toward the trio who were staring back.

"You guys mind if we watch the fights for a while?" the big guy asked.

"What you want to watch a spic and a nigger beating the shit out of each other for?" Norm asked. His voice had a sarcastic lilt to it. The other two snorted with laughter.

The big guy sat there, his expression unchanged. "You guys mind if we watch the fights for a while?"

The trio looked at each other and broke out in some alcohol-fueled laughter. Norm grinned widely and got up, ambling over toward the big man, obviously sizing him up.

"Tell you what, Larry," Norm said and he walked past Larry, "go ahead and turn the fights on."

Larry grabbed the remote and shook his head. "I wish you

guys would make up your mind." He pressed the buttons and the image of the two fighters came back on. Norm held out his hand and motioned for Larry to hand him the remote. Larry's head jerked slightly. Christ, he didn't like where this was heading, yet it was like riding a train down a track toward an inevitable wreck. Still, with Norm at the controls there wasn't much anybody could do to stop it, let alone him. He was just the bartender, after all.

Norm's face twisted into an unfriendly scowl and he snapped his fingers. "Gimme it, asshole."

Larry sighed and handed him the remote. He moved to the area by the phone to call the cops if another fight broke out. He just hoped no one would get hurt like the last time Norm bullied some poor fucker into a fist fight. He'd broken the guy's nose and knocked out three of his teeth and claimed it had been self defense. Norm was big and mean and quick. A triple threat. Of course, he'd sucker punched the guy first to set him up.

The big man was transfixed on the screen again, watching the fighters. Norm sat down on the stool next to him and leaned close.

"You look familiar," he said. "I know you?"

The big man didn't answer.

Norm punched the guy's shoulder lightly. "Hey, I'm talking to you."

The big man's head turned toward Norm, his expression still blank.

"I asked if I knew you," Norm said.

The big man shook his head and sipped his beer. He went back to watching the fight.

Norm glanced up at the television, then back to his buddies with a "watch this" wink. He held the remote up and flipped the buttons. The fighters disappeared, replaced by the ball game again.

The big man squinted, then blinked. He turned to Larry. After a few seconds, he said, "Hey, buddy, what day is this?"

Larry eyed the guy, his face cocked to one side. "I told you, it's Thursday."

The big man nodded. "You mind turning on the *Thursday Night Fights*?"

"No, we don't mind," Norm said in a loud voice. "Do we fellas?"

His two companions roared with laughter and agreement. They came sauntering over and stood next to Norm like two smiling goons.

Norm flipped the channel back to the fight. They were between rounds now and one fighter was getting wiped down by his cornermen. The big man's face creased slightly. A commercial came on.

"Hey what day is this?" one of Norm's buddies asked, his voice affecting a gravelly imitation of the big man's.

"I don't know," the other one said in an equally distorted tone. "You know what day it is?"

Norm grinned and tapped the big man on the shoulder again. "Hey, buddy, where I know you from?"

The big man glanced at him and shook his head.

"You understand English?" one of Norm's buddies asked. He moved around to the opposite side of the big man.

The commercials ended and the two fighters came back on. Norm grinned again and held up the remote. The channel switched back to the baseball game.

It seemed like it took the big man a few seconds to realize the channel had changed. He took a long swig of his beer, licked his lips, then called to Larry. "Say, what day is this?"

Norm and his buddies burst into a spasm of laughter. Larry edged closer to them and whispered, "Hey I don't want no trouble here."

"Trouble?" Norm said in a loud voice. "No trouble here. Just a couple of buddies watching the *Thursday Night Fights*." He slapped the big man's shoulder, a bit harder than before. "You want to watch the fights, buddy?"

The big man nodded.

"Well, why didn't you just say so?" Norm asked. He held up

the remote and with a flourish, changed the channel back to the boxing.

Larry tried to read the big man's expression as he debated whether to call the cops now and lose what little business he had, or wait until the trouble really started. The big guy looked totally relaxed, unaffected by the other men. Maybe he could avoid the trouble. Maybe not. Larry backed off, and began polishing the glasses.

"What day is this?" one of Norm's buddies asked.

"I dunno," the other one said. "You know what day it is?"

"It's fucking Thursday," Norm yelled. "Remember? The ball game's on tonight."

"It is? No shit. Let's watch it."

"Yeah, let's watch it."

Norm nodded and flipped the channel back to baseball, eying the big man as he did so. Norm picked up the big man's cap and put it on his own head.

The big man started to say something but Norm interrupted him. "What day is it?"

The question seemed to stun the big man. His mouth gaped slightly.

"It's fucking Thursday," one of Norm's buddies said.

"You want to watch the *Thursday Night Fights*?" the other guy asked.

"Yeah, how bout it?" Norm said. "Want to watch the fights?"

The big man nodded.

Norm started to hold up the remote, then stopped. He turned to the big man and studied him closely, tracing a fingertip over the big man's right eyebrow. The big man's head pulled away from the probing finger.

"Hey, don't," he said.

"What's the matter? You used to be a fighter, right?"

The big man nodded slowly. "Yeah."

"What weight?" Norm asked.

"Heavy."

"Heavy," Norm said, looking the big man up and down.

"You're what.... About two-ten, two-twenty?"

The big man nodded again.

"What about your record? You a winner or a loser?"

The big man didn't answer.

"I think you're a loser." Norm leaned close. "What's your name, pug?"

The big man glanced back up at the television, staring at the images of the baseball players.

"I asked you what your name was, loser," Norm said.

Larry straightened up. He'd seen this same scene played out so many times before, always ending the same way: Norm and his buddies egging some poor bastard on, goading him into a fight so Norm could get his kicks busting somebody up. But this guy didn't seem right. Like he was mentally challenged, or something. What sport could punching out a retard give Norm? Larry cleared his throat and said, "Hey, I told ya I don't want no trouble, didn't I?"

"Blow it out yer ass," one of the buddies said.

Norm chastised the man with a harsh look. He turned to Larry. "No trouble. Just a little harmless fun is all. Right?" He turned back to the big man. "What you say your name was?"

The big man blinked a few times. "Harry. Harry Gant."

"Harry Gant," Norm repeated. "What did they call you when you were fighting? Hammering Harry?"

The big man shook his head.

"What then?" Norm asked.

The big man shook his head again.

"Well, that's what I'm gonna call you," Norm said.

"Call me what?" the big man said.

"Hammering Harry," Norm said. "In fact, I think I seen you fight before, didn't I?"

"You seen me fight?"

"Oh yeah," Norm said, giving an exaggerated wink to his buddies. "Hey, Lar, give Hammering Harry here another beer, on me."

Larry's face pulled into a frown, but a mean look from Norm

and he filled up another stein.

Norm slapped the big man on the back. "Here you go, Harry."

"I know you?" the big man asked, nodded a thanks. ""How you know my name?"

"I seen you fight, remember?" Norm said. "Who'd you fight? Tyson?"

The big man shook his head. "Never fought him. Fought Greg Page once. And Big Eddie Johnson."

"Big Eddie," Norm said "You won that fight, didn't ya?"

If the big man was cognizant of Norm's sarcastic tone he didn't show it. He just shook his head. "Lost a close one. Shoulda gone to the body more." He shrugged. "Maybe I'll beat him next time."

"Next time? *You?*" Norm laughed. "Next time ain't gonna happen, pops." He held up the remote and the fight disappeared, replaced by the baseball game once more. "Fight's over."

The big man stared at the TV. "Hey, you mind if we watch the fights?"

One of Norm's buddies chimed in: "What day is this?"

The other two jerked with spasms of drunken laughter.

The big man sipped his beer.

Norm took off the cap and fingered it. "Nice cap."

The big man nodded and reached for it. Norm moved it out of the other man's reach, shaking his head. "What you doing reaching for my cap?"

The big man looked perplexed. "Thought it was mine." He looked up and down the bar. "You guys seen my cap?"

Norm held it up. "This *your* cap?"

The big man nodded.

Norm grinned. "Well, it's mine now." He held up the remote. "See, it's a baseball cap."

The ball game appeared back on the TV. Larry looked up toward the screen then back to the unlikely quartet. He leaned forward and said in a quiet voice, "Why don't you guys leave the man alone, huh?"

"Leave who alone?" Norm said in a loud voice. "Hammering

Harry here?"

"He was a professional fighter," one of the buddies chimed in.

"Fought Big Eddie Johnson."

"Almost beat him, too," Norm said, smacking the big man on the arm with his fist.

The big man's head turned toward him. "Don't do that."

"Do what?" Norm asked, then sent a slightly harder punch to the big man's shoulder. "That?"

"Don't."

Norm smirked, shrugged, and then smacked the big man with a harder punch, saying, "Why don't you make me?"

"Come on, Norm," one of the buddies said. "Deck that fucking loser."

Norm made a hocking sound with his mouth, brought the big man's cap up and spat inside it. He tossed it on the floor. When the big man's eyes followed the movement, Norm slammed his fist onto the side of the man's head, sucker-punching him hard.

The punch caused the big man to shift forward overturning his stein of beer onto the bar.

"Hey now," Larry said. "I already told you guys I don't want no trouble."

"Hey, fuck you," Norm said, his mouth twisting into an ugly scowl. He slid off the bar stool and shoved the big man hard. "Come on, pops, make me."

The two friends egged him on, using taunt after taunt. The big man's expression seemed blank for a moment, then he blinked twice. Larry wondered if the poor guy knew what was actually happening. He moved for the phone to dial nine-one-one and saw Norm's reflection in the mirror pointing at him.

"You touch that fucking phone and I'll be coming for you next, asshole. And you know I will. This is gonna be self-defense, just like all the others." He raised his clenched fists and turned back toward the big man. "Make me, pops."

The big guy rotated on the stool, his face a mask of confusion. He brought up his hands in a defensive posture as his feet hit the floor.

Norm grinned and moved in.

"Watch this," he said, and threw a powerful looking right.

The big man stepped inside the punch and ducked, coming up with a one-two combination to Norm's midsection. Norm shoved him back against the bar and grabbed his face with his left hand, bringing his right down on the big man's forehead with tremendous force.

The big man shifted to the side, rolling with the blow, which buckled his knees slightly. He turned and faced Norm in a fighter's stance once again.

"You like that, pops?" Norm said as he lumbered forward again, tossing a looping right hand again.

This time the big man leaned back almost imperceptibly, letting the punch sail past his face. He twisted landing a left hook to Norm's exposed ribcage, then clipping his face with a short right.

Norm whirled, trying to land a wide left hook. The big man stepped in and blocked it, then countered with a left uppercut to Norm's solar plexus.

Norm took two steps back, hitting the edge of the bar. Larry, frozen by the phone, watched in wonderment. The big man moved forward with the grace of a cat, his left hand shooting out in perfect rhythm, snapping one punch, two punches, three punches into Norm's face.

One of Norm's buddies jumped behind the big man and tried grabbing both his arms. The big man's body jerked with a sudden, powerful shrug and the buddy lost his grip. The big man whirled to face him and two quick punches to the buddy's gut and jaw dropped the guy. The big man turned back just in time to catch Norm lumbering toward him.

Larry watched the big man's feet as they seemed to glide across the floor, shuffling like he was on ice skates, avoiding the fallen buddy and staying just out of range of Norm's powerful, but slow punches.

More jabs popped Norm in the face. He spit blood. Lurched

forward. Left jab, left jab, right cross. A stream of crimson ran from his nose.

The big man stepped inside and delivered a perfectly timed left hook into Norm's gut. He grunted as he went to his knees, his muscular arms sagging at his sides.

"No more," he gasped. "No more."

Then his upper body curled into a ball on the floor, blood oozing from his nose and now gaping mouth.

The big guy looked at the final buddy who raised his hands, palms outward and shook his head. A nervous grin spread over his face as he glanced toward the door. "I don't want no part of you, man."

"I'm calling the fucking cops now," Larry said. He picked up the phone and started to press in the numbers.

"Hey," the big man said, his voice raspy with exertion.

Larry's hand froze over the phone.

"What round was that?" the big man asked.

Before Larry could answer the door slammed open. A young guy strode in. He was tall and rangy looking, and appeared to be half black, half white. His eyes shot around the room and settled on the big man.

"Dad, what's going on?" he said.

The big man turned toward him, cocking his head to the side. "Who're you?"

"Dad, it's me. We been looking all over for you." The young guy glanced toward Larry, then at the two men on the floor. "What happened?"

Larry shook his head.

"Who're you?" the big man asked.

"Dad," the younger guy said, moving forward and putting a hand on the big man's shoulder. "It's Nick."

"Nick?" The big man's voice was a husky whisper.

The young guy nodded.

"You...you can't be Nick," the big man said. "He's just a little.... He's my boy. He's only ten."

"It's me, dad. Come on. Let's go home."

"Home?"

"Yeah, dad. We found your car in front. Time to go home now." The young guy surveyed the scene once more, then looked toward Larry again. "He owe you anything?"

Larry shook his head. "Huh-un."

"So we good?" The young guy jerked his head in the direction of the two prostrate bodies.

"Self-defense," Larry said.

The young guy nodded and steered his father toward the exit, stopping to pick up his cap from the floor. As they walked Larry watched them, their movements jerking like a movie that was caught in one of those fluttering, endless loops: the big man seeming to struggle against being forced to leave, his son trying to maneuver him toward the door. As they slowed to open the door, the big man looked back toward the bar.

"Hey," he said, "what round was that?"

DEMENTIA PUGILISTICA

BY LONNI LEES

THEN

Soldier's Field was packed, filled with smoke and sweat and angry yells echoing from ringside. Cigar smoke and cheers and jeers permeated the darkness as the spotlight shone down on the ring, and me. Most of the crowd had placed their bets on me, just waiting for the pleasure of cashing in on a sure win, but ain't nothing beats the feel of being up there taking what's mine. He kept throwing punches at me but I was swimming without getting wet, each punch missing me, just the feel of the air whooshing past as his fist missed the mark. He made one hell of a punching bag but the dope just kept coming back for more. I was giving the audience the show of their lives, ducking and punching and never missing my target. I was stirring up more excitement than Joe Lewis when his paralyzing punches knocked out Jack Kracken in the first round. First round—shit. I wanted to give them what they paid for before I clocked the guy.

Fourth round I decided it was time to give 'em what they wanted. The guy had been a real punch-out, giving me the stink-eye and taunting me before the fight. The bastard called me a bog-trotter and I called him a stupid guinea and the press ate it up like salted pretzels. There'd been lots of boasting and hot air in his foreplay but he couldn't hold his own in the ring. Especially against the likes of me. The bell rang and the dumb wop came straight at me. I wondered if my glove would just slide off that grease ball, but before he could blink I had him against the ropes. I was hitting him with a left, then a right, then with a series of lightening punches to his head that left him dazed. I danced him away from the ropes like we were lovers and landed the final one-two that left him hugging the canvas. He never heard them count to ten. I was giving my fellow Micks what King Levinski had given the west side Jews 'til Joe Louis knocked him out.

I was giving them a big dose of pride.

It gave me a high like a sax player's heroin only I didn't need no drugs to get there. And there was no Joe Louis on the planet who could stop me. I was on top of my game and soaring into the stratosphere and enjoying every minute of the ride.

I was on top of the world. Everywhere I looked my name was up on posters; on walls, on the sides of buildings, on fences. Irish Danny Sullivan against the sap of the month. Strangers would pass me on the street with a smile and a big thumbs up. I never touched the hard stuff myself, but any pub I'd enter, in any Chicago neighborhood, the drinks were always on the house. I got more respect than all the Irish gangsters and politicians in town put together. Even they looked up to me.

Miami, Hoboken, Reno and Comisky Park, every place I had a match I came up a winner. I was the best and I was rising fast and now I was only three fights away from the championship. Life was good but I never once lost track of who to thank. If it hadn't been for Father Devlin at St. Patrick's I'd have just been another Irish thug from the wrong side of town headed on a downward spiral. And going down wasn't easy when you were born at the bottom. How much farther down can you go when you're already in the gutter? The good Father saw something in me early on and dragged me to the gym, defiant and with a chip on my shoulder the size of the Blarney Stone. But first time in the ring I knew I'd found my calling. I lived in the gym instead of on the streets and I'll always be grateful for that. Manny Santini ran the gym and I guess he was okay enough. The guy was a Jew-talian who couldn't tell *ravioli* from *kreplach*, but he ran a clean place and was a fun guy who always had a good joke or story to tell. He had a great sense of humor. Every Christmas he'd put up a little tree and trim it with blue and white decorations, then top it off with a Star of David. It made me wonder if there might be a good drop of Irish in him somewhere. Father Devlin, who thought of Manny's soul as half saved and half damned, introduced me to Bingo Malone who started managing me before I'd finished school. He molded me from a wet-behind-the-ears sparring partner into a headliner in no time flat.

I lucked out in the mother department, too. She wasn't like rest of 'em in the neighborhood who'd just as soon clobber you alongside the head as look at you. She'd even block my father's fists when he was on a drunk and aiming at me. A veritable saint she was. Life had short-changed her and I wanted to make up for it. Things were harder on us after he died, but easier too. We didn't have to duck no more. She always told me there was a better world out there. A place with food on the table and hope and respect.

A place where dreams come true.

Her words never left me. On sunny days I'd drive my '36 Auburn Boat Tail Speedster down Lakeshore Drive. Heads would turn and I'd always have a beautiful dame perched next to me. Just me and my red and white Auburn and a pretty girl with the wind blowing through her hair. And I wasn't one of those love 'em and leave 'em guys either. I always treated the ladies with respect, just like I was taught. They appreciated that. Mom would'a been proud. In so many ways. I found that other world and just wish she'd lived long enough share in it.

Damn but life was perfect.

NOW

When I wake up I don't remember how I got here, but it looks like I got a room to sleep in. I hardly even notice the rats, vermin or human, that I'm sharing my digs with. There's a roof and a bed and somehow my bursting bladder remembers there's a toilet down the hall. I flip back the blanket and head out of the room. I'm one lucky lad because I'm first in line for the crapper. I do my business, then stand in front of the mirror to smooth my hair and splash some cold water on my mug to try and clear the fog out of my brain. A stranger looks back at me. The only thing I recognize are those grey Irish eyes. My sandy curls have been replaced by greasy strands and my custom tailored silk shirt has been replaced with something worn and stained and smelly.

Who is that staring back at me?

Why does his tongue dart in and out of his mouth like that, flipping beads of spit onto the mirror?

He scares the bejeebers out of me.

I'm confused.

THEN

The first time I noticed Norma I was sitting in my corner spitting into the pail. She was strutting around the ring holding up a sign that read Round Three. She was Jean Harlow blonde with skin white as ivory piano keys and legs as long as an Arlington Park race horse and the most kissable red lips I'd ever laid eyes on. Damn, but she was a sight to behold. I'd seen some beauties in my day but she took the cake. The expression in her baby blues told me she got hot from the aroma of blood and perspiration that filled the ring. In that split second I knew that I would be her perfect aphrodisiac, the two of us mixing into the perfect cocktail. She made concentrating on my opponent hard. But, even with the distraction, the guy was easy. Some spick from the east who lead with his chin despite having a glass jaw. Well, I gave the guy the old one-two and had him down for the count before the bell. As the ref held up my arm and declared me the winner, I turned and gave Norma a wink and a smile and the rest was history.

Back in the locker room, I was toweling off my sweat, ready to head for the showers.

"Great fight," said Bingo, but he seemed distracted. He was acting kinda squirrely and his eyes kept darting around like he had something on his mind besides the win.

"You okay?" I asked him.

"S'sure, sure kid," he stuttered. "Nothin' I can't handle."

So I took his word for it. In a way, I suppose I was glad I didn't push him. It might'a really put a damper on things if I'd known what was eating him. About all I wanted to think about was basking in the glory of my latest win with that beautiful blonde on my arm.

"I got a hot date waiting for me, Bingo," I said and walked out the door.

It was already late, so I just took Norma out for a couple of drinks so we could get the feel for each other. She was easy to talk to and I was really relaxed, like I'd known her for a long time. We could almost read each others thoughts, like an old married couple who could carry on a whole conversation with grunts and nods and never miss exactly what the other was saying. Ends up she was some kind of Norsky from Wisconsin farm country and a Lutheran to boot. My mother might not have approved, but I could see now how Manny happened. When the right one shows up it's easy to make concessions, tradition be damned. I didn't doubt for a second we could figure things out.

* * * * * * *

We made a date for the very next night.

And the night after that. And the night after that. Well, you get the picture.

One night we drove up to the Belmont Theater because Norma wanted to see Camille. I have to admit that Greta Garbo and Robert Taylor made one handsome couple. Damn near as good looking as Norma and me. Norma was mesmerized and couldn't stop talking about Garbo's beautiful gowns. I told her that after the next fight I'd take her to Paris and buy her dresses that would make Garbo's look like rags she'd bought from some sheeny down on Maxwell Street. She liked that and let loose with little giggles that lasted until the people behind us impatiently told us to hush up so they could hear the movie.

Garbo's husky voice filled the theater as the actress said, "Nobody could ever love me for thirty years."

"I could love you for a hundred," I whispered into Norma's ear.

"Oh, Danny," she said, tears glistening in her pale blue eyes. "I love you oodles and then some."

A week later, we were dressed to the nines when we walked into the Willowbrook Ballroom. Heads turned, as much for the beautiful dame on my arm as for Irish Danny Sullivan, local hero. The band played romantic songs as we danced, holding each other close, never wanting to let go. Everybody in the place must have wished they were us. I'd never felt so close to heaven as I did that night. As we sat at our table Benny Goodman let go with his latest hit, soft and sad and beautiful in its Lorenz Hart lyrics.

> *It seems we stood and talked like this before*
> *We looked at each other in the same way then*
> *But I can't remember where or when.*

We rose and worked our way onto the dance floor. My fingers traced her back, the fabric of her white satin gown whispering promises against my fingertips. It fit her like she'd been poured into it by some fairy godmother and I could feel her every move, her every muscle, her soft skin beneath the exotic fabric as we floated across the floor in perfect unison. We were smoother than Astaire and Rogers in The Gay Divorcee and twice as pretty.

> *The clothes you're wearing are the clothes you wore*
> *The smiling you are smiling you were smiling then*

But I can't remember where or when.

"It's like they wrote this song just for us," she said. "It's just how I feel. Like we've known each other forever."

> *Some things that happen for the first time*
> *Seem to be happening again*
> *And so it seems that we have met before*
> *And laughed before*
> *And loved before*
> *But who knows where or when*

"That's our song," we both said at the same time, then laughed and held each other even closer, if that was possible.

That was the night I asked Norma to marry me.

And she said yes.

NOW

It feels like bugs crawling all over my face and it wakes me up. I open my eyes to raindrops falling on me. Raindrops are better than bugs any day. I'm lying in an alley next to a dumpster and by the stink of rotting fish and God knows what, I must be by a Chinese restaurant. I can't figure how they can make such a stink but serve up such good eats. It don't make any sense to me but it makes me hungry.

When I blink to squeeze the sleep from my eyes I look over and there's this dame squatting next to me with a bottle in her hand. She ain't no beauty like that long-legged blonde that keeps tip-toeing around the edges of my brain. Even though she's sitting down, I can see that this redhead has those "peasant Irish" gams that look more like tree trunks than legs. A good, sturdy lass, one might say. She's looking at me with admiration, like I'm Rudolph Valentino or something. Her hair is auburn, or maybe it's just the grime makes it look that dark. She might have been pretty before the booze started writing sad stories all over her face. Puffy, dark circles accentuate the green of her eyes and there's lines that should only be on a face twice her age. She smiles at me and I can see a gentleness about her. Why does she keep grinning at me like that? Geez, but she's got cute dimples. She looks kinda like Shirley Temple on a toot.

"Who are you?" I ask, morning gravel in my voice.

"Oh, Danny," she says. "It's me. It's your Rose."

"Sure, Rosie, I knew that," I say. I didn't want to make her feel bad. And besides, it's been a long time since a dame looked at me like that. We sat there in the alley looking at each other and pretty soon I started to remember. Just a little. She took a long drink from the bottle, emptying it, then stood up and tossed it into the dumpster.

"Time to rise and shine, sweetie," she says. "There's a wonderful new day waiting for us."

As I stood up she hooked her arm into mine. We walked from the alley to the street and towards a fresh, new day. The rain was soft, like little angels pissing down from the clouds. As we walked I remembered bits and pieces about her. She liked her drink and sometimes I'd panhandle and buy her a bottle and it made her happy like I'd bought her a dozen roses. I never touched the stuff, but she needed it. I know first hand that life can be mean sometimes. Hootch helps some people forget. I don't need nothin' to help me forget. My problem is remembering. But I still remember my mother telling me whiskey was the curse of the Irish and it'd be best to never take the first taste. So I never did. One time, when my Da wasn't home, I opened his bottle of Old Bushmills and inhaled the fumes. Damn, but it smelled swell. I never wanted to become him, so I recapped it and walked away.

We're walking along the sidewalk, Rosie and me, and when people see me they avert their eyes. But she just struts along, proud to be with me, and it don't even bother her when my mouth dribbles a little or I lose my balance and need to lean against her for support.

"Let's go to Grant Park," she says. Her eyes light up like a kid's on Christmas. "You know how I love sitting next to those big lions outside the Art Institute. They're so swell, Danny. Can we go there? Can we?"

It's a long walk but when we get there the rain has stopped and the sun is peeking through. I sit with Rosie under one of the statues, watching people walk by in their fancy clothes with someplace dreamy to go. I might'a been one of them once, but hard as I try I can't quite remember. Flashes of a beautiful blonde in a satin dress. *I'll take you to Paris.* I know she was special, because my heart aches way down deep when I think of her. I can't remember her name. Things come in pieces and I never put them together so's they make any sense. It's like when you work on a jigsaw puzzle and it's half done, but the damn cat keeps messing it up, and you have to start over from scratch every day. *Nadine, Nola, Nancy, no.* If her name would come, I tell myself maybe things would be right again.

Occasionally, as someone ascends the Institute's steps, they toss a few coins our way and Rosie picks them up and puts them in her pocket. Pretty soon she runs over to a vendor and comes back with a hot dog for each of us. We gobble them down like we haven't eaten in a week. Maybe we haven't. I don't know. People pass and cars pass and the occasional push cart squeaks by. One of the vendors rings his bell and....

> *"Round three," the announcer calls.*
> *I'm up and out of my corner like a bolt. Dancing my fancy footwork around some other Irishman and throwing phantom punches his way. I keep pulling my punches and he keeps striking out and missing. I like toying with the guy, but the crowd is getting impatient so I close in and hit him hard. He reels backwards from the sheer force of it.*
> *Clear as a bell, I hear a voice in my head. It says: First you kill the body, the head will follow. I know it means something....*

Some copper's got my hands behind my back and I feel the cold steel as he cuffs me. I hear Rosie yelling at him and stirring it up as a small crowd looks on from a safe distance.

"He ain't drunk, I tell ya!" she yells at the cop. "He don't even touch the stuff."

"He's drunk as a Mick at a wake," says the cop, "and it's down to Summerdale Station 'til he sleeps it off."

But Rosie keeps right on yelling as she tries to pull me away from him.

"He's putting the scare in decent folks, dancing around and waving his arms and mumblin' his nonsense." The cop gives her a shove and she loses her balance, falling to the ground. "You want a pair of matching bracelets, Missy? I'd be more than glad to accommodate you."

"Don't ya know who he is?" She asks, defeat in her voice. "He's the champ, damn you."

"Right so, and I'm the bloody King of England."

So I'm taken down to the station and thrown in a cell. It ain't too bad really. They fed me warm food and the cot's a damn sight softer than sleeping in the alley. I shut my mouth and mind my own business and sleep like a baby. Next morning I wake up and there's this old guy in my cell, just sitting on his mattress looking at me all puzzled like. He's got marshmallow skin and little red veins march across his pudgy cheeks and over his beezer-nose. Then his bloodshot eyes get all big and round like a light went off.

"I knew I know'd you from somewhere," he says. "You're Danny Sullivan! Hey, lads," he yells out to the other cells, "you know who we got here? It's Irish Danny Sullivan himself."

First it's dead silent, then I hear someone clapping. Then somebody else joins in and before ya know it the cell block is filled with applause.

"You was the best," someone yells out.

"We love ya, Danny," says another.

Pretty soon the guard comes in, keys jangling as he scuffles down the hall. "What's all the ruckus about?" he asks. "And quiet down in here! This ain't supposed to be no party."

He comes over to our cell and my whiskey-nosed cell mate tells him I was somebody. That I'm Irish Danny, the best damn boxer Chicago's ever seen and ever will, like I'm some sorta legend or somethin'.

The guard studies my face, trying to match up the who was with the who is. "Well, I'll be damned," he finally says. "Come on, lad. Your time's up and you can go now." He opened the cell door and I walked down the hall towards freedom. "I used to watch you in the ring," he says. "Let me escort you to the door myself," he says, like I'm really somebody special and he ain't ashamed to be with me. As I walk out into the sunlight the guard slips me a fin and says, "Now you take care of yerself, Danny, you hear me?"

I maneuver down the precinct steps and sitting there at the bottom is Rosie. I remember who she is, so the day's starting out with promise. She looks like she'd waited there all night and looks up with that same big smile. I'll bet there was a time she was a real looker. She ran up and gave me a hug that could'a broken a lesser man's ribs, but it felt damn good. I might be a nobody, but I had somebody, and that was worth a pot o' gold. Like they say in the old country, it warmed the cockles o' me heart. It sure did.

"Did I take you to Paris?" I ask her.

Why did I say that? Sometimes I confuse her with somebody else. But who?

"In my dreams, Danny." She squeezes my hand. "Only in my dreams."

"I don't get it, Rosie," I say. "Why do you even hang around for a broken palooka like me?"

"Because I love ya, Danny," she grins, "and you always treat me like a lady."

"And a fine lady you are."

THEN

"We g'gotta t't'talk," said Bingo. I can tell something's wrong by the way he's jittery and his lids are twitchy and his stammering is worse than usual, so I sit down next to him.

"So talk," I said, "I'm all ears."

"I'm in a world of sh'shit," he said. "I'm in so d'da'd'deep to the bosses I just can't see any other way out."

He told me he'd been betting on a lot more than the fights and he'd been losing and can't win enough to pay back all he owes. The more he bet the deeper a hole he dug. He'd been playing the horses and the numbers and anything else he could. Ends up he owes. A lot. And it's way more loot than I have. I kinda spend it as fast as I make it. I can't see no way to get him out of the mess he's made for himself. If I had it I'd give him every penny, and I told him as much.

"There's one way you can h'help," he said. "You know I la-la-love you like my own son, Danny, and I'd never ask if there was any other way."

"What are you asking me?"

He was quiet for a long time and I could see tears welling in his eyes. I'd seen him bad but never this bad. We just sat there in silence for what seemed forever, me figuring he'd spit it out when he was good and ready. Finally, he took a deep breath, then spoke. I wished he hadn't.

"You know we've got a f'fight coming up," he began. "Every fight the money's on you and every f'fight they clean up. But the odds are so much in your favor...."

"Go on."

"Most of the money will be on you, as always. If the bosses were to bet on the other guy, and let's s'say the other guy wins, it'll be a huge clean up and they'll be willing to cancel my debt. There, I said it."

"You're my best friend in the world, Bingo. How can you even ask that? I'm only a few fights from number one and you want me to throw it?"

"If we both b'bet against you, we'll clean up too."

"If it's such a win-win, why do I feel like you just handed me a turd and told me it was a T-bone?"

He thought a little before he spoke again, but he couldn't look me in the eye. He hadn't been able to since this whole conversation started.

"You'll still be champ, we all know you're heading for it. It'll just take one extra f'fight to get there, that's all. God, it's damn near k'killing me having to beg like this, but...."

"But what?"

"If the fix isn't in they're going to kill me."

* * * * * * *

Norma knew something was bothering me, but she never asked and I never told. How could I? I just kept smiling and reminding her that after the fight we'd go to Paris. That seemed to distract her some. What would she think of me if she knew I was supposed to work something crooked? What would she think if I let my friend get killed just so I could win? What will I think of myself regardless of which decision I make? I was trapped in a no-win and it was eating me alive.

I finally told Bingo I'd throw the fight, but he'd better not ever do anything like that to me again or I'd gladly kill him myself. And I meant it, friend or not, there are some lines you just don't cross. I wanted to beat the shit out of him for putting me in the middle of his mess and I told him as much. But making him feel bad didn't make me feel one bit better.

By the night of the fight I was feeling worse than I'd ever felt in my life. I sat in my corner like nothin' was wrong, but things could never be more wrong than they were now. I looked across to my opponent, Jack Clancy, and wondered if he knew the fix was in. Would it matter to him that he didn't win it fair and square or was winning all that mattered? Well, at least the win would go to another Irishman, if that was any consolation.

We walked to the center of the ring, Clancy and me, and touched gloves. The bell rang and the fight began. At first we just danced around a bit, getting the feel for each other, then went into a series of punches. Pretty soon Clancy got serious and I got three hard ones in the gut that damn near knocked the wind out of me. The guy was tougher than I thought, but I knew I could have beat him easy. But that wasn't in the plan, not tonight anyway. It hurt me through and through to be pulling my punches instead of playing it straight.

By round three the crowd was acting like it knew what was up. Hissing and booing and yelling their curses into the ring. Round Five and Clancy just kept hitting me. Hard. To the head. I hit him back a few times, sure, but not with the force I should have. One, two, three, four more hard hits to my head. My brain felt like it exploded, like somebody had set off a deadly charge. It felt like it was on fire and for a second everything went black and I forgot where I was.

Clancy slammed me with two more fast ones and something snapped. I must've forgotten I was supposed to take a fall, because I flew at the guy with a succession of blows that caught him by surprise. I was Irish Danny Sullivan and nobody was gonna take that away from me. I just kept hitting, my head hurting far worse than the blows he was getting, and next thing I knew he was down for the count and the crowd was going wild.

"That's our Danny!" Somebody yelled.

"What took ya so long?"

I vaguely remember the ref holding my hand up, declaring me the winner. I must'a danced around the ring and done all the usual malarky, but next thing I knew I was flat on my back in the locker room with a headache the size of Texas. Bingo and Norma were standing over me, and I didn't even know who else but there was a crowd of 'em.

"Look at his eyes," somebody said. "Somethin' ain't right."

"Watch my finger," said somebody else, waving his hand back and forth in front of my face.

"Get him to the hospital!"

* * * * * * *

I don't know how much time had passed, but I woke up in a hospital room hurting from head to toe, but mostly my head. In the corner Manny from the gym and a beautiful blonde were talking to a doctor in whispers. I couldn't help but notice her long legs so I figured I must be on the mend.

"Irreparable brain damage," I heard the doc whisper.

Are they talking about me?

"I won, didn't I?" I said, the words coming out like I'm under water. My lips felt parched and my throat felt like it'd been scratched by cat claws. "I did, didn't I?"

Manny and the woman walked over to my bedside.

"He's awake," she said.

"You got the guy—big time," said Manny.

I figured as much. Danny Sullivan ain't got the word lose in his vocabulary.

"Where's Bingo?" I asked and the two of them look at each other.

"Just tell him," said the pretty lady.

"Danny," Manny said, "they found Bingo dead in the alley. We don't know what happened. If he got mugged or what the shit happened, but whoever it was did a real number on him. He's gone."

It's a mystery to me what happened in the ring that night. I only remember my head was killing me. I don't know, after so many head blows, if I forgot I was supposed to lose or I just couldn't take a dive or what. All I know is I won, but winning didn't make any difference because my best friend was dead. And I'm the one who killed him.

The blonde leaned over me and kissed me on the cheek, then turned and walked towards the door with Manny. I heard her whisper as they walked out the door:

"I feel bad, Manny, but I just can't deal with it. I can't look at him like that."

Something felt empty inside me, like I was losing something

special.

And they left.

We looked at each other in the same way then
But I don't remember where or when.

I left the hospital a few weeks later and by then everything I
had was eaten up to pay the bills. I even had to sell the Auburn
and there was no place left to go. I found my way back to the
gym. When you're on top everybody loves you but when you
fall they disappear like snow flakes melting on the sidewalk. I
was alone and Manny was my only hope. I asked him to hire me
on as a sparring partner for the young kids just coming up, but
he said no. Something about one more blow to the head would
kill me. He let me work for awhile cleaning up around the place
and folding towels, but pretty soon the day came that he called
me aside.

"I gotta let you go, Danny." He sighed. "You just make people
uneasy. They look at you and it scares them that someday they
might end up like you. I'm sorry, but that's the way it is."

So I packed up the few things I could call mine and head to
the door, any remnants of my old life that I'd been hanging on
to dead forever. It was one hell of a ride while it lasted. All's I
know is that I'd been on top of the world once, and that's more
than most can say, right?

I turned and faced Manny.

"Where am I gonna to go? What am I gonna do?"

"Maybe you'll just have to be a schnorrer," he said.

"A what?"

"A beggar, Danny. A beggar. But you should praise God that
you're still alive and breathing. I'm sorry, but I can't be responsible for your life. I've got my own business to take care of."

NOW

Every day starts the same. In my mind I see a sexy blonde dame in a white satin dress and my heart aches to the core. Nora, Natalie, Naomi, no. If I could piece it all together I'm sure things would be right again. If I could only think of her name, but it never comes. An 'N', I'm sure it starts with an 'N'...is it Norsky? No, that ain't right either.

So I shake the cobwebs from my head and start the day.

That night I'm walking with my Rosie. She's the redhead, not the blonde, I tell myself. She's my Rosie. And I'm starting to remember that damn near every time I see her now. The neon from the bars and dives reflects on the pavement like a beautiful rainbow beneath our feet. We're just moseying along, enjoying the night and each other. Rosie is happy as a kitten with a teat as she sucks on her bottle of whiskey. I bought her a good one today, not the rotgut I usually have to settle for. It's been one hell of a glorious day, the best I can remember in a long time. My head hardly hurts at all. We pause under a streetlight and kiss each other like we was Romeo and Juliet. We're standing in front of some dive and the music drifts out its door and out onto the street, like romantic background music from a movie.

Our movie.

I feel at peace.

A figure steps out of the shadows. I hear laughter echoing from within the dive. The sounds of happy voices. Two more figures follow closely behind the first as they saunter towards us.

"Hey, look at the stumble-bums, Vinny," one of them says. "Ain't they just the cat's meow?"

"Looks to me like they're trashin' up our street," says another one.

"Yeah," says the first guy. "Think maybe we ought'a clean things up?"

He walks over to where we're standing and pushes his hairy

wop chest up against me, so close I can smell the garlic and the rage that ooze from his pores.

"It's getting too crowded here," he says and punches me in the stomach.

"Get lost," says Rosie, as feisty as ever, but the guy gives her a shove then hits me again.

You might hit Irish Danny once, but you sure as hell ain't gonna get away with it twice. I haul off and punch the wop right in the kisser and he reels backwards, surprise on his face, like he's just been hit by a truck. But he comes right back for more and I give it to him again. I haven't felt this alive in a long time and I'm savoring the moment and giving it all I've got. Five more gut punches before the other two decide it's time to join in. So now it's me against three punk Italians, all three of them bent on beating the crap out of me. I get in a few more good ones before they knock me to the ground and start to kick me. I find my way back on my feet and go for all three of them. Next thing I know I'm on the mat, *no not the mat, the sidewalk,* and I can hear ribs crack and I'm hurting from head to toe as they kick and punch. *And he's down for the count, says the ref.* I gotta get up before they count to ten.

"No, not in the head!" I hear Rosie scream. "Oh, God, don't kick him in the head! He can't take it. Stop, stop...."

She wails like a banshee, racing over and trying to pull them off me with all the wonderful craziness she's got. She's one helluva woman, that Rosie. But they shove her away again and just keep pounding on me.

Something in my head explodes. Pain shoots through me like a million needles and a thousand brilliant stars scream across my brain.

One more brutal kick in my head and things go black.

"Let's get the fuck outta here," says a voice and then I hear footsteps running away into the darkness of the night.

I can hear my own death rattles and I'm praying to the good Lord that Rosie can't hear them too as she kneels beside me and holds my head in her lap.

Music pours out from the gin joint behind us, soft and sad and beautiful.

> *It seems we stood and talked like this before*
> *We look at each other in the same way then*
> *But I can't remember where or when.*

But I can remember.

I can remember now.

Her name was Norma and I loved her. But it ended up she was like every other Good Time Charlie, latching on to my gravy train then turning tail and taking a powder as soon as the chips were down. That aching in my heart wasn't love at all, just the deep hurt that's left behind once a heart's been broken.

"Norma," I say, and I'm kinda laughing. "Norma."

"Oh, Danny," says Rosie, holding me close. "I'll be anybody you want me to be, anybody at all. Just please don't go. I love you Danny. Please hang on, hang on for me Danny."

I open my eyes and see my broken angel.

"You're a real lady, Rosie my love. And you never once walked away."

I can still feel the warmth of her arms around me, but I'm growing colder . Her sobs sound farther and farther away, whispering their prayers into the darkness.

"Don't leave me."

ZERO AT THE BONE

BY WILLIAM BOYLE

"Don't listen to them, Clip," the old cut man said.

"Got to listen," Tommy said. "They're right. He beat me here. If he had beat me over there, it'd be different. But he beat me here. I got to listen, Willie."

"You fought your best. I was there. It's not he's a better fighter. Just you were slow tonight. The Scotsman got lucky."

"Slow?"

"Slow."

"Three goddamn rounds. I didn't even get a punch off in the third. He was too fast. Had me tied up."

"Ref stopped the fight too early. You weren't even hurt."

"I felt like about a pound of shit."

"Don't talk down."

"I'm shit."

"There's still Giles. And Deen. You'll work your way back up to Guthrie."

"Yeah."

"I guarantee it. December. January. You'll be ready by then."

Tommy took the tape off of his hands and massaged his raw knuckles. He had thrown seventy punches and only landed ten. One had been a good jab to Guthrie's face. That was in the first round. Almost all of Tommy's landed punches had come in the first round. In the second, Guthrie had overpowered him and run him ragged. In the third, Guthrie had shut him down completely. The old cut man was trying to convince him that he had fought his best, but he hadn't. It had been ugly, and Tommy didn't care. The truth was he was sorry the referee had stopped the fight so early. He was hoping that Guthrie knocked him out cold and he woke up the next day in a hospital somewhere with a big-titted nurse hovering over him. It wasn't happening that way, though. He was leaving the Coliseum quietly through a service exit. Just him and Willie the cut man. His trainer—who was also his old man—was meeting them out back with the car.

They got in the car—Tommy in the front, Willie in the back—and his old man turned and put a hand on Tommy's shoulder. "Don't worry, kiddo. You did okay."

"Okay?" Tommy said.

"Okay. The Scotsman's too fast for you, that's all. We'll work on it. You'll figure out a way."

"Yeah."

"Chin up, Clip."

Tommy couldn't listen to the shit anymore. You gave it your best shot. Chin up. Get him next time. He wanted to be back in his apartment, staring at the wall. To hell with the heavybag. To hell with running. To hell with working out. To hell with all the fighters he had ever wanted to be like. To hell with his old man. Tommy was done.

"Clip, you look like you got the weight of the world on your shoulders," his old man said, starting the car and taking them away from the Coliseum. "You got nothing to be ashamed of. Every fighter gets his ass handed to him a few times."

"Yeah," Tommy said.

Willie the cut man lit a cigarillo in the back and filled the car up with thick smoke. Tommy rolled down the window.

"You think you had a better shot with Ferranti?" his old man asked.

Ferranti had been his trainer for three years, but he had left to work with Bernie Rodriguez in Queens. Tommy had hired on his old man out of desperation. There had been no one else. "No," Tommy said. "It's not that, Pa."

"I know I'm smalltime, kiddo."

"Pa. You're fine. You're a good trainer. Ferranti was washed up." He was lying to his old man. Ferranti was the best. Tommy had been twenty-three and three under Ferranti. With nine KOs. The big guns had all been talking about Tommy "The Clipper" Fitzgerald as a contender. He was even on the undercard at a Mackey-Sorensen bout at Madison Square Garden. With his old man as his trainer, he had one win and five losses. But that wasn't the whole story. It wasn't just his old man. The fire had gone all the way out of him since Ferranti had walked. Nothing his old man did could help.

His old man dropped him outside of his apartment, telling him again not to worry about anything. Tommy nodded and said goodbye to his old man and Willie. He stopped at the corner store and bought *The Daily News*. The guy behind the counter looked at him and shook his head.

Tommy said nothing.

He went up to his apartment and looked at himself in the small mirror on the wall in the kitchen. His chin was bruised, soft to the touch, but that was it. Guthrie hadn't hurt him all that bad. He cracked a cold beer, sat down on the couch, and flipped through the newspaper. The stories seemed to go through him. There was a big piece on Sorensen organizing a charity bout to raise dough for an orphanage. Read all about it. Sorensen's a goddamn saint.

After a while, Tommy decided to go to Casey's. He was pretty sure Sally Unitas would be bartending. Sally was about the only person he wanted to see. She was always good for a laugh. She had big knockers that were always popping out when she bent over to get beers out of the cooler.

When he got to Casey's, he was sad to see Bald Nick behind the bar. Bald Nick never shut up. He talked through the butt end of a black cigar and sweated like a hairy wrestler in a B-movie.

"Clip," Bald Nick said. "Bad luck. Bad damn luck. But things are looking up. Bald Nick's pouring. Forget all your troubles. Bald Nick is pouring tonight, Clip."

Tommy ordered a beer and sat there. Bald Nick put the beer

in front of him, and Tommy got to thinking about how it would be nice to take a woman home. Some nights he just wanted to be alone. Other nights he wanted to find a woman to take home. Tonight was one of those nights. He looked across the bar. There was Emily Vincente. She was married. He had made it with her once and vowed he would never sink that low again. There was also Edna. Nobody knew Edna's last name, but she was a pretty mean lay when she wasn't hammered flat as elephant shit. And there was Ginny Carter, who looked to be paired up already with Mikey Elizondo. At the back of the bar, though, Tommy noticed someone new. She was sitting alone at a corner booth, fingering the rim of her beer bottle. Her hair was platinum blonde, and she was pretty in a slutty yet saintly sort of way. There was one thing about her that set her apart from the other women in the bar. She had one arm. One long right arm poking out of a blood red blouse. Where the left arm should have been, there was nothing. Just space. The sleeve of the blouse was pinned up on that side. The fact that she was missing an arm made her more appealing to Tommy. He ordered a shot of bourbon and two beers. He downed the shot and then carried the beers over to her. "I'm Tommy," he said.

She said, "My name's Reilly."

"Reilly?"

"Reilly."

"That's nice."

"Thanks."

"I bought you a beer. You mind if I sit down?"

"Thanks. No. Go ahead."

Tommy settled in across from her.

"What do you do, Tommy?" she asked.

"I'm a fighter."

"Fancy."

"Not at all. Turns out I'm no good at it."

"I'm a dental hygienist," she said.

"Isn't that tough with only one wing?"

"I manage."

"It's pretty sexy," he said.

"What?"

"The thought of you cleaning teeth with just the one arm."

She laughed. "You're something, Tommy."

"Let's finish these beers and get out of here," Tommy said.

"Okay," Reilly said. "I'll take a chance."

* * * * * * *

Later, sitting on the couch in his living room still wearing most of their clothes, Tommy reached out, unpinned Reilly's left sleeve, and touched the stump. He expected it to be hard and sharp, but it was soft.

"So, how'd you lose it?" Tommy asked.

"In the war."

"What war?"

"I'm just kidding. In a car accident."

"It's really something." The stump fascinated him. He traced his finger from the bottom of the stump up to her shoulder.

"It doesn't make you sick?" Reilly asked.

"No."

"A lot of guys, it makes them sick."

"Sure, I guess. But I'm in love with it."

"That's nice."

"It really is something, Reilly."

"Thanks."

"Listen."

"What?"

"I'm in love with you."

"You've known me an hour."

"I'm nuts."

"You're punchy, that's what it is."

He went over and got a bottle of Irish whiskey out from under the sink. He took a long drink. "I'm not."

"You are."

"Marry me, Reilly." He sat back down next to her.

"You don't know the first thing about me."

"I lost my fight tonight, Reilly. And I'm in love with you. That's all. Now I'm in the mood to get married."

"You're just in love with my stump."

"That too."

"Hell."

"Marry me."

"We've known each other about an hour. And you only want to get married because you lost and you're drunk."

"I always lose now, and I'm always drunk. Take a chance."

"You're definitely punchy." She laughed. "I could have the clap. Or cancer. Or twelve kids."

"I don't care if you have cancer of the clap. Or herpes of the kids. That stump trumps everything."

"You're sick."

"Maybe."

"And punchy."

"Sure."

She lit a cigarette. It fascinated Tommy, the way she did it all with just the one arm. "You have any music?" she asked.

"I have some old country and blues."

"I don't like any of that."

"What do you like?"

"I like classical music."

"When are we gonna get married?"

"Soon, Tommy."

"When are you gonna clean my teeth?"

"Whenever you want. I'll slip you in the back door. Doctor Andersen doesn't need to know. Let me see your teeth."

Tommy opened his mouth, and Reilly looked inside.

"Jesus," Reilly said. "Don't you brush or anything?"

"Sometimes I brush with my finger."

"You don't floss?"

"No. I use toothpicks."

"It's scary, Tommy."

"Funny."

"I'm gonna clean your teeth."

"You make it sound sexy."

"It can be."

"God, you're the best."

She laughed.

"Listen," he said. "Do you have a car?"

"Yeah, why?"

"Let's go for a ride."

"I don't think so."

He downed the rest of the whiskey.

"It's not a good idea," she said.

"Reilly, we've got to do it. Let's drive to Orchard Beach."

"Not now, Tommy."

He went over to the sink and looked in the cabinet for more whiskey. There was a pint of Seagram's hidden under a pot. He took it out and held it up. "Let's go, Reilly."

Reilly had parked her car on Logan. They walked there. Tommy got under the wheel of the car and turned the radio on. He had the pint of whiskey in his lap. Reilly, sitting crookedly in the passenger seat, had her head in her hand. Tommy fiddled with the radio knob and cursed when he slipped past the station he wanted. He finally found it.

"Can you make it lower?" Reilly said over the music.

Tommy turned the volume down. He put the car in gear and took it away from the curb. It was late, and the streets were quiet. "Classical," Tommy said. "I can't get over it." He felt good, but he also felt terrible. He took a slug of whiskey. He liked Reilly. He liked her very much. He liked his old man, too. And, once, he had liked fighting. He almost remembered what it was like. He remembered, as a kid, keeping clippings on his favorite fighters. A shoebox full of them. He had liked that. He would take out the box and read the clippings over and over. He also used to enjoy his long morning runs to Orchard Beach. Back when it was new to him.

They approached Orchard Beach. "I run here every morning," Tommy said. "This is where I go."

Reilly, more relaxed now, said, "Yeah. I've got places like that."

Tommy parked in a dark corner of the lot next to a tree. He left the lights and the radio on, and he got out from under the wheel. "Come on," he said.

There was a picnic table under the tree. Tommy sat down on the bench.

Reilly got out of the car and sat next to him. She lit a cigarette.

"I sit at this table every morning," he said. "I take a long break. I just sit here."

Reilly passed him the cigarette. He took a drag.

"You're really something," he said. "The way you work things. Lighting cigarettes. You don't seem to have any problem."

"I've been doing it a long time now. Almost fifteen years."

"And you drive that rig like that without any problems?"

"Yeah."

"Pretty good."

"I don't think we should be here," Reilly said.

"I know."

"It's dark."

"But we're here."

"I want to go, Tommy."

"In a little while. Let's just sit here."

"Just for a couple of minutes."

"Okay." He took a long pull of the whiskey. "You don't like me anymore, do you?"

"I like you, Tommy. I just don't want to be here. I'm nervous."

"You don't want to marry me."

"We'll figure it all out tomorrow."

"Sure. Tomorrow. I guess I was just kidding about all of that anyway."

"I figured that."

"Yeah." He finished the whiskey, stood up on the table and threw the bottle into a distant patch of weeds. It made a loud thump against the hard ground. Tommy laughed and sat back down.

"Let's go," Reilly said. "I'll drive." She got up and went over to the driver's side of the car.

"Okay," he said.

Reilly got in the car. She stuck her head out the window and said, "Come on, Tommy."

He got in the car on the passenger side and slumped down.

He fell asleep for a little while. When he woke up, they were passing St. Raymond Cemetery. There was a bar across from the cemetery that was still open. "Stop," he said.

"What?" Reilly asked.

"Pull over."

She yanked the car to the side of the road, kicking up dust. Tommy got out.

"Where are you going?" Reilly asked.

"I'll see you tomorrow, kiddo," he said.

Reilly drove away. Tommy went over to the bar and had a few shots of bourbon. The bartender did not know him. He was glad. He did not want to go home. After forty-five minutes, he left the bar and crossed the street. He climbed over the cemetery gate. He walked deep into the cemetery and sat down at the base of a tombstone that said something about the dead guy falling asleep in Jesus. This made Tommy angry. He tried to kick the tombstone over, but it wouldn't budge. He left the cemetery and went back to the bar. "You got a payphone here?" he asked the bartender.

The bartender shook his head.

Tommy thought about how no one had payphones anymore. He thought it was sad. "House phone?" Tommy asked.

The bartender sighed. "Local?"

"Yeah."

He got the phone from under the bar and handed it to Tommy. "Keep it short."

Tommy called his old man and asked him for a ride. His old man said he'd be right over. Tommy hung up the phone and ordered a double shot of bourbon with a beer back. The bartender poured. Tommy emptied his pockets on the bar.

Ten minutes later, his old man showed up. He was wearing sweatpants and a heavy coat. "Pa!" Tommy said. "Have a drink. Have a goddamn drink."

His old man sat next to him at the bar and ordered a glass of beer.

"Take me to the fuckin bridge, Pa," he said and laughed. "I'm gonna jump." He ordered another drink.

"I'll say a prayer for you, Tommy," his old man said. "All I can do."

"Yeah. Pray up a storm."

They sat at the bar for a while longer, and Tommy's old man bought him a round. When they left, Tommy got into the backseat of his old man's car. "Driver," he said, "take me anywhere but here."

They drove around the neighborhood with the radio on. Tommy's old man pointed out the house on Country Club where he grew up. He stopped the car in front of the house. "This place, Tommy. The people who live there now, they're loaded. They put a pool in the yard. A big addition on the back."

Tommy shrugged.

"We had nothing back then. Eight of us living in the house. Eating goddamn oatmeal for breakfast every morning. Potatoes for dinner. I can't even look at a goddamn potato anymore."

"Rough," Tommy said.

"Listen, you're gonna fight again, Tommy. You're gonna be good again. You're not just gonna be an opponent. I'm working on a fight now for you with Fitzgerald. In Bay Ridge."

Tommy shook his head. His old man started the car and drove away. When they got back to Tommy's place, his old man helped him inside.

* * * * * * *

The next morning Tommy woke up and saw his old man sleeping on the couch. He drank some tomato juice dosed with

Tabasco, black pepper, and chunks of jalapeno and then went for a run.

At Orchard Beach, he sat on the picnic table and thought about Reilly. He thought about going back to Casey's to find her that night. He thought about the fight with Fitzgerald his old man had set up for him. It was a sure loss. Four rounds on Fitzgerald's turf. It was the point he'd come to in his career. He probably wouldn't win again. He'd fight four-rounders on enemy turf and lose the decision every time because home judges would never go against their guy.

He stopped at a bodega for a bagel on the way home. He also bought a pack of Marlboros, a twelve pack of Budweiser, an issue of *Hustler*, and *The Daily News*. When he got home, his old man was gone. An envelope containing forty dollars was on the kitchen table with a note that said: *Chin up.*

Tommy ate, thumbed through the *Hustler*, got changed, and went to Casey's. Sally Unitas was bartending. She bought him a beer and he watched her as she bent over to pluck it out of the cooler. There was an OTB next door, and he went over and placed a couple of bets. He lost. He went back and bought another beer and watched Sally get it again. He sat there and hoped Reilly would come in.

He sat there for a few hours and drank eight beers, every other one on the arm. He watched the races and then asked Sally to change the channel and put on the Yankee pre-game.

Reilly finally came in and sat down next to him. He bought her a beer. "I apologize," he said. "Reilly, forgive me. I got a little too drunk on you."

She smiled.

"Run away with me. Key West. What do you say?"

"Okay, Tommy," she said. "Let's get a table in the back and talk about it."

Tommy ordered a couple of shots of bourbon and a couple more beers and told Sally he was out of cash and needed a line of credit. She said it was no problem. He and Reilly took the drinks to a back table and sat down. "So, shit, let's get serious,"

Tommy said.

"Let's," Reilly said.

"Key West. Mojitos. Let's do it."

"Let's," she said. "First—"

"First what?"

"A proposition."

"Okay. Shoot."

"The dentist I work for."

"I'm with you."

"He's got a safe in the office. Keeps ten grand in it."

"Guy's what, a jerk?"

"No, it's just I'm sick of living the way I live. It's just for the money. I got the building alarm code and I think I know where the combination for the safe is."

"Why don't you do it alone? Why bring someone in you gotta worry about splitting the dough with?"

"I can't do it alone. It's easy, but not that easy. Especially with my disability."

"Playing the old disability card, huh?"

"It's a good card."

"I'm in. What the hell. I'd say shake on it, but you drink your beer, kiddo. Let's do the heist and head south. Get conch fritters in Key West. Spend what we steal."

* * * * * * *

They went straight to the office. Reilly punched in the alarm code and left the lights off when they got inside. She used a little penlight to guide him around some chairs and a desk. She had the penlight in her mouth and was feeling around with her hand.

"I didn't figure you for a thief, Reilly," Tommy said and laughed.

"I'm no thief," she said.

"You're a bandit. A goddamn one-armed bandit."

They went into the back office and she turned on the light. There was a guy in there. He was wearing a white coat. The dentist, Tommy figured. It was a frame. Had to be.

"Hey, chump," the guy said.

Reilly went over and stood by him. "Sorry, Tommy," she said. "You're sweet. Really."

"You're the dentist?" Tommy asked.

The guy grinned big. Had terrible teeth for a dentist.

"So, what's the frame?"

"Need a fall guy, that's all."

"Insurance?"

The dentist showed him a stubby little gun. "Pretty much. You've got a partner. Your partner cleans the office out, turns on you. Reilly's here working late, gets knocked out cold. Payday's big. Hundred grand in the safe goes missing. Plus other stuff that's broken, gone. You, you're just a means to end, a loser who gets to play the part of loser."

Tommy laughed. "What I was born for, I guess." He looked at Reilly. "Kiddo, you really are a one-armed bandit." He thought it'd probably be good to get shot, less like a punch, more like an earthquake in his gut. Least it would feel like something. The big knockout.

Reilly said, "Nothing personal."

"Never was much for things working out." Tommy paused. "A dentist. You could do better."

"I've got three cars," the dentist said. "A condo downtown Brooklyn."

"Beautiful," Tommy said.

"I like it, you knowing what I have, you not having anything."

"Sure you do."

"I feel bad for you."

"You're lucky, that's all."

"Maybe."

The dentist pulled the trigger, and Tommy felt it go in right above his hipbone. He looked at Reilly as he went down face first. Bested by a woman with one arm. His whole life had been about bastards with two arms throwing punches at him and now here was this woman with one arm, teaching him about betrayal and bad goddamn luck. He saw feet moving around him, heard things being lifted. He was pretty sure he wouldn't die. He felt alive. The bullet wasn't lodged in there, he was sure. He was letting plenty of blood go, but soon there would be sirens. But what if he did just bleed out on the floor of the dentist's office? That was too funny to think about. Read all about it. Tommy Fitzgerald, done wrong, dead at the dentist's. Tommy Fitzgerald, sad sack of shit right to the goddamn end.

ABOUT THE AUTHORS

WAYNE W. DUNDEE lives in the once-notorious old cowtown of Ogallala, on the hinge of Nebraska's panhandle. To date, Dundee has had ten novels, five novellas, and over two dozen short stories published. Much of his work has featured his private eye, Joe Hannibal. *Goshen Hole*, the seventh and latest novel-length Hannibal mystery, came out in December, 2011. He recently has also been gaining notice in the Western genre. His 2010 Western short story, "This Old Star," won a Peacemaker Award from the Western Fictioneers writer's organization; and his first novel-length Westerns, *Dismal River* and *Hard Trail to Socorro*, appeared in 2011. Titles in his Hannibal crime series have been nominated for an Edgar, an Anthony, and six Shamus Awards. Dundee is also the founder and original editor of *Hardboiled* magazine.

STAN TRYBULSKI is a Columbia University alum and was a felony trial prosecutor for the D.A.'s office in Brooklyn. Prior to becoming an attorney he was a newspaper reporter, sports writer, college administrator and bartender. He has published four novels, *The Gendarme*, and three Doherty mysteries: *The Ides of June*, *Forty-Deuce*, and *One-Trick Pony*. His short stories have appeared in recent issues of *Hardboiled* and *Sherlock Holmes Mystery Magazine*. *Casemaker* and *Slam Dunk*, his next two Doherty mysteries, will be published in 2012 and 2013. His website is www.stantrybulski.com.

RON FORTIER has been writing for over thirty-five years. He is best known for his work on the Green Hornet comic series for Now Comics and writing Alex Ross' first comic project, *Terminator: Burning Earth* for the same company. He co-founded Airship 27 Productions with artist Rob Davis. The company produces brand new novels and anthologies featuring classic pulp heroes from the 1930s, to include Ron's revival of *Captain Hazzard: Champion of Justice*. Ron also maintains a weekly blog at his website www.Airship27.com and writes a review column, *Pulp Fictions Reviews* found at http://www. pulpfictionreviews.blogspot.com.

ROBERT S. P. LEE is the designer and publisher of *Blazing Adventures Magazine* still up at www.blazingadventuresmaga-zine.com. He has worn many hats having been published over the years in *Plots with Guns*, *Thrilling Detective*, *CrimeSpree Magazine*, *Thuglit*, as well as in *Hardboiled*. Currently, Robert has gone back to his first love of illustration, having earned a certificate from Famous Artist School, he is now working on a certificate in penciling from the Joe Kubert School of Art.

G. D. MCFETRIDGE touts himself as an iconoclast, mountain man, working-class philosopher who writes from Montana's Sapphire Mountains. He is a tremendously talented writer. His short stories and essays have appeared in many venues in the US, UK and Canada as well in *Hardboiled* magazine. His email is willy.montana@yahoo.com.

ARLETTE LEES is one of the two very talented Lees Sisters, and she has had her stories published in *Hardboiled* magazine and the crime anthology *Deadly Dames*. She lives and writes in California. Her latest book is *Cold Bullets and Hot Babes* (Borgo Press) a detour into the dark alleys and twisted cul-de-sacs of the human heart.

TERENCE BUTLER lives and works in Hollister, California. He likes to read, and usually to write, and he enjoys taking care of his and his wife's horses. He's also addicted to Nikons and modern art. Recently his stories have appeared in the magazines *Yellow Mama*, *Shot of Ink*, and the anthology *Deadly Dames*. He has upcoming stories in *Plots with Guns* and *Cemetery Dance*.

MARC SPITZER is a New York author who teaches special education at a preschool in Brooklyn. He says he is addicted to reading, writing and watching his two favorite sports, ice hockey, and, of course, boxing.

C. J. HENDERSON is the creator of both the Jack Hagee hard-boiled detective series and the Piers Knight supernatural investigator series. He is the author of some seventy books or novels and has written hundreds of short stories and non-fiction pieces. You can learn more about him and his work at his website www.cjhenderson.com.

GARY LOVISI lives in Brooklyn, New York and is a MWA Edgar Award nominated author, publisher of Gryphon Books, and current editor of *Hardboiled* magazine. He is the author of over twenty-five books, the latest include *More Secret Adventures of Sherlock Holmes* (Ramble House); *Murder of A Bookman* (Borgo Press); and his collection of twenty-three hard crime stories, *Ultra-Boiled* (Ramble House). His latest book is the dark science fiction novel *Mars Needs Books!* (Borgo Press). Forthcoming is a new novel, *Sherlock Holmes: The Baron's Revenge* (Airship 27 Productions). You can find out more or contact him at his website: www.gryphonbooks.com.

GARNETT ELLIOTT lives and works in Tucson, Arizona. He's had stories published in *Alfred Hitchcock's Mystery Magazine*, *Beat to a Pulp*, *Round One Round Two*, *Pulp Modern* #1 and *Needle*. His novella "The Shunned Highway" will be featured in an anthology called *Drive-in Fiction*.

PENELOPE STANHOPE is a British pulp author who has had work published in the UK magazines of the '40s and '50s.

MICHAEL A. BLACK is the author of sixteen books and over seventy short stories. He has a BA in English from Northern Illinois University and a MFA from Columbia College Chicago. He was a police officer in the south suburbs of Chicago for over thirty years and worked in various capacities in police work including patrol supervisor, SWAT team leader, and investigations. He has also written two novels with TV star Richard Belzer of *Law & Order SVU*. His most recent books include *The Incredible Adventures of Doc Atlas* and his third Leal and Hart novel, *Sacrificial Offerings*. In 2011 the second Leal and Hart book, *Hostile Takeovers*, won the Readers' Choice Award for Best Police Procedural Novel. His hobbies include the martial arts, running, and weight lifting.

LONNI LEES is the other half of the Lees Sisters writing duo. Her stories appear regularly in *Hardboiled*, *Yellow Mama*, and she has had stories in the anthologies *Deadly Dames* and *More Whodunits*. Her short story collection, *Crawlspace,* and her first novel, *Deranged* (both published by Borgo Press), are also now available from Amazon, and she's completed another novel, *The Mosaic Murder*. Lonni has won awards for her writing as well as her art and has illustrated for books and magazines. She was twice selected as Writer in Residence at Hedgebrook, a writers retreat and has lived in several states and traveled to many countries. She currently resides in Tucson, Arizona with her scientist husband, Jonathan and shows her art at a Tucson gallery.

WILLIAM BOYLE is originally from Brooklyn, New York but now lives in Oxford, Mississippi. He received his MFA at the University of Mississippi and has published stories in *Chiron Review*, *Aethlon*, *Plots with Guns*, *Out of the Gutter* and other magazines and journals. He has recently completed a novel. His email is williamboyle4444@yahoo.com.

ACKNOWLEDGMENTS

"Introduction: Battling Boxers" by Gary Lovisi appears here for the first time. Copyright © 2012 by Gary Lovisi.

"Quick Hands" by Wayne D. Dundee appears here for the first time. Copyright © 2012 by Wayne D. Dundee.

"A Little Too Much Heart" by Stan Trybulski appears here for the first time. Copyright © 2012 by Stan Trybulski.

"Blood Feud" by Ron Fortier appears here for the first time. Copyright © 2012 by Ron Fortier.

"Tango" by Robert S. P. Lee appears here for the first time. Copyright © 2012 by Robert S. P. Lee.

"Battling Benny" by G. D. McFetridge appears here for the first time. Copyright © 2012 by G. D. McFetridge.

"Bullet for a Boxer" by Arlette Lees appears here for the first time. Copyright © 2012 by Arlette Lees.

"The Bloody Mirror" by Terence Butler appears here for the first time. Copyright © 2012 by Terence Butler.

"A Nice Jewish Boy" by Marc Spitzer appears here for the first time. Copyright © 2012 by Marc Spitzer.

"Bet Your Own Man" by C. J. Henderson originally appeared in *Karate/Kung-Fu Illustrated Magazine*, March 1989. Copyright © 1989, 2012 by C. J. Henderson.

"Boxing, Babes, & Bullets" by Gary Lovisi originally appeared in *Blazing Adventures Magazine* #9, 2008. Copyright © 2008, 2012 by Gary Lovisi.

"First Man Falling" by Garnett Elliott originally appeared in the online magazine *Beat to a Pulp*, Nov. 2010; this is its

www.ingramcontent.com/pod-product-compliance
Lightning Source LLC
Chambersburg PA
CBHW020751250626
47155CB00003B/1024